D0397327

NOW ENTERING ADDAMSVILLE

Francesca Zappia

NOW
ENTERING
ADDAMSVILLE

Greenwillow Books
An Imprint of HarperCollins Publishers

FOR MY BROTHER AND SISTER.
THIS IS ALL YOUR FAULT.

Now Entering Addamsville
Text and illustrations copyright © 2019 by Francesca Zappia

The text of this book is set in Janson MT. Book design by Sylvie Le Floc'h

Library of Congress Cataloging-in-Publication Data

Names: Zappia, Francesca, author.
Title: Now entering Addamsville / Francesca Zappia.
Description: First edition. | New York, NY : Greenwillow Books, an imprint of
  HarperCollins Publishers, [2019] | Summary: "Zora Novak is framed for a crime she
  didn't commit—in a town obsessed with ghosts, will she be able to find the culprit and
  clear her name before it's too late?"— Provided by publisher.
Identifiers: LCCN 2019016991 | ISBN 9780062935274 (hardback)
Subjects: | CYAC: Psychic ability—Fiction. | Murder—Fiction. | Ghosts—Fiction. |
  Haunted places—Fiction. | Mystery and detective stories.
Classification: LCC PZ7.1.Z36 Now 2019 | DDC [Fic]—dc23
  LC record available at https://lccn.loc.gov/2019016991

19 20 21 22 23 PC/LSCH 10 9 8 7 6 5 4 3 2 1
First Edition
Greenwillow Books

There are mysteries within mystery, gods above gods.
We have our gods, they have theirs.
That's what is called infinity.
—Jean Cocteau, *The Infernal Machine*

"That wasn't any act of God.
That was an act of pure human fuckery."
—from Stephen King's *The Stand*

HAL-LORELEI-MADS

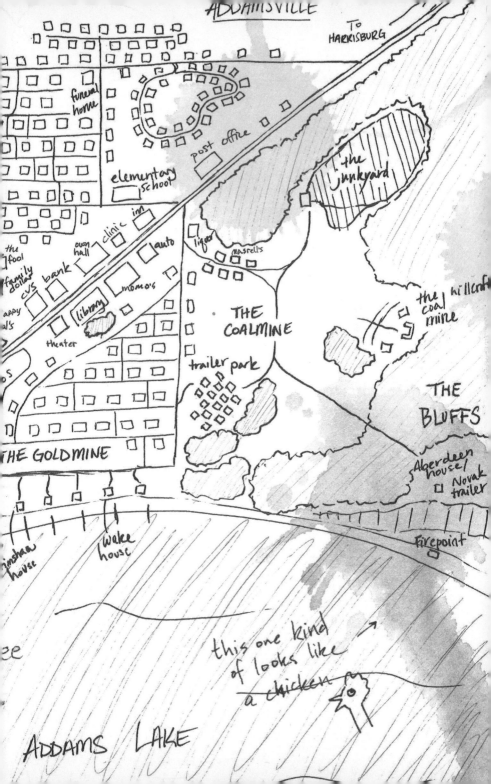

1

George Masrell's house went up in flames at 2:59 a.m. on a frost-tipped October morning. Masrell was eighty, lived alone on the northeast side of town, and spent his days cleaning the bathrooms at Addamsville High. He was liked in the way outdoor art installations are liked: for his quirks and his reliable permanence.

His permanence ended while Addamsville slept. In an hour or two, news crews would arrive, suburbanites would wake for their morning routines, and stories would begin to form. How it happened. Why it happened. Whether or not Masrell would—or was already—haunting the ashes of his house or the hallways of the high school, because Addamsville was so obsessed with its ghosts it couldn't even hold off for a couple of hours after an old man died.

I was the first one to know something had happened, because at 2:55 that morning, all the ghosts in town looked to the northeast, toward Masrell's house. In the street and in yards, peering out windows and patrolling the sidewalks. They stopped. They turned. They stared. Mom had always told me to pay attention when the ghosts reacted, because they rarely reacted to things in our world but they always reacted to things in theirs. I paused in the driveway, skin crawling on the back of my neck.

Then I heard footsteps coming toward me, and a faint voice said, "Zora?"

It was 2:56 when I jumped inside a plastic garbage can to hide from my cousin.

I stifled my breath with the fraying hood of my sweatshirt so I could track her footsteps coming toward me. The can had wheels on one side and wasn't designed to hold a hundred and sixty pounds of living human on a sloped driveway, so I had to shift on the damp bag of trash to keep the whole thing from tipping over. The smell stung my nose. Bootheels tapped lightly on the asphalt. She, like everyone else in town, couldn't see our spectral neighbors and wouldn't have noticed anything was wrong.

"Zora?" Her whisper trailed through the cold darkness. I pressed my lips together to keep the swearing and the gagging inside. Trust *her* to be out at this time of the morning, doing her research. The footsteps moved around the can and stopped. The strap of her backpack rustled against her peacoat. "Zora? Are you—please don't tell me you got in there."

She would never hide in the trash, the elitist. She only hid in luxury cars and walk-in closets.

She sighed, paused, and then said somewhat reluctantly, "I'm on my period and my mom brought out the bathroom garbage today."

I shot off the bag. The can tilted on its wheels, spun, and crashed down the driveway, spilling me out on the asphalt with a disgraceful squawk. The black trash bag tangled around my legs. I kicked it away, growling, as I got my bearings and scrambled to my feet.

"Gross!" I hissed at her. "So gross!"

Artemis put her hands on her hips and gave me her best look of disapproval. Her shiny blond hair was pulled back in a stick-straight ponytail, and her eyes looked like black pools in the automatic light above her garage. I glanced up at the towering Victorian—none of the lights had come on inside at the sound of the disturbance, thankfully, which meant my Aunt Greta was still asleep. The ghosts had disappeared from the driveway and the yard.

"Periods are not gross," Artemis said. "They're natural. And the waste has to go somewhere."

"I have them, too, and I say they're gross."

"Why are you hiding in our garbage cans? You're not rooting through our garbage, are you? If you need food or something, just *ask*, my mom isn't as bad as you think—"

"Oh my god, how poor do you think I am?" I pulled my messenger bag back into place on my shoulder, swiped the trash water off the flap, and began backing down the driveway. I never felt grungier than when I was standing next to Artemis, and soaking in garbage did not help. "I don't need to dig in your trash. And if you tell your mom I was here, I'll cut all your hair off. I know where you sleep."

She rolled her eyes and followed me. I walked faster. Artemis and her mother lived at the top of a hill on the southwest side, where they could oversee all parts of Addamsville: the town to the north, the woods to the west, the bluffs and the mines to the east, and Addams Lake to the south. This meant their twisting driveway, descending through the broad maples and oaks that dotted their front lawn, made my escape from Artemis more difficult than I would have liked. The ghosts had all trailed to the street, their forms shivering and disappearing into the shadows of houses and trees. Hiding from something I hadn't seen yet.

"Why are you out so early in the morning?" Artemis asked, tailing me as I dipped onto the lawn and skirted around a particularly gnarly maple tree. "Why were you all the way up at my house? And where is your car? Are you hunting again? I've been trying to talk to you about that—I know what happened was awful, but this is so important, and if you're back on the hunt, I can help you even better than before."

I didn't say anything. She could follow me for a while, at least as long as we were on the safe streets lit by warm wrought-iron lampposts, but once we hit the east side of town, her propriety would keep her from going any farther. We reached the sidewalk and I turned east.

"This is kind of creepy, Zora, you know that? What are you *doing*? If you're hunting, you should have told me. You shouldn't do it by yourself. People might think you're stealing. You aren't stealing, are you?"

My shoulders prickled. I'd been very careful about what hours of the morning I conducted my business. From two to four a.m., Addamsville was as silent as it would ever get, inhabited only by the dead, and since the weather had taken a turn, the hours and my freedom to roam unnoticed grew longer. If people caught me skulking around when it was dark, of course they would think I was doing something illegal—I was Zora Novak, after all, arsonist and delinquent.

"Zora, come on, I don't want to call the police on you."

I stopped, teeth clenched together, and turned. She stopped, too, and for the first time that night she met my stare with a look of trepidation. Besides our height, the only similarity between us was our eyes, and I'd spent a lot of time learning how to make mine as terrifying as possible. Even when I tried to soften my expression, it didn't always work. *Ten, nine, eight, seven, six, five, four, three, two, one.* "I wasn't going to break into your house. I wasn't stealing from anyone. And I'm *not* hunting."

Her chin turtled into her cashmere scarf. "Then what were you doing?"

"You're not going to believe me if I tell you."

"I might. I believe a lot of things, after all." She held up the Moleskine notebook she'd been carrying under one arm. It was the notebook she always wrote in, the one that held all of Addamsville's stories.

"Why are *you* out this early?" I asked. "Are *you* hunting alone?"

"Kind of. Not hunting, exactly, just researching. I wanted to check a few locations before the *Dead Men Walking* crew gets here tomorrow." She checked her phone. "Well, today, I guess. I don't know where they're filming, and I wanted to make sure the hot spots were safe for them. It's not going to do anyone any good if they run into a firestarter while they're here. Now will you please tell me what you're doing?"

I thought of not telling her. Going home to my sister and a shower and what little sleep I could get before school. Artemis wouldn't call the cops on me, whether or not she knew why I was out here. She wasn't a troublemaker, and she wasn't one to report troublemakers, especially me. She kept her nose deep in her ghost research and minded her own business.

But I had no doubt she would tell her mother, and that was worse than her calling the cops.

"The mums by your front porch looked ratty," I said.

"So?"

I sighed, undid the flap of my messenger bag, and turned it upside down. Flower trimmings scattered to the sidewalk along with a few crumpled geometry worksheets, an empty light bulb package, and a handful of pens. I picked up the pens, the worksheet, and the cardboard packaging and shoved them back into the bag.

Artemis's eyebrows knotted in confusion. "You pruned our mums?"

"They looked ratty," I repeated, glancing around. Almost all the ghosts were gone. "Will you leave me alone now?"

"But—why—" Then her expression lifted, and a manicured finger shot out to point at me. "It's you! You're the one who's been going around fixing things for people and cleaning their yards and—"

"Keep it down!" I darted toward her, hoping to shut her up; my sudden movement seemed to do the trick. The old Victorian houses on her street were all far back from the road and hidden by trees, so at least there was no one around to hear us. "Don't tell anyone! You'll get me arrested."

Artemis's brows furrowed again. "Is this supposed to be some kind of repentance?" she asked, head cocked with a historian's curiosity. "For what? You didn't set the fires a year ago. And besides, people won't forgive you if they don't know you're the one doing all the nice things for them."

"I tried asking," I said, "but surprise, nobody wants help from a Novak. Is that enough explanation for you? Go away." I flicked my hand, peppering her with the garbage water, and started east again.

Bootsteps clopped up the sidewalk behind me.

"Zora, wait! The hunting—Addamsville needs more help than just pruned mums—"

I spun, the old anger bubbling in my throat. She didn't understand how this worked, between her family and mine. She didn't understand what hunting firestarters took from you. And she didn't understand me.

The northeast sky stopped me. A pillar of smoke curled into the air, visible only because of the floodlights of the distant junkyard polluting the dark behind it. Artemis stopped, too, her hand inches from my arm.

"What is that?" she asked.

There was only one thing it could be. I had never set a fire that gave off that much smoke, but I'd seen it on television and in pictures. It spilled black and angry from the doors and windows of houses while their roofs caved in and their walls cracked. It was the fire of buildings being devoured. My heart skittered into the lowest reaches of my chest. The blistering heat. The deadly light. The stumps on my ring and pinkie fingers of my right hand ached under their prosthetics.

The wail of a fire truck started on the opposite side of town.

I took off. Away from Artemis, away from the wide-open spaces where I might be seen. Had I been thinking straight at the time, I might have turned to Artemis and calmly confirmed her as my alibi. I might not have immediately run away from her. I might have paid more attention to the ghosts, because for them all to disappear as they had meant there was something very wrong going on in their world. It meant there was a firestarter nearby.

But I never thought straight when it came to fire. Losing two fingers because of it will do that to you.

So I ran until I was alone, until I met the protective covering of the trees and hills of the east side, where the trailer park nestled quietly in the early morning. There were no dead here, though there should have been. They'd made themselves scarce. I hiked up the curving trail to the top of the bluffs to find the Novak trailer sitting dark and still. Artemis hadn't followed.

The trees hid the town from here, but sirens still rang in my ears. They'd rattle in my head until six a.m., when I pretended to wake up and found my sister Sadie watching the news. Milk from her cereal spoon dripped unnoticed onto her thick afghan. The reporter standing before the blackened ruins of Masrell's house detailed the two-and-a-half-hour struggle of the firefighters who extinguished the inferno and the unfortunate scene they'd found inside.

George Masrell was dead. The fire had burned too fast and too hot to have started accidentally. The police were now looking for an arsonist.

The people of Addamsville would know what this meant. Who had a record of setting fires? Who had shown disregard and even outright disdain for other locals in the past? Who might have had a slight beef with George Masrell because he yelled at her for dumping cold coffee in the school trash a couple of times?

I'd been the center of an Addamsville story before, but never like this.

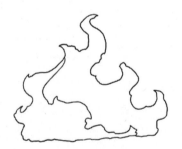

2

Addamsville was a small town where everyone knew everyone, and everyone's parents knew everyone else's parents, and grandparents, and great grandparents, and all the way back to the founding of the town at the dawn of mankind. We were big enough for our own movie theater, a CVS pharmacy, and a dog park, otherwise known as the Happiest Place on Earth. There was a poor part of town and a rich part of town, and one part never let the other forget where it stood. If you had been here long enough, your last name was a status symbol. It was currency.

I was a Novak, and we paid in blood money.

Our trailer was the only one in town not in the trailer park. Sadie told me it was once, before I was born, but then Mom got tired of our neighbors and worked some magic to get it moved to the bluffs, where we could hide in the trees and on clear days look down at Addams Lake. When the town council tried to get Mom to move it back, they found Dad standing by the front door, leaning on his wood axe and chomping what looked like a lot of tobacco but was actually a cheek of Sour Apple Big League Chew, and Mom squatting on top of the trailer.

I like to imagine that was what frightened them off: Mom on the roof like an evil crow, dark hair damp with early spring mist, black eyes flashing in the gloom of the trees. Maybe they didn't see her until she moved.

It was only a scare tactic, of course, but Mom was known around town as a weirdo anyway, so the story grew. She was a witch. She saw ghosts. No one really believed that, and she didn't want them to, because it was true. I used to walk with her to Momo's General Store at town center, where she'd explain the dead to me and buy me fresh-sliced Colby cheese to eat on the way home, and the owner, Maurice Moseley, looked at us like we'd crawled out of the sewers. There and back, passersby stared at Mom as we walked. *There's that Dasree Novak,* they'd say. *Get the children away before she steals their youth.*

Mom was already famous. The story of Mom and Aunt Greta, the Aberdeen girls, who disappeared in Black Creek Woods as children and returned months later unharmed and without memories, was one of the jewels in Addamsville's crown of creepy tales. As an adult, Mom often wandered the town at night. Hunting, but no one knew that. She didn't have friends. She only had us. When she went missing in the woods the second time, a lot of people said they felt terrible for us and hoped she came back safe, but I think they expected it out of her.

Dad was a little better. He didn't see ghosts and no one thought he did, and while his marriage to Mom planted doubt in plenty of minds, his charm let him wiggle past it. Even if you started out on the wrong side of unsure about him, by the end of the conversation he'd have you handing over your wallet and keys for safekeeping. Despite the questionable reputations of the Novaks who had lived in Addamsville before us, most people considered Dad a pretty nice guy.

That was because no one realized he was also the slickest thief east of the Mississippi, and his fingers were stickier than flypaper in June. That got out a year after Mom's second disappearance, when I was fifteen and he was sent to prison for an elaborate Ponzi scheme, and any tolerance or sympathy our family might have found burned up in the blazing inferno of town judgment.

So then you had me and Sadie. Sadie, five years older, had gone through high school as Sadie, Queen of the Undying and leader of the Birdies, the local gang of juvenile delinquents. She still had her favorite pair of combat boots, though they hadn't seen the light of day in many a moon. Like Mom, Sadie scared most people who looked at her just by the soulless depths of her eyes, and unlike Dad, she owned a temper that could raze small buildings.

Now her hair was brown instead of black, and she kept it cut to her chin. She liked afghans, cheap drugstore reading glasses, and sweatpants that had words like TOUGH and FUN stenciled across the butt. She had never seen ghosts or firestarters, and Mom had never told her about them. She worked in Harrisburg, the larger town about thirty minutes to the northeast. People in Harrisburg didn't care about the families of Addamsville, though Lazarus and Dasree Novak's names came up occasionally, and Sadie had to deflect interest before someone made too many connections.

"I love our parents, really," she told me one night as her unquenchable anger battled her need for sleep over her bowl of instant ramen, "but Jesus, all my good customers will leave if they find out who we are. I'll end up cutting hair for the people who run true-crime podcasts."

I was born *Sadie 2.0: Zora Edition.* I stole her dye and colored a fat swatch of my hair platinum blonde. I found a chain to wear around my wrist so I clanked when I walked. I annoyed her until she finally taught me how to do makeup like hers. I learned how to turn my eyes into soul-sucking pits of terror. On top of all that, I could see the dead, and Mom knew it. She taught me what they were. How they worked. She taught me that it was her job to protect the living and the dead against firestarters, the creatures that killed with fire and fed off the human spirit. I wasn't allowed to tell Dad or Sadie about this, because they wouldn't understand.

I improved on Sadie in other ways, too. I mean, if you want to use the word *improved*. You could also call it evolving further into the Novak stereotype. I was taller, I was smarter, and I was angrier.

And when your mom disappears, your dad goes to jail, and the whole town hates you on sight, sometimes you get it in your head to start doing stupid things to ease that anger.

Stupid things like hunting firestarters alone.

3

The morning of the Masrell fire, I arrived at school smelling vaguely of water that has been sitting too long on the trash from a teenage girl's bathroom. There had been no time for a shower after Sadie saw the news; she spent the next hour freaking out, trying to get ready for work at the same time she grilled me about where I had been.

"You were out again, weren't you?" she'd said, combing frantically at the tangles on the ends of her hair, working her way up the strands. "You didn't take the Chevelle, but I know you were, because otherwise you'd be yelling about how you were asleep the whole time."

I could have pointed out that there was no way she could ever really know because she slept like a rock, but she was right, so all I said was, "When it happened, I was with Artemis. I have an alibi."

"With Artemis? Like, our cousin Artemis?"

"Do you know another Artemis?"

"What were you doing?"

"Trying to get away from her. I swear I didn't do anything. I wasn't even near Masrell's house."

Sadie had given me a skeptical look, then seemed to remember that she still had her reading glasses on and tossed them onto the countertop in our trailer's kitchen nook before she reached for her shoes. "The police are going to be looking for the person who did this—"

"I know, I heard the television."

"—which means they're going to want to talk to you. Tell them the truth—"

"*Yes*, that's what I was already planning to do."

"—because if they find out you're lying, it's only going to be worse. Okay? Ugh, that stupid TV crew coming here today; their fans are going to be all over the place, and they'll make this fire even bigger news than it would have been otherwise. *And* Dad is coming home soon. What's he going to say when he finds out?" She had stopped with only one shoe on and rubbed her forehead. "He shouldn't have to deal with this now, not so soon after getting out—"

I didn't know why she was protecting him; it was partially his fault the town would blame this on us. But Sadie's steamroller tendencies only got worse when let loose, and they were already making me grind my teeth. I couldn't afford to be angry, so I said, "He won't have to deal with it, because I didn't do anything. If I have to talk to the cops I will, and I'll tell them the truth. It's not difficult. Go to work and chill out."

"Chill out" wasn't in Sadie's vocabulary, especially if she was outside the trailer, but she did relent and leave for Harrisburg. That left me to cover myself in deodorant and dollar-store body spray and head to school, knowing there was no way on god's green earth I'd be overlooked by any police officer.

Addamsville sits in a curved basin of green hills in southern Indiana, bordered to the east by the bluffs and to the west by the thick crush of Black Creek Woods, which skirt the base of Piper Mountain. Handack Street and Valleywine Road, the two roads into town, intersect at a jackknife, making an arrowhead that points south toward the blue expanse of Addams Lake. The side streets crisscross in a neat little lattice pattern, littered with cute tourist shops and local landmarks. Toss a rock and you'll hit a historical house. In the winter, the homeowners compete to see who has the best Christmas light display. In the spring, families in their Sunday best crawl from their homes like the undead to talk about the weather. In the summer, kids develop sunburns while splashing around in the lake. And now, in the fall, the trees turn all shades of gold and red, and the haunted hayride goes up in the Denfords' cornfield. To the tourists, Addamsville was a pretty painting on the wall, and all its ugly parts had been cropped out of the frame.

My mom's 1970 Chevelle, prowling the streets like a rusty shadow, destroyed the ambiance nicely.

This wasn't any black-and-white 1970 Chevelle. This was *Dasree Novak's* 1970 Chevelle, and everyone knew it. Pitch-black with two thick white stripes running down the hood. Rust eating at its underbelly. Growling like an angry alligator. Mom had done something to it to make it resistant to fire—like Mom and me—and she'd made it her first weapon against firestarters. I had no idea what she'd done to it, or how, but I imagined it added to the town's mystique for the tourists. Look, the haunted Chevelle! Run if you see it—the driver hates tourists.

There was once a time when the Chevelle made me fiercely happy, like I was ripping an oily, ragged hole in that pretty painting. But in the past year, the Chevelle had felt more like a beacon drawing all eyes to me wherever I went, from both the living and the dead. I needed a car, though, and Sadie wouldn't let me drive her old Camry, we didn't have any other vehicles, and none of us would ever in a million years sell or trade it in. It was the one beloved thing of Mom's we still had.

A police cruiser with a dent in the fender sat outside the front entrance of the high school, so I curled around the parking lot and hid the Chevelle on the other side, between the gym and the football field. A quarterback with an Addamsville jersey circa 1960 watched me from the other side of the field's chain-link fence, but the two linebackers normally with him were gone. The bell for first period had already rung; the hallways were empty, and though I managed to keep my face straight, my pulse jumped and my battered coffee thermos rattled in my hand. Teenagers texting on iPhones passed, unsuspecting, by teenagers listening to Walkmans. George Masrell had yelled at me just yesterday for dumping my coffee in the trash can outside the janitor's office. He'd had a spot on his collar and he smelled like the soap from the restrooms. He was dead now.

I went to the janitor's office to check. The only ghost there was old Principal Harris, fading around the edges like a blurry photo, looking down the English hallway. He turned to stare at me, the way they all did, as if he expected something from me.

"Do you know what happened to Masrell?" I asked.

Principal Harris floated a little to the left, then back. Trying to figure out what had happened was difficult when your suspects couldn't communicate. I left the good principal there and hurried on.

For the past few years I had a litany of excuses prepared for tardiness to class. Not because I was out hunting firestarters, though; I just thought school was stupid. I'd forgotten them all by the time I made it to first period geometry, and that left me standing in the doorway with twenty-eight pairs of eyes on me. Mr. Gerwijk paused midsentence at the whiteboard, his mouth slightly open.

"What?" I snapped.

"Zora," Gerwijk said, "you were called to the office several minutes ago."

At least I still had my sunglasses on. Fear shows in the eyes.

There's no point walking slowly to your doom; if you know it's coming, you might as well jump into the dragon's mouth. As I passed the library, one of the student aides stepped out carrying a stack of books and saw me. She squeaked and dropped the books in her rush to get back through the library doors.

"Are you serious?" I yelled back to her.

I'd never set anything on fire. Firestarters did. Creatures with bodies like black tar, sharp claws and bird talons, horns curving over their heads and red pinpricks for eyes. If they were allowed to run free for too long, they could possess human bodies and hide inside them. The easiest way to find a firestarter was to pay attention when the ghosts acted strangely—or to follow the fires. After you found them, the solution was straightforward: lure them into the open, run them over with the Chevelle, and chop their heads off. Incapacitate, behead. It was the way Mom had done it, so it was the way I did it.

But one time last year, just *one time*, I let a firestarter get the better of me. I was found unconscious in the Denfords' cornfield with two fingers cut off and my head sliced open, and half the field was up in flames. From then on it was Zora Novak, arsonist, and no one in Addamsville would believe differently.

I stomped on to the office. If there was another firestarter in town, I had more to worry about than just clearing my name.

Principal Sutherland—the current, living principal—stood by the administrative assistant's desk in the front office with two of Addamsville's three cops, one stout and brown-skinned and one lanky and pale. They saw me through the office windows before I walked in, and I knew, I *knew*, I was right screwed.

"Stormin' Norman and Captain Jack," I said as I pushed my way through the office doors. "What can I help you gentlemen with?"

Norm Newall—the short, grumpy cop with the little notebook—and Jack Lansing—the tall, red-cheeked one—both shuffled on the spot, but for different reasons. One in obvious impending frustration, the other in discomfort.

"Enough, Miss Novak," Principal Sutherland said. I hadn't even been flippant. "Officers Newall and Lansing would like to speak to you. You'll go into my office. Since you're eighteen, you don't need a parent or guardian present."

I didn't move. "Speak to me about what?"

Here's a thing about cops: *always* make them tell you what they're coming after you for. Never guess. It makes you seem more suspicious.

"Don't play with us, Novak," said Norm. "Haven't you seen the news today?"

"Which part?"

"About George Masrell," Jack said, and Norm scowled at him.

"Please, into my office." Principal Sutherland's tone was short.

I pushed my sunglasses on top of my head—maybe some fear would make them believe me—as I followed them into the office

"We all know you like to set fires on public property," Norm said to me as I dropped into a straight-backed chair in front of Principal Sutherland's desk. Norm and Jack flanked the door. "We haven't had an arson like this in town for plenty long enough, and lines can be drawn."

"I didn't set any fires," I said.

All three adults gave me that *look*, the one that says they know you're full of it. They had no real evidence I set any of the fires from the last firestarter, but they were damn sure the cornfield had been my doing, and my amputated fingers were all the evidence they needed.

I rubbed my forehead. "Seriously. Even if I had done it then—which I didn't—I wouldn't do it now." I held up my right hand. I wore the black gloves on both hands, but the ring and pinkie fingers on my right stood up, stiff and odd, when the other fingers curled. "I don't do fire."

The *look* softened, but not a lot. People feel sorry for you when two of your fingers get cut off and your head gets sliced open, but they don't feel too sorry if they think it was your fault.

"We're not accusin' you of anything, Zora," Jack said, "but we've been checkin' the school security tapes for the past few hours, and you're the last person Mr. Masrell talked to on 'em. Outside the janitor's office yesterday, after school let out."

"Yes, I did. He was yelling at me for throwing away coffee and making the hallway smell like Starbucks. I don't even drink Starbucks. Too expensive."

"And you yelled back?"

"Of course I did! He was being a jerk."

"Was he only yellin' at you about the coffee, Zora?" Jack said. "Seems like a lot to get that angry over."

"All he yelled about was coffee," I said, "but no, he was probably angry at me about, like, the fact that I exist."

"What do you mean?"

"My dad took all his money, like he did to everyone else in this town. You might have heard about it. Was a bit of a headline."

Okay, that was a little sarcastic.

Norm stood in stony silence. Jack looked uncomfortable. Dad was in prison, so it wasn't like they could do anything else to him.

Finally Norm said, "Can you tell us what you did from

the time you spoke to Mr. Masrell yesterday to the time you arrived at school this morning?"

Well, here it was.

"After the coffee thing, I left school and went to the dog park for a while. Then I went to work for the rest of the night. Captain Jack here knows—he stopped by for the Chocolate Killer Sundae."

Jack beamed. Norm glared at him.

"It's fall," Norm said. "What are you doing getting ice cream? It's too cold."

"They only serve it till the end of October." Jack shrugged. "Gotta get it while it's there."

Norm made a noise of discontent and turned back to me. "Why were you at the dog park?"

I shifted in my seat and crossed my arms. "Because I like dogs."

"What time did you leave there?"

"Around five."

"And when did you get to work?"

"Five ten."

"Was there anyone there who can confirm that?"

"Yeah, everyone else working that night. Hal, Mads, Lorelei. They're all working tonight, too. And Bach was there. He ordered his usual; we talked for a bit. Ask him."

"Bach. Forester's Bach? You friends with him?"

"We don't hang out."

"What about after work?"

"I went home and watched *Cheers*." I paused for a heartbeat, glancing between Jack and Norm, thinking how I probably still smelled like trash. "Then I waited until Sadie fell asleep, then went out. I was on the west side of town until three a.m., fixing porch lights and pruning flowers. Around three I went home and went to bed. My alarm went off this morning, I ate breakfast, got dressed, and came to school."

All three adults stared.

"Excuse me?" Norm said. "You admit you were out last night?"

"You know the person who's been going around fixing things for people overnight? Broken fences, lights, things like that? That's me."

Norm and Jack looked at each other. "Can anyone confirm this?

"My cousin Artemis."

"Greta's daughter?"

"Do you know another Artemis?" I snapped, then took a sharp breath and forced down my rising annoyance. "I was passing her house as she came home from some ghost hunt. We talked for a bit and noticed the fire—we could see it. I can give you a list of all the things I did last night, and you can go check with the owners of the houses. I promise you I couldn't have been on the east side."

Norm looked at Principal Sutherland. "I'll have them call her down," she said, ducking out of the room to tell the office assistant, then returning.

"Let's assume you're telling the truth for now," Norm said. "Why were you late getting here today?"

I shrugged. "Sadie kept me. You know, giving me a speech about being a good person and doing the right things."

"Speakin' of your sister," Jack said, "we've tried contacting her. Do you know when she'll be home?"

"She gets off work around five today, but she might go out with her boyfriend after that."

"Who's her boyfriend?"

"Grim."

Norm and Jack both looked confused for a moment. Then Norm scowled. Jack snapped his fingers and said, "You mean Gavin Grimshaw?"

"That's the one."

A look flashed across Norm's face that made me suspect Grim was another of their suspects. If an eerie, overcast day could take human form, it would look a lot like Grim. Despite all his melancholy, Grimmie wasn't dangerous. Weird for sure, but docile as a rag doll and sweet as all get out. And he was one of the few people who could get Sadie out of the trailer.

"Could you tell me your sister's or Mr. Grimshaw's whereabouts yesterday evening?" Norm said.

Even Sadie wasn't immune to this witch hunt. Although she, too, had been known to commit the occasional misdemeanor, Grim was pure as a dove.

"I don't know what they were doing while I was at work," I said, "but after that they watched TV with me. They passed out before I did. Around nine thirty." I folded my arms and clenched my jaw to keep everything else inside. I wanted to say so many things. I wanted words to make them understand. That I would never do something like this, and neither would Sadie. That despite what happened to Mom, and what Dad did afterward, Sadie and I weren't bad people.

No anger or ranting or threat would make them believe it. So I pushed down the burn in my chest, forced myself to unfold my arms, and said, "I didn't like him very much, but I'm sorry this happened to Mr. Masrell. I didn't have anything to do with it. I don't like fire now"—my voice shook—"and I don't want to hurt people."

They stonewalled me, all three of them, with faces that said clearly that my past was still counting against me. I understood why I was their first suspect. I'd be my first suspect, too, if I was running the case. But did they have to make it so obvious they were coming after me because I was *me?*

Finally Norm broke the silence. "Do you know anyone else who might have done this, or had a problem with Masrell?"

Anyone who had a problem with Masrell and could make

all the ghosts on a street flee for cover?

"As far as I know, nobody's set a house on fire since Hermit Forester," I said. "Have you talked to him yet?"

Jack's expression turned sour. That was all the answer I needed.

"We're going to find out who did this," Norm said, flipping his notebook closed and stuffing it in his breast pocket. "A man died last night, and all this town can talk about is ghost hunters and television shows. If you know or find out anything about what happened, you come tell us. Understand? *Anything.*"

"Understood."

"I need to speak to the officers now, Zora," Principal Sutherland said. "I want you to go straight back to first period. If you don't, I will find out, and you'll have detention for the rest of the semester."

I stopped outside the office with my skin tingling. Artemis was in the waiting area. Her phone was open on her lap and her fingers flipped through the pages of her Moleskine notebook. Of course she couldn't use the regular-ass spiral notebooks. She had to get the pretty, expensive ones for her ghost research.

She didn't look tired at all. She looked like a princess with a fairy godmother who could magic her into made-up cleanliness every morning.

"Hey, slugger, you're up."

She looked at me. She had more fat on her cheeks than I did, but Dad always said he could see the family resemblance because we both kind of looked like our moms. The Aberdeen girls.

Her pretty cherubic face sank into a scowl. "What did you tell them about last night?"

I glanced around; the office assistant was in the break room, making coffee.

"I told them the truth. They want to confirm with you. And probably talk to you because you're into death, or whatever."

"I'm not *into death*." Any of the sympathy that had tempered Artemis's reactions to me this morning was gone. "I'm into uncovering the history of this town, you effing raccoon." She stood and snapped her notebook shut.

"You still say 'effing'?"

Artemis rolled her eyes and strode past me. "I don't have time for this. The *Dead Men Walking* crew is coming this afternoon, and I have about a million things I need to put together before they get here. I know you don't care about protecting anyone, but I do."

"They're still coming? After Masrell?"

"Of course. You think my mom would stop a nationally aired television show from filming in town?"

So Sadie was right—they were still going to bring *Dead Men Walking* here, which meant the show's fans would come, too, and the story of Masrell's murder would spread. The last time firestarter attacks had hit headlines this big was thirty years ago, when Hermit Forester was still out and active.

"Whatever." I pushed the office door open. "See you, buttface."

"You're the worst," Artemis called back.

Instead of going straight back to class, I stopped in the restroom and shut myself in the third stall. The first stall was occupied by a blank-faced girl in a floral-print dress, staring into the toilet and flickering at her edges. I needed the second stall as a buffer.

If the police thought Artemis might know something more about me than where I'd been last night, they were really scraping the bottom of the barrel. Artemis and I were branches of a tree that had forked off in wildly different directions. Sometimes we weren't part of the same tree at all. Sometimes I thought maybe we weren't even the same species.

Artemis was *into death*, but not the way I'd implied. She'd been trained by her mother to help me hunt the way Aunt Greta had once helped my mom, though she could only sense the presence of ghosts, not see them. She'd been mentioned on the local news a few times for her research into historical sites around Addamsville and Harrisburg. Just looking at her, with her cashmere scarves and sleek, shiny hair and designer boots, you'd never guess she was into the supernatural at all. She looked more like a social media star.

No one would ever suspect Artemis of arson, despite that she'd been out last night, too. Even if they never found any evidence I'd set the fire at Masrell's house, they'd still suspect me, because *fire* and *Novak* were the only things most people knew about me. They never tried to dig deeper, even when I went straight up to their doors and asked if they'd like me to show them myself.

I slumped against the scuffed stall wall. A rising tension headache pounded in my temple. Artemis was right. Protecting people was more important than what the town thought of me. It was exactly what Mom would have said, if she was around. I uncurled my right hand; only then did the prosthetics look natural under the glove. If Mom was around, I wouldn't have lost any fingers. If Mom was around, she could tell me how to handle all of this, what to say, where to start.

But it had been five years since she disappeared. There was no telling when she would come back, which meant I had to deal with this firestarter myself before it hurt anyone else.

4

After a day of eavesdropping, I'd heard three decent theories about who had set the fire—besides myself—but only one of them was close to right.

The first was Pastor Keller. I totally believed Pastor Keller might emerge from Black Creek Church one day to burn people with the fires of heaven and cleanse them for their sins, but even if he was possessed by a firestarter, I'd seen him at 2:20 that morning, digging around in his trash with his usual audience of ghosts. The guy threw his glasses away once a week, minimum. He lived in an old house behind the veterinarian, across town from George Masrell, and ghosts didn't hang out around firestarters.

The second suspects were the Birdies, who were on

people's lists for the same reason I was. They had a reputation for wrecking things. They weren't known for fires, though. They took baseball bats to mailboxes, graffitied concession stands, and once put dead bluegills in all the air ducts in the high school. None of them were possessed, either. I'd seen them around school, and they'd been just as interested in the rumors as anyone else, and causing no trouble with the ghosts.

The third suspect, and the one who came the closest, was Hermit Forester. Thirty years ago, the Foresters had lived in a mansion in the woods, bigger even than the Goldmine houses. One night the mansion caught on fire, killing the oldest son and sending the rest of the family to live in town while their house was rebuilt. Kids nicknamed them "the Firestarters," because it sounded close to "Foresters," and kids can be so clever sometimes.

While they were here, a rash of arsons swept through Addamsville, killing some teenagers, an auto mechanic, five people in the old town hall, and three more members of the Forester family. That left only one of them to return to the woods and the rebuilt mansion, suspected but never convicted of any crime. Hermit Forester holed himself up while Addamsville dealt with the fallout of what the media dubbed "the Firestarter Murders."

That was where Mom had gotten the name for the creatures. When I'd asked Jack and Norm if they'd talked to Hermit Forester, I hadn't been kidding. Forester wasn't a firestarter, but his assistant, Bach, was. The ghosts had pointed Mom toward Forester and Bach when she'd gone hunting for the culprits of the Firestarter Murders, but she couldn't get rid of them. Cutting off a firestarter's head would neutralize the threat it posed, but then you had a head. To get rid of it for good, you had to send it back through the entrance it used to get into Addamsville. Mom had never found Bach's entrance.

The fires had ended when Forester returned to his home in the woods, and in all the time I'd known Bach, he had never given off a whiff of danger. Mom had always said firestarters weren't inherently evil creatures; we were their prey, like any other animal relationship, and Bach was like a fox adopted by a pack of rabbits. He had killed in the past, and there was no forgiving him for that. But I wasn't sure he'd done this.

I sat in the Chevelle, tapping on the steering wheel while I waited for the parking lot to empty. One person was already dead. The firestarter that did it would be feeding on Masrell's ghost right now, and would continue to do so for as long as it was allowed to remain in Addamsville. With one dead under its belt, it would easily have enough power to possess someone else. I squeezed my prosthetics through my glove. It was already worse than the last one I'd taken out, which hadn't even killed one person.

I prowled through town with my gut doing somersaults.

Even the Chevelle's growling seemed a little subdued, like it knew where we were going and was trying to warn me what a bad idea it was.

George Masrell lived off a dirt road that trailed northeast, toward the junkyard. A long strand of trees had been planted to shield the junkyard and the east side from the tourists who drove into town on Valleywine Road.

I parked the Chevelle two streets away from Masrell's house so the engine wouldn't attract attention from the people still gathered outside. As I approached, my stomach turned over again, my hands tingled, and a small voice in the back of my head said *Get away get away get away from this place there was FIRE HERE.* I tucked my hands into my jacket pockets, curling my prosthetics around so they fit, and pushed on.

The ruin of the house, still slightly smoking, was visible from the end of the street. Police tape cordoned off the yard. The roof and half the outer wall had gone down, leaving a gaping, blackened corpse. Withered beams speared out of the rubble like broken bones. The smell was the worst part of it, the part that had all my hairs standing on end and made me want to run for the hills. Burned wood, burned rubber, burned plastic. *Fire lived here,* it said. *Fire destroyed here.*

A fire truck and a police cruiser sat by the curb. A few firefighters poked in the wreckage. One spoke with Chief Rivera. The Chief was a short lady with a heavy brown coat, dark hair up in a bun, and aviators hiding her eyes despite the heavy cloud cover. I had literally never seen her crack a smile, and she definitely wouldn't if she saw me lurking around, so I hunched my shoulders and ducked behind the cars lining the opposite side of the street.

I wasn't alone. People I didn't recognize loitered on the sidewalk. Some had their phones out. Some had camera bags. Some carried whole backpacks bursting with equipment. A few wore *Dead Men Walking* sweatshirts. There were only a handful of ghosts among them, and all hid near the houses, away from the street. They watched Masrell's. A host of blackbirds weighed down the power lines overhead, like vultures waiting for predators to vacate a recent kill. I hid myself near two women and a man wearing the sweatshirts.

The police knew this was arson and not just Masrell falling asleep with a lit cigarette. If they were interviewing me, they hadn't found much evidence, if any. They hadn't asked any specifics about fire, hadn't tried to find out if I knew what accelerants were used, nothing like that. Because they knew none *had* been used, just like in the Firestarter Murders. Those fires had burned hot and fast, and sometimes right in the middle of the day, in front of witnesses. No accelerants, because firestarters didn't need them. The house looked like it had burned for hours. There was barely a skeleton left.

One of the women from the group I'd hidden behind

glanced back at me once, then again. I didn't like the look, so I moved on to the next gathering of onlookers and positioned myself behind them and a car. Chief Rivera had finished talking to the firefighter and now paced around the heap that used to be the front porch.

She stepped on dry grass. Dry and brown from the uncharacteristic drought we'd had through the fall. I scanned the lawn in front and to the sides of the house. All dry, none burned. The trunks of the trees near the house didn't look as if they'd been touched by the fire, nor did the sides of the houses on either side of Masrell's. A fire that hot and that big, and nothing nearby had been burned. Another firestarter staple. The porch roof had squashed a few bushes, and the branches of those that peeked out from underneath waved in the breeze, rustling yellow leaves.

A firefighter stepped from the wreckage of the house. There was movement in the doorframe behind him. A man appeared, wearing a white T-shirt and boxer shorts. George Masrell. Potbellied and stick-limbed, wrinkles of skin pulling his face into a frown. Everything about him was slightly red, like an oven coil still glowing. There were ragged black holes where his eyes should have been. The firefighter stepped back into the house, right through him.

My gut lurched. Even ghosts who'd died in the most tragic accidents and the most gruesome murders appeared as whole as they'd been in life. They had color, and eyes. I saw ghosts like Masrell on a regular basis, but that never made it easier to look at them and know the remains of their spirits were being eaten away. There were twelve from the Firestarter Murders, nine I saw often: five town council members, on the lot where the old town hall once stood; the auto mechanic, in the middle of Elmwood Lane; Yvette Forester in the grocery store parking lot; Lenore Forester, under a beech tree in the neighborhood near the Goldmine; and Valerie Forester, the pale-haired sentinel of Valleywine Road.

Masrell turned toward me. I knew he sensed me there, the way all the ghosts did. He knew I could see him. *Which way,* I thought. *Which way is the one who killed you?* Ghosts couldn't speak, but they could still move their bodies, and the ghosts made by firestarters always knew where their predators lived. He faced me for a moment, and then he turned just slightly, toward the east, and he pointed. I followed his finger to a swatch of trees hiding the old coal mine.

I looked back, heart pounding, but Masrell was gone. I was sure he hadn't meant the junkyard or the bluffs: the junkyard was too far north, the bluffs too far south. The mine was possible; that place spawned ghost stories for a reason. And it was on the opposite side of town from Forester's house.

I turned to go, sure that my luck avoiding Chief Rivera would run out soon, and met the gaze of a woman standing thirty yards down the sidewalk. I froze on the spot. She was tall and blond and had eyes like the pits of hell.

Aunt Greta.

Greta Wake was what you got if a Greek statue had sex with the Williams-Sonoma catalog. She wore a green blouse under a neat white cardigan, white pants, and spring-mint Crocs that clopped as she started toward me. She was Artemis's evolved form, divine judgment in a woman's body, sainted protector of Addamsville, and the unspoken leader of the new town council.

Two men flanked her: Pastor Keller, with the cobwebs of Black Creek Church still hanging from his shoulders, and Buster Gates, the pig-faced owner of the junkyard. Both town council members. Neither big fans of the Novaks.

They were the ones I should have checked for before I visited the crime scene. Hindsight's 20/20.

"Zora Novak." Greta's voice was low, but it carried across the distance between us. "What are you doing here?"

The group of onlookers I'd hidden behind scooted out of her way. Running wasn't an option, so I planted myself where I was and stood to my full height.

"I figured if the cops were going to accuse me of something, I should find out exactly what I supposedly did." I gestured toward the house. There was no sign of Masrell or any other ghosts.

"And you thought it would be *wise* to show your face

here?" All three of them were on me now. It felt like they all loomed over me, even though I was taller than everyone but Buster. Greta put her hands on her hips. "George Masrell was a respected member of this community, one who your father cheated nearly into poverty—"

"Oh man, *poor*, that's like the worst thing to be!"

She powered right through me. "—and you think it's okay to come here? When the whole town has seen your family show hostility toward him?"

"Are you still talking about my dad, or do you mean when I yelled at Masrell about the coffee? Because he yelled at me *first*—"

"There is a history of bad blood between you, a known habit for starting dangerous fires, and clear motivation!"

I had trained myself well this past year, but Aunt Greta was my kryptonite. Forget ghosts, forget the people nearby; everything inside me went brittle when she was around, ready to shatter on first impact.

"Yes," I said through my teeth. "There's a whole Novak family mafia running the Addamsville underground. We get rid of anyone we don't like, and we do it in the most horrific ways possible." I put my hands on her hips to mirror her, and by the twitch in her cheek, she hadn't missed it. "We're *your* family, too, don't forget. The police talked to Artemis, you know."

That didn't seem to faze her. Aunt Greta shouldn't have been acting like this. She had helped Mom with the firestarters once, the way Artemis wanted to help me. She could sense them, too—she had to sense what was going on here.

Greta seemed to ignore it all, though. She and I stood toe-to-toe, and she smelled overwhelmingly of lavender.

"Yes, we share a family," she snapped back, head held high. "Which is why it's so important that I *stop* my family from trespassing on private property and getting their fingers cut off—"

"You old hag! I didn't do anything wrong, and I didn't hurt anyone!"

"Like hell you didn't." Buster stepped up. Color flushed his cheeks and forehead. His hands balled into fists the size of Christmas hams. "And your old man didn't take all our money, neither."

"Screw you, Buster," I snapped. "It's your own damn fault you bought into that scheme so hard. Thought it would help you get a Goldmine house, right?"

Buster inflated like a hot-air balloon. He'd been one of many to donate to Lazarus Novak's Fund for the Establishment of Historical Landmarks in Addamsville and was its biggest supporter until it all turned out to be a lie. But he, unlike George Masrell, would be more hurt by his stolen dignity than his stolen money.

Greta put a hand up, warding Buster off. "What would your mother say if she could hear you now?" Her voice was calm. "Justifying theft? Making flippant comments about a man's murder?"

Something in my jaw cracked. "I wouldn't know. She's not here."

"She would say this is not like you," Pastor Keller said, his voice deep and sad, his eyes tired. "She would say you've lost your way."

I threw my hands up. "Oh my *god*, you nutcase, what are you even talking about? You don't know my mom *or* me! You have no idea what she'd say, and you don't care! None of you do. You called her a witch when she was here, and when she went missing *you all* decided not to look for her." I turned to Greta again. "You're her *sister* and you didn't even care. You want to talk to me about making flippant comments? You treated her like *garbage*—you abandoned her—"

"Now, wait a second—" Buster started in.

Pastor Keller held up an accusing finger. "Young lady, this is—"

Aunt Greta stared at me, silent, as the two men spoke over each other, chastising and berating. She didn't have to say anything. My mother hung between us, that invisible tether, the one even she wouldn't dare cut.

"Hey! Hey, break it up!"

Chief Rivera came jogging across the street, her dark bun bouncing with her strides. Her aviators now hung on the breast pocket of her uniform. She planted herself in front of me and faced the three adults. Pastor Keller and Buster finally shut up.

"Is there a problem, Greta?" the Chief asked.

"I was asking why she was here," Greta said, clearly doing her best to control her anger.

"She was accusing me of setting the fire," I said. Greta's nostrils flared. The Chief glanced at me over her shoulder, then turned back.

"You three are threatening a minor. Not only a minor, Greta—your niece. The only person she ever hurt was herself. What's gotten into you? What would Dasree say?"

"Twice in one day my mom's name gets invoked," I said. "You'd think that meant someone here actually liked her."

Only Pastor Keller and Buster seemed to hear me, because they both shot looks my way. Greta only sniffed at Chief Rivera and pulled herself up a little higher.

"I need all three of you to calm down and step away," Rivera said.

"Abby, don't you think—"

"Step *away*, Greta."

Aunt Greta's eyes flashed. For all her bluster, she was scarier when she was silent, and she didn't say a word as she spun and clip-clopped back to her car. Buster Gates and Pastor Keller followed, Buster with a few choice words to Chief Rivera, Pastor Keller with a too-long look at me and a promise that he would pray for George Masrell.

Chief Rivera let out a weary sigh.

"What are you doing here, Zora?"

I leveled a quick glare at the onlookers nearby, then lowered my voice and said, "What's anyone else doing here?" I motioned to the tourists. "I wanted to see what was going on."

"You're not anyone else," she said. "With your family's reputation, you know that. And you're not a minor anymore, so be glad they didn't call me out on that. You know how this town gets with rumors. Until we can figure out what happened, I need you to keep your head down. Don't go causing any more trouble. Can you do that for me?"

"Yes, ma'am." Blowing up at Aunt Greta wouldn't help that sterling Novak reputation. I crossed my arms, tucking my hands into my armpits. "I just don't want to be blamed for this. Did Jack and Norm tell you about what I said? My alibi? Can't you—"

"The word already got out that you were the one fixing things. A lot of people are talking about—well . . ." Another pause. "I know your family, and I know you. I don't believe you'd do something like this, but I've got no evidence. You're a good kid. I'm going to do everything I can to make sure this town doesn't run away with its rumors. Okay?" She glanced at her watch. "Don't you have to get to work? Jack's always talking about those damn sundaes."

I did need to go home and change clothes. I looked over Chief Rivera's shoulder, where Greta, Buster, and Pastor Keller now stood by Greta's Lexus, clearly waiting for the Chief to finish talking to me.

"You let me worry about them," Chief Rivera said. "Go on now."

"Fine. Thanks."

"Thank me by staying out of trouble."

I stuffed my hands back into my pockets and retreated. I circled around the opposite end of the street to get back to the Chevelle.

Rivera must have seen what I had. Not Masrell's ghost, but the pristine yard, the way Masrell's house had burned so completely. She must have drawn the connection between the Firestarter Murders and this one.

But even she couldn't stand up to the town council if they decided I was the one who'd started the fire. What Greta said was gospel truth, and Pastor Keller and Buster had plenty of pull, too. Buster's lackeys were the kind of people who'd run you over with their trucks if you had a haircut they didn't like. Mom had always said the town's opinion of her wasn't as important as her responsibility to the dead, but this kind of opinion was going to interfere with hunting. If Greta said I was guilty, Addamsville would believe it, and my job would get a whole lot harder.

But Aunt Greta *knew.* She knew about Mom, and

firestarters, and ghosts. She was one of the Aberdeen Girls—
she knew strange things happened in Addamsville. She'd never
been overly friendly to me, never stopped by our trailer, never
invited us to their house, at least not since I was really little.
And she'd only gotten worse since Mom disappeared.

I'd just have to avoid her while I found the firestarter who
did this.

I stopped the Chevelle at the corner and looked back one
last time at the burned husk of the house. A man in a white
shirt stood among the black char.

5

I won't lie and say I took Chief Rivera's advice to lay low, because I'm me, and we all know better than that by now.

Happy Hal's Ice Cream Parlor had risen from the ashes of the old town hall. A bronze statue of Sylvester Hillcroft, the founder of Addamsville, stood at the tip of the jackknife at Valleywine and the Goldmine, the only reminder of the building. All five of the previous Addamsville town council members had died in the old town hall fire, and their spirits were said to wander the premises of Happy Hal's, searching for the hallways and rooms that no longer existed.

They didn't wander Happy Hal's. They stood at the base of the Hillcroft statue, eyeless and glazed red, feeding Bach and Hermit Forester, who had killed them.

From April to October, a red-and-white–striped awning invited customers to come on down and try Hal's Happy Summer Sundaes. It was a walk-up shop, a semicircle structure with a patio in the front. Customers ate on picnic benches beneath wide striped umbrellas. Four windows looked out along the curving wall of the shop, where employees waited to take orders, the ice cream machines on the countertops behind us. Inside the shop, hanging between the two middle windows, was a bronze bell with a pull string that we called "the Bell of Shame." It was pulled seldom, and usually by me.

We'd met the end of our season, but tourists are weird about ice cream in cold weather—especially when the ice cream place is supposedly haunted—and business hadn't slowed yet.

I pulled into the parking lot at 4:58 and yanked on my red polo. The foremost requirement of all Happy Hal's employees was a striped visor bearing our logo, so I scraped my hair up into a two-toned ponytail and tugged the visor on with a begrudging sigh. I checked that my gloves were securely on, then kicked my way through the employee entrance.

"And she appears—Lady Firestarter herself!"

Hal Haynes III stood at the soft-serve machine, swirling up a large chocolate chip freezie and shooting me a playful grin that said *please do not hurt me.* As usual, even when I was minutes early, I was still later than everyone else. A short line had formed outside the first window despite the chill in the autumn air, and Madhuri Bakshi was busy taking orders while Hal made the ice cream. Hal turned the freezie upside down to carry it to the window, to show the little boy outside that it wouldn't fall. The boy looked stunned.

"Ha ha," I said, moving past both of them to open the second window. "Sales are either going up or down tonight because I'm here, so either you're welcome or I'm sorry."

"So many rumors going around," Mads said, switching places with Hal so he could take the next customer. Her black ponytail swished over the Velcro clasp of her visor. "A lot of vultures circling."

I slid my window open. "Which vultures? The ones with cameras or the ones with money?"

"The ones with social media accounts," Mads replied.

A man moved from the end of the first line over to my window. I put on my customer service voice. "Welcome to Happy Hal's! What can I get for you?"

His eyes went first to my gloved hands resting on the countertop, then to Mads and Hal.

"Uh—can I get two large cookies 'n' cream freezies?"

"Sure, no problem."

I lined up next to Mads at the soft-serve machine.

"What did the vultures say?"

"It hardly matters at this point." Mads shook her head. "It's out, so—"

"What did they say?"

"That you totally did it," Hal chimed in cheerily. "That'll be eight fifty-two. Yeah, Zo, according to the Harrisburg news, the Novaks are some kind of mobster family and they're getting back at George Masrell for that stuff your dad did, and for you yelling at him. There's a video."

I slammed one of the freezie cups down. "Why would we be getting back at him for the Ponzi scheme? *We were the ones stealing* his *money!* What video is this? Someone show me."

"Get a smartphone," Mads said.

"Flip phones still work perfectly fine."

"I can show you, Zora."

A pale waif of a girl slid from Mads's shadow. I jumped high enough to drip cookies 'n' cream up my arm.

"Jesus, Lorelei."

"Sorry," Lorelei said. Her pale cheeks flushed with brilliant color. She had a habit of coming out of nowhere, but I don't think she meant to do it. You probably get pretty good at being quiet and sneaking around when your dad is pig-face-on-a-rampage Buster Gates. Only her ability to talk helped me pick her out from the actual ghosts. She pushed her glasses up her nose. "You c-can borrow my phone, if you want to see what got posted."

"Yeah, in a minute. Thanks." I cleaned up the mess and ran the cups back to the man at the window. "Twelve twenty-five, please."

"You didn't deliver them upside down," he said, looking smug. "I get them for free if you don't deliver them upside down, right?"

"That's Dairy Queen," I said. "We just do it for the kids. Twelve twenty-five."

He scowled but handed over the cash. When he reached for the cups, he brushed my prosthetic fingers. He froze and stared long enough to make anger flush over me. I let it pass right through. *Ten, nine, eight, seven, six, five, four, three, two, one.* I let go of my desire to ring the Bell of Shame.

"Is there something wrong with my hand?" I asked, voice flat.

"Oh. No. Sorry." He hurried away without waiting for his change.

The same stares and mild hesitation happened with the next five customers, until an older woman came up with her granddaughter, an adorably runty little girl who squealed with delight when I leaned out of the window with the freezie upside down. Not a blink from that old lady. Classy as hell.

I didn't get a chance to take Lorelei up on the video offer until an hour later. The weather shifted from chilly breeze to warm stagnation. In Indiana you learn not to rely on consistency from the weather. As the lines died, we settled into our routines: Mads cleaned up spills around the machines and topping dispensers; Hal sorted through receipts at the counter; Lorelei gathered up a trash bag to take out back.

At different points I caught each one of them glancing at me. I didn't say anything about it, and neither did they. The three of them were the closest thing I had to friends, so if they believed I had anything to do with the fire, there was no hope for anyone else.

"Here, Zora," Lorelei said once she'd come back from taking out the trash. She handed me her phone. "Just . . . don't get mad enough to throw it, okay?"

"I'm not gonna throw your phone." I took it from her. "I don't break other people's property."

The video was of me and Greta arguing outside George Masrell's house. The person shooting the video had been nearby, in one of the groups I'd hidden behind. *Tourists.* The jerks always had their phones out. We hadn't been yelling, but everything we said came through loud and clear.

It didn't look good. The only thing that gave me any sympathy was my age—it clearly looked like an older woman accosting a teenage girl. But next to Greta, I looked grungy, and I blew up so fast it looked like I'd done something wrong.

The comments were all accusations. I started counting down from ten. One near the top said *I go to school with her!* Some had my name. One recounted my family's highlights from the last ten years: Mom going missing, Dad going to prison, me going to the hospital. Laid out for the Internet to see, forever. *Zora did it, Zora's the worst, Zora sets fires.*

The pressure of the day finally snapped my resolve.

"Fu—" I began, then caught Hal's pointed glance out the shop windows at the customers, and bit off my sweet release. "—dgecakes!"

"The news got ahold of this," Mads said. "I don't think it's going to die down now."

"Aren't there laws about showing people being wrongfully accused of things on video?"

Hal shrugged. So did Mads. Lorelei gave me a scared-mouse look and slipped her phone from my clawed hand.

If the Harrisburg news crews had gotten ahold of that video, that meant my name—and probably my image—was past Addamsville's borders. People would look me up. They'd make connections. Sadie would have to deal with it at work. All I could do about that was pray it brought her more customers, even if it was only the true-crime podcasters.

Almost as soon as I thought of her, Sadie pulled up in the parking lot.

I waited at the window for her, arms hanging out and head poking through. She was wearing the neon orange top and black pants she'd worn to the salon that morning. Her hair was still up and her black-frame glasses still perched on her nose. That was about par for the course; no time to go home and shower or change her clothes. And once she did go back home, she wasn't leaving again. She looked angry, like she almost always did outside the bluffs—angry and distracted, rubbing at her ears.

Her boyfriend Grim trailed behind her. He wore a dark-blue jumpsuit with the words GATES AUTOMOTIVE SCRAPYARD printed across the breast pocket. Grim didn't walk anywhere; he loped. Lanky and long, hands in his pockets, his wild tangle of dark hair bouncing with him as he went. He could pass for a stoner, but even the stoners in town thought he was weird.

Sadie's lips drew into a thin line. Grim looked worried, but he always looked like that.

"Hey," I said as they drew near. "What's the matter, Grimmie?"

Grim gave me a sad smile. "You've probably had a rough day, huh?"

"Not the best."

"Hey, Lo," Grim said through the window. Lorelei appeared behind me, a white shadow, and smiled. Her answering "Hi" was so soft it could have been another breeze. Lorelei and Grim were cousins, though the way they acted, you'd swear Grim was her older brother.

"Hey." Sadie leaned over the outside counter until I had to

back up. "You don't know what happened to Masrell, do you? Seriously? You have no idea?"

I paused. Even Sadie had to ask twice, because my word wasn't enough. My own sister, who knew exactly what kind of shape I was in after I lost my fingers. Who *knew* how I reacted to fire now. Even she couldn't completely believe I hadn't killed someone.

I clamped down on the hollow feeling in my chest and said, "He yelled at me for throwing coffee away. I yelled at him for being the cryptkeeper. That was it."

"Did the cops talk to you this morning?"

"At school. I said I didn't have anything to do with it. They said they were going to talk to you."

Sadie rubbed her forehead, looking the picture of the young bedraggled mother. She always looked like a young bedraggled mother after she got off work. She'd been talked at all day and she'd be talked at all night, until sleep finally let her escape, and even that was temporary. I was glad she didn't know about ghosts or firestarters; it would just be another thing for her to worry about. "All right, well, it's not like we actually did anything."

"Hey, Sadie." Hal slid an orange cream freezie and a tall chocolate swirl cone across the counter between us. "Sorry you guys have to deal with this."

Grim took the chocolate and sucked contentedly on the

top curl of ice cream. Sadie shook her head while she pulled a twenty from her purse. "It's fine, it'll pass. I do feel terrible, though. There are plenty of people who didn't like Masrell, but murder? Who would hate him enough to kill him?"

"Everyone I know thinks it's Hermit Forester, emerging from the woods after thirty years," Hal said. "Like the clown from *It.*"

"Or a copycat," Mads said. "That's what the marching band thinks right now. A twenty-something running around with a boner for the Firestarter Murders."

Except Forester was too far from the coal mine. More likely a new firestarter had opened a gateway—its entrance—in the mines and had retreated there after killing Masrell to build up power until it could possess someone. Much easier to set more fires when you could walk among humans undetected.

Sadie jammed a plastic spoon into her orange cream, brows furrowed and mouth turned down.

"I saw the video," she said quietly. "One of my regulars showed me. She recognized you from the picture on my counter. Why would you go anywhere near his house? And *why* would you stick around if you saw Aunt Greta there?"

"I know it was a bad idea. I wanted to—to prove I hadn't done it, and I needed to know more about the fire. I didn't see her. I think they pulled up afterward. *They* were the ones who came up to *me*—"

"Zora, please *think* for, like, *two seconds* before you do something next time. There is always someone around to film something, especially at a place like that. We can't afford this kind of attention, not when Dad is getting out of prison in two days. Let Rivera do her job."

Heat pooled in my face. It was *Dad's* fault we were getting so much of this attention, and she could only talk about *his* feelings, and *his* reactions. But worse, she said it like I didn't know what was happening, like I was too stupid to see how my actions affected the situation. Like I wasn't smart enough to figure out for myself that this was pretty near a worst-case scenario. I try to make things right, and everyone tells me to sit down, shut up, let the adults handle it. I wished I could. I would have handed all of this back to Mom in a heartbeat, if it was possible. But I was the one here, and I had to do *something*.

I lowered my voice. "It's not even your problem."

"It *is* my problem," she hissed back. "I'm responsible for you until Dad comes home."

"Eat your fu—fudging ice cream, Sadie."

"Let's go sit," Grim said gently, rubbing Sadie's back and looking strangely like some kind of druid in a jumpsuit, put on Earth to heal weariness. "We can talk to the police later and tell them what we know. Everything will be okay."

Sadie huffed, gave me a look halfway between reproach and apology, and let Grim pull her to one of the patio tables.

She ate her ice cream with a hand covering one ear, the other open to Grim.

I busied myself getting more spoons and napkins to refill the holders by the windows and slammed the spoons down so hard the cup fell over and rolled onto the floor. I bit my tongue to keep from swearing. I was always the one who had to be careful, and the only thing I'd ever done wrong was underestimate one little firestarter. Dad had been the thief. Mom had been the witch. All the Novaks before me had been the trailer dogs of this town, and thanks to them, we always would be. I was trying to make things *right*.

Even Sadie had to ask if I'd killed George Masrell. If I'd *killed* someone.

Mads's voice rose. "Why would an old hermit kill a janitor? And *don't* say because he—"

"Because he murdered twelve people," Hal finished.

"He was only suspected of that." Lorelei appeared by the soft-serve machine. "Never convicted."

"His whole family dies in different mysterious fires within a week and he comes out totally unscathed, but somehow the police never find out who did it?" Hal shrugged. "I'm just saying, looks suspicious. Start your investigations with the most obvious. Maybe George Masrell knew something."

Mads looked like she'd just realized she was in an argument with a ten-year-old. "The Forester mansion gets used for ghost tours now. He doesn't even live there anymore."

"Sure he does. Bach works for him, doesn't he? And he's always lurking around town. Forester lives in the upper floors, where they don't take the tours." Hal clapped a hand against the countertop. "Maybe he had *Bach* do it."

"The most obvious," I repeated as I picked up spoons. "Me and the weird hermit from the woods are the most obvious options. Cool, thanks Hal. Also, Bach might look like a vampire, but I'm pretty sure he doesn't kill people." *Anymore* was the very important missing word. Truthfully, I wasn't sure what Bach did with most of his free time, but if he'd killed anyone in the past thirty years, I couldn't find any record of it.

Mads snorted. "A vampire with a greaser fetish."

"You should be honored to be among such company as Hermit Forester and his Lost Boy," Hal said to me. "Keep it up and you'll be a town legend."

"Yes, because that's an accomplishment." Everything became a legend here if it had once been alive and something bad had happened to it. Sometimes the *alive* part wasn't even necessary.

"Speak of the devil." Hal laughed and motioned out the windows. "Your vampire's here, Zora. And he brought some friends."

I shot up as a pitch-black Mustang turned off the street. It was long and sleek and made barely any noise, impressive for a muscle car of its age. There wasn't a speck of dirt on it. Like a beautiful, evil version of the Chevelle. Bach's pale hands on the steering wheel were visible as he passed under the parking lot lights. Three other cars followed him in.

The first: Artemis's powder-blue Prius.

The second: a gray SUV with dark rims and silver detailing.

And the third: a white panel van with a huge text logo painted on the side in black and red, the words as obnoxious and as visible as possible.

DEAD MEN WALKING

6

Dead Men Walking had become an Addamsville favorite in the two months since it was announced that the show would be filming here. I'd seen only one episode, in which they went near Chernobyl, and I was less concerned with learning the cast's names and more with the fact that they were wandering around a *literally radioactive area* looking for ghosts.

How stupid did you have to be to put yourself at physical risk to search for a truth that would never be accepted? Even money didn't seem like a good enough reason for it.

The cast climbed out of the SUV. The leader, the sidekick, the tech guy, and the girl. The only one whose name I remembered was the leader, Tad Thompson. The intro to the show was him explaining how he'd had some kind of revelatory incident as a child that put him on the search for signs of life after death. He looked like your run-of-the-mill white guy in a T-shirt and cargo pants. As soon as he appeared, a smattering of applause broke out among our customers, starting with a table where a man wore a *Dead Men Walking* baseball hat. Tad Thompson gave a big smile and waved.

The five dead town council members stood twenty feet away, unimpressed.

The cast members milled around their SUV and their van while a couple of cameramen and production assistants got equipment ready. Everyone on the patio had turned to watch them.

"Did you know they were coming here?" I asked Hal. "Don't they need permission to shoot on your property?"

"It's my dad's property, not mine," Hal said. He leaned out the window to get a better look. "Doesn't matter anyway. Even if I said no, the town council would overrule it."

"Can they do that?"

"Would *you* get in a fight with Greta Wake?"

"Already did once today, will pass."

Artemis had left her Prius and now stood off to the side of the camera crew, looking made up and ready to be interviewed. There was a man wearing khakis, a blue button-down, and a lanyard with an ID tag, directing the crew with their equipment; Artemis was trying to speak with him and he didn't seem to hear her. His eyes scanned the patio, the front of Happy Hal's, then settled on Bach's Mustang as Bach climbed out of the driver's seat. The man's face lit up.

"Vampire with a greaser fetish" was, I hated to say it, not an entirely incorrect description of Bach. He was too trim and put together to be a punk rocker, too casual to be an aristocrat. It was like Hermit Forester had hired a bouncer who used to guard a castle and drink the guests' blood. Dark T-shirt, dark jeans, dark boots. Black hair. Pale skin. A jawline that could cut diamonds. Firestarters tended to pick who to possess for a reason, and Bach clearly had not been trying to lie low when he'd taken that one.

The man with the ID tag went up to him. As he spoke, Bach looked him up and down, expression flat. The man stopped talking. Bach smiled a bit and said something. The man's face fell. Bach turned away and started toward Hal's again.

"Get your jaw off the floor," Hal said. "It's unsanitary."

I already held the tray for the double-size Happy Summer Sundae. Frozen banana, frozen cherries, no hot fudge. One spoon. Bach ordered the same thing every time he came around, so I'd gotten good at having it already made when he got to the window.

Hal and Mads thought this was hilarious. Everyone did, when you're known for your lack of interest in any other human person. Lorelei had already faded into the background in extreme secondhand embarrassment. I slowed down so Hal wouldn't lay it on any thicker. I wasn't interested in anyone because I had a very specific set of aesthetics that appealed to me, and two of them were "old-world vampire" and "*Outsiders*-style greaser." It wasn't my fault Bach managed to land in the center of that Venn diagram.

Besides, this wasn't a *I want to look at your face* sundae. It was a *I need to question you about your employer's homicidal tendencies and connections to Addamsville's paranormal happenings* sundae.

But Bach didn't make it to my window. Tad Thompson slid in front of him first.

Bach and I both blinked in surprise, and Tad, leader of this ghost-hunting pack of scavengers, smiled and leaned through my window like he'd been in line the whole time.

"Hey there," he said, extending a hand for me to shake. I shook it. He glanced down but didn't say anything about the prosthetics. "I'm Tad Thompson, part of the crew from *Dead Men Walking*." When I didn't respond, he motioned toward the van with the logo. "The TV show."

"I know who you are," I said.

"Yeah, but it's bumming me out that *I* don't know *you*."

There are few things in this life for which I have real patience, and being hit on is not one of them. "Wrong tree, dog. Bark elsewhere."

"Lesbian?" he said.

"None of your business," I replied.

His smile widened. "I don't believe it until I see proof."

Hal watched from the other window, but said nothing, because he knew I could handle this. Mads stood somewhere behind my left shoulder; the stone silence from her direction was enough to know she was listening and probably also rankled. Lorelei still hadn't reappeared. I glanced at the Bell of Shame.

Behind Tad, Bach raised his eyebrows. I pinched my leg through my jeans to keep my temper in check. No more incidents today. I had to behave. Even if it was for a misogynist asshole.

I put on my sweetest smile and said, "What can I get for you?"

"Depends," Tad said, "are you on the menu?"

I grabbed the string on the Bell of Shame and yanked as hard as I could. Hal and Mads cheered. Tad Thompson sprang back from the window as the bell let loose its cantankerous cry. He ran into Bach, who looked down at him with his hands in his pockets and his lips curling up. Several hoots went through the crowd gathered on the patio. I kept ringing the bell.

"Shame on those who come to Happy Hal's and hit on the employees!" I yelled with vicious glee. "Shame on those who do it *so badly*! Shame! Shame!"

"Shame!" Hal and Mads joined in. Sadie whistled from her table. Tad looked at all of us like we'd lost our minds. The crowd cheered. I let the string go and the ringing faded.

"Now," I said, as quiet descended. "If you'd like ice cream, you can move to the back of the line, wait your turn, and ask for it like a real human being."

Tad glanced around the patio. Customers watched with ice cream dripping from cones and off spoons; the *DMW* crew stood motionless with their equipment; Bach took a deep, contented breath. Finally, face flaming, Tad stepped out of the way and let Bach approach the window.

"Hello, sir," I said, putting on that winning smile again. It wasn't so difficult this time. "What can I get for you?"

Bach's black eyes shone with mirth as he gave me an equally sweet smile back. The way his lips formed around his teeth always gave me the impression of fangs. "Hello, ma'am. I'll have the Happy Summer Sundae, bananas, cherries, hold the fudge. Nice weather we're having, isn't it?"

"Just beautiful."

"Beautiful," Bach said. "Not only is the service here top of the line, the ice cream is great, too. You are a fine server, ma'am; may I get your name?"

"Oh, why thank you, sir. My name is Zora Novak. It's very nice to meet you."

We shook hands. Bach never flinched at my fingers. I made a point to meet Tad's gaze over Bach's shoulder, hoping my eyes felt like lasers searing into his gross soul.

Bach stepped off to the side, and Tad approached the window a second time.

"Hello again," I said. "What can I get for you?"

"One medium chocolate cone."

I got Tad his stupid cone and took his stupid money. By now it was late enough that the only new people showing up were *Dead Men Walking* fans who'd heard that the cast was here. Many of our customers had stuck around to watch the filming. The dead town council members had disappeared shortly after the *DMW* cast had arrived, and I hadn't seen them since. A lot of ghosts had disappeared, but they tended to do that when tourists were around.

I volunteered to sweep the patio, where Bach leaned against the counter with his sundae, watching the crew set up. Through the window behind him, Hal mimicked Bach's posture and Mads mimed sweeping past him. Then they pretended to make out.

I didn't want to make out with Bach. I just liked the way he looked, and sometimes it was easier to talk to him than to anyone else. He knew who I was. I knew who he was. He'd murdered people on Hermit Forester's order and he'd possessed a human for a body, so there would come a day when I had to chop his head off and send him back through his entrance, but until then, we had an understanding.

I ignored Hal and Mads and leaned against the counter. Bach glanced at me but didn't move away.

"I hear we get to suffer through a week of this." I pointed to Tad and his three team members trying out different poses along the curb.

"I'll give them four days," Bach said, spooning frozen banana into his mouth.

"Four?" I snorted. "You going to scare them out of here?"

"Oh no. I'm on a loose leash these days; I'm not going to ruin that freedom."

"So it wasn't you who set the fire at Masrell's?" I said it so only he would hear.

"No," he replied, just as quietly, "but it was one of us. Sammy's lying low—he knows the rumors are going to come up again and doesn't want anyone bothering him."

Hermit Forester—Sam Forester—didn't want anyone bothering him so *I* wouldn't look into Bach's entrance again, so *I* wouldn't ruin the little farming operation they'd had here for the past thirty years. Twelve ghosts they were feeding off of.

"How does it work?" I asked him, glancing around to make sure no one was paying too close attention to us. "I know Forester pulls strength from the people you kill, but he's human."

"Partly," Bach said. "His mother was a firestarter."

"Lenore Forester?"

"No. His other mother. My mother. Hildegard."

"So he's *half* human."

Bach made a noise. He didn't look happy; he had told me before that his mother—if that was really what firestarters called them, the things that spawned more firestarters—had shackled him to Sam Forester, and Sam was the one who made him kill. I wasn't sure I believed him yet, but everything I knew about firestarters had come from Mom, and they hadn't exactly been spilling their secrets to her. Bach told me things, but only a little bit at a time, to keep Hermit Forester from finding out he was doing it and going on another rampage.

The audience at Hal's was turned now, facing the street, where the camera crew had set up. Lamps lit the long line of quaint, touristy buildings down Valleywine. Tad handed his cone to the one girl in the group—her name was Leila, according to the white block letters on the back of her sweatshirt—slopping melted chocolate over her fingers. Then Tad took his power stance with his hands clasped in front of him.

The producer quieted the crowd at Hal's. Customers and fans alike already had their phones out. The cameras started rolling.

"Tonight," Tad's voice was low and serious, "we arrive in the sleepy town of Addamsville, Indiana, to investigate some of the grisliest murders ever seen in small-town America.

Collapsed coal mines, missing children, a family of killers, and a mysterious spree of fires—believed by many in the town to be the work of the devil himself—have plagued this midwestern hamlet for years."

I cupped my hands around my mouth and yelled, "A hamlet is smaller than a town!"

Heads turned. Sadie, at a nearby table with Grim, gave me a look that could have stripped paint off a speedboat. The producer held up his hands and called back, "Quiet, please!"

I sank against the counter. Even correcting a bunch of jerks couldn't help me relax. My only small consolation was that these hacks would never know the dead were here.

"The town itself is overflowing with stories," Tad continued, "but we've narrowed our investigation to a few specific locations. The first: the abandoned coal mine where the son of the town's founder died tragically more than one hundred years ago. The second: Maple Hills Campground, where two teenagers perished in 1990. And the third location, the focus of all of Addamsville's dark energy: the Forester mansion, hidden in the woods to the west of town. It is in this house where the fires began; is it also where the spirits of Addamsville draw their power? That's what we're here to find out."

I looked for Artemis; she was already looking at me. Worry laced her features. The coal mine. She wouldn't know about the firestarter there yet—but going to Forester House was bad enough. I nudged Bach with my elbow. "Did you know that? That they're going to Forester's?"

He nodded, mouth full of ice cream. "I knew. They're filming that one last. A couple days from now. They already knew I worked for Forester, big shocker. I think Greta Wake told them. She e-mailed Sam about it, and he didn't want to comment. I had to turn down an interview request from that producer when I got here, too."

Greta told them. Greta okayed it. Did she not think Forester would do anything? If he was trying to lie low, he wouldn't, so maybe Forester House was safe. Then what did Artemis look so worried about?

"Don't want to be on TV?" I asked.

"I'm not big on spreading rumors."

"So Forester really had nothing to do with Masrell's fire?"

Bach looked at me, taking on the preternatural stillness firestarters could manage in a human body. His gaze jumped down to my hand, then back to my face. "He didn't. Neither did I. And I thought you gave up hunting, after the last one."

"Yeah, well." I swallowed against a dry throat. "One person is already dead. I have to do something until my mom gets back."

Bach gave me a look I couldn't decipher and went back to his sundae. Artemis had shuffled closer to us, watching the filming with her face screwed up. Artemis usually looked like she was two steps from having a frustrated meltdown, but this was from worry, not anger.

When the *DMW* crew finished with the shots away from the building, they came in close.

"Could we borrow this spot?" the producer asked in a saccharine way that clearly meant *move your asses*. Bach wedged his spoon in his mouth and we stepped to the nearest empty table. The other three members of *DMW* went back to the van while Tad stood where Bach and I had been. The producer then motioned Artemis over. She jumped and hurried past us.

"Keep it short," the producer told Tad. "But make sure it's usable."

Tad waved a hand. "I know the drill." He turned to Artemis. "What's your name again?"

"Artemis Wake."

"What—seriously?"

"Yes."

"Are you out of a comic book or something? That name is ridiculous."

Artemis bristled.

"Tad," the producer said.

"Okay, look," Tad said. "There's no introduction. We do that in post. I'm going to start asking you questions."

Tad turned to the camera. Artemis patted her hair down

and smoothed her expression. She had to know how red her cheeks were.

"Artemis, what can you tell us about the ghosts of Addamsville?" Tad's voice resonated over the patio.

Artemis didn't look at the camera even once, bless her heart. "We've had ghost stories as long as we've been a town. Ghosts built this place—ghosts keep it alive now. Most of the stories are meant to scare people, but when you dig into the history, the truth behind the myth is often sad, or even something completely normal that got twisted over time. What's interesting, though, is that most of the stories are about white townspeople, when there's an admittedly scant but still documented history of slavery and abuse of native peoples—"

She lost Tad at "white townspeople." He let her go on for a bit until she finally registered his expression and her voice died off.

"Great," Tad said flatly. He paused for a moment. "What's it like to live in such a deeply haunted town?"

"Like living anywhere else. It has its history. I think of myself as a historian—we have just as much to learn from our ghost stories as we do from artifacts and old journals. Addamsville is a good place for that."

Still no life in Tad Thompson.

"You've conducted investigations into locations here yourself?"

"Oh yes. I camped overnight in Maple Hills once." Artemis had been to a lot of places, but she'd managed to keep this answer to something a general audience would find interesting. Points for Artemis!

"Could you tell us the story behind Maple Hills?"

"It was part of the Firestarter Murders," Artemis said. "Twenty-eight years ago, an arsonist burned down several houses in town, the old town hall, and one of the cabins in Maple Hills. It was during the off-season, and the only people inside were two local teenagers, Michelle Garrington and Elton Holly. The campground was closed off after that. The burned cabin is only a foundation now, but there are stories that say you can sometimes hear a girl and boy talking quietly to each other nearby. Or, late at night, moans and screams coming from the campground. The police have also gotten calls from residents on the far side of the lake who say they saw what appeared to be a very large fire in the woods, where the cabins are."

Tad leaned in, one arm crossed over his chest, the other hand at his chin, contemplative.

"What did you experience while you were there?"

"Not much."

Tad stared at her. Artemis cleared her throat.

"A few orbs," she said. "And a dark feeling? Like I was being watched."

Tad nodded his head seriously. Waited a few seconds. Looked at the producer.

"Sure," the producer said.

Tad broke his pose. "Awesome, thanks." He slapped Artemis on the shoulder. She watched him walk away with the cameraman and sound guys and the producer, her mouth hanging open and her face beet red.

"Woof," I said, loud enough for her to hear me. "That was rough, eh?"

"Shut up, Zora," she snapped.

Bach shook his head, smiling, and drank the last of his ice cream straight out of the bowl.

"Thieves!"

Artemis's ranting carried across the empty parking lot.

"They come here asking for truth, but they only want what looks good and sounds edgy! Did you see the way he looked at me when I said the word *history?* He fell asleep standing up! They don't even know this town, but they're going to come in and stomp all over it like everyone else!"

I'd never in my life seen Artemis so incensed. I leaned against the Chevelle's bumper, parked by Sadie's Camry, where she and Grim sat on the trunk. Lorelei stood in Grim's shadow. Hal was next to me, yawning, and Mads flipped through an app on her phone. The dead town council members had returned to their statue, and a few other ghosts wandered around the parking lot. I needed to talk to Artemis alone, but she was ranting too much.

Artemis marched back and forth, breath coming out in streams of fog.

"Yell louder," I said. "I don't think they heard you in Harrisburg."

Artemis sneered at me. "Zora, for once in your life, will you think of someone other than yourself?"

I ignored the sneer. "What are you talking about? I think of other people all the time." I counted off on my fingers. "When I'm making fun of them, when I'm keying their cars, when I'm—what's that look for?"

Artemis spun away from me, hair trailing her like a blond curtain. "I can't believe we're related."

The others didn't laugh, either.

"They're here for money," Sadie said. "They'll get their stories and go, and we'll have a little more foot traffic for a while."

Artemis scoffed. "For a while. We already get enough foot traffic. Tourists keep scratching up the antique wallpaper in Newman's, trying to find the etched initials of the lost lovers who stayed in the east room. They punch holes through the rotting parts of the covered bridge to try to see the ghost of Roadspike Stevens climbing out of Black Creek. Pastor Keller even said he found a few people *literally digging up graves* to find out if it was true that there were no real bodies buried in the church graveyard. But all this is okay with all of you? They're tearing our town apart piece by piece to sate their curiosity and get *money*, and that's okay?"

Mads glanced up, eyebrows raised. Hal scratched at his neck. Lorelei had disappeared behind Grim, who stared absently northwest, toward Piper Mountain. Sadie took her hands away from her ears. "Of course I'm not okay with it," she said. "But my life isn't going to end if some wallpaper gets scratched up or a bridge has to be repaired. The gravedigging thing is . . . upsetting. But whatever the case, I have a few priorities that are higher on the list than saving this whole town. Food, for one. Health insurance. Making sure my car keeps working. Keeping *this one* out of juvie." She jabbed a finger at me.

"Excuse you," I mumbled. "I'm old enough to get sent to *real* prison now."

"Arty, look," Mads said. Artemis jerked to a halt. "If it bothers you so much, why not talk to your mom about it? She's the one who started all this stuff. She's the one who can do something about it."

It took a second for Artemis to break her wide-eyed stare at Mads, and when she spoke, it was with all the previous bluster blown out of her. "I've tried. It only gave her the idea to make the town more 'interactive.'"

"Jesus Christ," I said. "She really is turning it into Conner Prairie for the Afterlife."

"Pretty much."

"It sucks," Hal said, "but my dad's gung ho for it, too. When he found out they wanted to film at the shop, he told me to put signs up in every window so our logo gets on TV. I'll ask around and see if anyone else is unhappy with it, and maybe we can get a town assembly called. Until then I think we're going to have to suffer." He shrugged. "Anyway, it's freezing balls out here, so I'm leaving."

"It's, like, fifty degrees," I said.

"My balls accept nothing less than sixty-five," he called back as he climbed into his Ford.

"I'm leaving, too." Mads slipped her phone into her pocket. "See you guys at school tomorrow."

"Bye, everyone." Lorelei hugged Grim quickly and disappeared for the last time that night.

Sadie and Grim slid from the Camry. "Grim's staying over with us tonight," Sadie said to me.

"The more the merrier." I held a hand up. Grim gave me a high-five, then caught my hand and patted it between both of his, a monk on a mountainside offering a prayer. "Just don't eat all my Fruity Pebbles, okay?"

"I have two boxes in my car for you," Grim said.

"God bless you, Grimmie!"

After they'd all left, Artemis stood there looking lost.

"Why does it feel like I'm the only one insulted by those

guys?" She motioned to the spot where the *DMW* van had parked.

"Rest assured," I said, "I also thought Tad Thompson was a bag of dicks."

"But you don't care that they're using the town?"

"Yeah, of course I do. I hate tourists. And I hate people like Tad Thompson who think we should be throwing ourselves all over him. Where are they from? LA?"

"Seattle."

"Freaking city people think we're poor midwest bumpkins or something. Just because I grew up sticking cicada shells to my shirt and making mud pies doesn't mean I'm stupid. We don't have to like what they're doing, and we don't have to pretend to like it."

Artemis said nothing to this. She turned the other way, hands on her hips, scanning for something on the street. She could sense ghosts nearly as far away as I could see them.

"Is your mom really trying to get *more* tourists to come here?" I asked.

"It's her one goal in life," Artemis said. "She wants Addamsville to be the tourist capital of Indiana."

"That's certainly a title."

"The whole town council has been looking for ways to extend the tourist season."

I'd heard. The ghost of Harben Mill was now rumored to show up on clear spring nights, waiting for her boyfriend in the

Denfords' cornfields. Theater two at the Royal Six, believed to be haunted by Mr. Beverley, the building's original owner, now mysteriously echoed with the *Mary Poppins* soundtrack very very early on summer mornings. Coal miners could be seen walking the frozen lake in winter. Only the last one was kind of true.

It was bad enough just in the fall. Tourists had found our trailer on the bluffs before. They thought it was a meth lab. They nosed around our property until Sadie or I came out with Dad's wood-chopping axe and scared them off. We'd tried talking nicely before—well, Sadie had—but that just made them try to ask permission.

More tourists would come because of the George Masrell fire and *Dead Men Walking*. The two events happening so closely together was already state news. If we got any unluckier, it would be national news. And Addamsville was perpetually unlucky.

"Why'd you look worried earlier?" I asked. "The coal mine, Maple Hills, or Forester House?"

"I checked Maple Hills last night, and the ghosts there are calm. No firestarters there in a long time." Artemis turned. "And I figured Forester had to give permission for them to film at his house, so he's not planning to kill them. But I've never been in the coal mine. And it's a lot closer to Masrell's house. And you looked over at me, and I figured Masrell had told you where the firestarter was when you saw him today."

"Yeah. Bad news."

Artemis reached out for me, but didn't touch me. "Zora, we have to do something. We can't let them go in the mine if there's a firestarter down there."

"Yeah, I know. But they're not going to listen to either of us if we tell them not to go in, and if we damage the mine to make it seem unsafe, then we won't be able to get in and find that firestarter ourselves. I'm sure its entrance is down there."

Artemis's face lit up. "You want to—oh, Zora, that's great! We can start hunting again! And my research—I can learn so much more if you're there!"

I jabbed a warning finger at her chest. "This is *temporary*. Understand? A one-time deal. Someone has to take this thing out, and I'm the only one around to do it."

"So when are we going? Tonight? We have to get there before them."

"No. I can't take the Chevelle down in the mine, and I'm not fighting another firestarter hand to hand. We're focusing on making sure it doesn't attack the *DMW* crew first." I sat back against the Chevelle and thought. "All right. How about this. You're upset about the filming, right? That the show is going to bring a flood of tourists that are going to ruin the town?"

"Yes . . ."

"We screw up their filming. When those ghost-hunting shows get 'evidence' that turns out to be bored local teenagers, they can't use that as proof, and it makes the town look like a fraud. Might get them out of the mine faster, and while we're there we can keep an eye out for the firestarter. That's what, three or four birds with one stone?"

"How did you think of that so fast?"

"I'm always thinking about ways things could go badly for me. That means constantly thinking of terrible things I could be doing. Is it risky? Sure. Do I think I can pull it off? You bet. I wouldn't have suggested it if I couldn't."

"What do you plan on doing to them?"

"Uh"—I waved my hands in the air—"play tricks on them? Make them look like idiots? It happens all the time on ghost-hunting shows, right? Except we'll do it better."

"I am *not* damaging their equipment. We'll get sued."

"I didn't mean damaging equipment. Jesus. I meant faking evidence but making it obvious it's being faked. Then they can't use the footage. No one wants to watch a ghost-hunting show where the ghosts are annoying teenagers."

She looked like I'd kicked a kitten. "You want me to *fake evidence?*"

"You know all that paranormal stuff. You'd be good at it."

She was already shaking her head. "No. Nope. As an investigator of the paranormal, I *cannot—*"

"Now *I* can't believe we're related. Do you have a better idea? There's a firestarter in that mine, and if it's there when they go in and we aren't around to stop it, all those people are going to die. And besides—don't you want to preserve the sanctity of investigation by making those guys look like the hacks they are? Don't you want to show the world they can't come into Addamsville and stomp around because they think it's open for everyone?"

She hesitated. I knew that would work on her before she replied, before her expression even changed. I knew it because despite both our disbelief, we *were* related, and there was at least one thing, inherited from our mothers, that proved it.

We were Aberdeens.

"No destruction of property?" she said.

I held up a hand. "Scout's honor."

"No hurting people?"

"Nope."

"What happens if we get caught?"

"I take the fall, one hundo percent."

"Even though you're doing this to stop a firestarter?"

"Aw, that's so sweet, you care about me."

"If we get caught doing this together, then I'm in trouble, too. And if both of us are caught, that firestarter is going to run loose."

She wasn't wrong. I hated it when Artemis wasn't wrong.

"We could get Bach to help," I said. "Forester doesn't want this firestarter around, either. With a third person, we'd be more efficient. And safer."

"*No.* No extra people, and no Bach." She shuddered. "Why would you even suggest that?"

"Look," I finally said, "I am going to help you save this town. I'm going to help you get these mouth-breather tourists out of Addamsville, because I hate them as much as you do. Even if you get caught with me, you have your mom and a sterling reputation. Nothing's going to happen to you. I'm the trash in this situation. I'm the disposable one. We keep people safe now, worry about the consequences later."

She gave me another long, hard look.

I stared right back and said, "Either you come with me to help, or I go do it by myself. And you know how well that went last time."

We squared off in the Happy Hal's parking lot in the heart of autumn, with the dark and the ghosts. Artemis's gaze strayed to my hand. It was my fault I'd faced the last firestarter alone, and we both knew that. It was my fault Artemis hadn't been there to watch my back. She wasn't the bravest girl in Addamsville, my cousin, but she had a heart.

And finally, Artemis said, "I can't let you go by yourself."

8

That night, against all common sense, I went out to perform my good deeds. Pruning, fixing, mending. It wasn't to make up for the fires the town believed I'd set, like Artemis thought. If I couldn't hunt for them, I had to do something. I couldn't suffer the full weight of Mom's disappointment.

Just because people knew now that I'd been going out at night didn't mean I had to stop doing it. Who was going to be out in the freezing cold at one in the morning?

I got as far as the east side and was trying to right a tilted mailbox when headlights flooded the yard around me and hollering split the night.

"There she is!"

A truck roared down the street, barreling toward me. I

sprinted around the side of the house as the lights inside came on, then leaped over the back fence. I didn't stop until I was four streets away. I ducked down by a culvert at the end of a driveway as the roar of the truck and the hoots of the men riding in it faded away.

I knew that truck. Gargantuan, fire-engine red, with a massive steel grille guard. It was Buster Gates's truck, and I'd bet anything the guys riding in it were part of his usual crew of gun-toting vigilantes.

I'd starting doing nice things for people at night because they wouldn't let me do them during the day. I'd hoped raking and trimming and cleaning and fixing enough mailboxes would even out the Novaks' bad karma, even though no one knew who was doing the work. I'd hoped that the hatred toward us might lessen. A Novak doing good things and not taking credit for it? It had to count to someone, somewhere.

But no. Instead of some kind of understanding, I got Buster Gates in a truck, trying to run me down.

The first night of filming was the next day. The *DMW* crew was scheduled to visit the Hillcroft coal mine, not far from the bluffs, to investigate rumors of strange voices in the old tunnels, traces of demonic activity, and sightings of Salem Hillcroft, the son of the man who'd built this town. The mine opened up somewhere far below into a series of caves, and Salem was said to have died in a tragic fall into the depths when he was my age.

In my explorations of the mine, I'd never seen Salem, but I'd seen plenty of other ghosts. Usually miners. The mines went deep, and the ghosts seemed to follow them all the way down.

Every entrance had been closed off except the north one, the one the *DMW* crew would use. I'd found a second entrance down south when I was in middle school, boarded up and grown over with weeds and underbrush. The boards had rotted enough to pry them off with a crowbar. It was a creepy old place—chains hanging from the ceiling, water dripping somewhere, and the occasional dead miner—but I'd scared the bats out and peeked around. After a bit of walking, it connected to the other entrance, and by my best estimates, also to the cave system below. I explored enough times to get a feel for the upper layout, but after that I mostly hung around in the mouth of my secret entrance, burned whatever twigs and trash I could find, and complained about the lack of mine carts.

The second entrance would make it easy to fake the crew out. Noises echoed. Voices sounded spooky no matter what was said. And I knew the tunnels they would be using.

Filming started at ten. No one at school that day would shut up about it; it had beat out this weekend's homecoming as the topic of choice, a difficult feat in a town where homecoming was a headliner in every possible news outlet, including the barbershop and the drugstore. The information about the filming had not been released by the *Dead Men Walking* crew themselves, but, I was almost sure, by the kid of someone in close with the town council.

Artemis came close to talking to me a few times throughout the day, only changing course when I dialed my expression up to code red. If Artemis was seen talking to me at school, it would eventually get back to Greta, and I didn't need Greta getting up in my business again. Greta could not be allowed to interfere, and she would definitely try. I still didn't understand what she was doing, pretending like she didn't know about firestarters. If Artemis needed to say something to me, I *did* have a functioning cell phone capable of receiving text messages, and she knew the number for it.

I hadn't been joking when I'd suggested Bach to Artemis for our outing in the mines. He had motivation to join us on the hunt, he knew more about firestarters than any of us, and he was capable of the special type of shit-eating grin that said he was well versed in screwing with people.

Every Tuesday and Thursday, Bach hung out on a bench beneath a big maple tree in the park, listening to music and watching people play with their dogs. I knew this because I *also* spent a lot of time watching people play with dogs at the park. He was there when I arrived, a slash of black against the brown and orange. There were only a few ghosts here, and they stuck to the edges of the field where the dogs played, far from Bach. Five, six. Usually there were ten or more. They were running in the advent of another firestarter's arrival. I stuffed my hands into the pockets of my jacket and sidled up to the bench.

Bach looked up through his sunglasses and tugged out one earbud. "Hey, Zora."

I liked that he called me Zora when other people weren't around. Some days it was hard to remember he was a murderer, even if it had been against his will.

"What's going on?" I asked.

"Usual," he said. "Burger's not bringing the ball back, and Gracie and Tater are fighting over their Frisbee. Want to sit?"

I sat next to him. He offered me his other earbud. He was listening to something slow and chill, with a lot of guitar. A fluffy brown dog went galloping after a bright red ball that squeaked when it hit the ground.

Dogs are better than people. This is a complete and true verified fact. Dogs don't care what you look like. Dogs don't care what skeletons hide in your closet. They don't care what color you are, or what weight, or how rich, or how guilty. They don't care about your gender or your sexual orientation. They don't care if you have deformities or illnesses. They care about being fed and played with and petted. They'll lick your face because it's *your* face.

"I love dogs," I said.

"I'll agree with that," Bach said. He rested his elbows up on the back of the bench. "It must be nice, having such a simple life."

"Life with Hermit Forester getting you down?"

He smiled. "It's not bad. Definitely more chill than it used to be."

"How long have you worked for him?"

"Oh." He thought. "Awhile now."

I had no idea how old Bach was. I wasn't even sure firestarters had ages. The person whose body he wore was young, about my age, and his cover story was that he went to high school in Harrisburg. But firestarters essentially made their human bodies immortal; they hollowed out the insides and paraded them around as long as they liked. Bach could have looked like this for a very long time.

Bach's smile widened as he tilted his head toward me. He had killer cheekbones and a nose that could be used as a straightedge. "Did you come here to talk about dogs and ask how long I've been working?"

I took the earbud out. He took his out, too. "Fine, no. I came to ask if you wanted to help with the *DMW* crew."

"What about them?"

"They're filming at the mine. Masrell pointed me there yesterday. This new firestarter is down there, and Artemis and I are going into the mine tonight to try to get them out of there before it hurts them. Nothing illegal."

Bach's eyebrow lifted as I spoke. He slid his sunglasses off and hung them on his shirt collar. The shade from the trees and his brow made his eyes look as dark as mine. "Can I ask you a question?"

"Sure."

"Why are you really starting again? Hunting? You said before that you were done."

I blinked. "Oh. I thought you were going to ask me something like, 'Why are you doing something so stupid, Zora?' or 'Zora, aren't you worried about getting caught after being accused of killing a man?'"

"You told me why you were doing it," Bach said. "To keep people safe, which is the right answer. But I want to know if it's your *actual* answer—is that what you really feel? I've spent enough time around humans to know you're smart enough to give the right answer without really believing it, and I saw you after the last firestarter. You were so sure you'd never do any of this again. What changed?"

"People change their minds."

"Did you feel guilty?"

"What does it matter?"

He looked back out over the field. Gracie and Tater flew after their Frisbee. "Guilt is still new to me. I've been in a human body a long time, and it's the one thing I can't get used to. It's like the harder you try to throw it off, the heavier it becomes."

I looked sideways at him. "*You* feel guilty?"

He smiled sadly. "If I could release those ghosts, I would. If I could wiggle my way out of Sammy's control, I would. But I haven't tried very hard to do those things, either, because it's my duty to protect Sammy. Not doing it would mean betraying my mother. Hildegard. I know you think we're all animals, but we have our own sets of emotions and loyalties, and that's one I don't know if I can shake."

I didn't know what to say. Bach was usually friendly, but rarely so candid. "Moms, right?"

The smile curled up sharper. "Guilt tripping no matter where they are."

"So that's a *no* on the mine?"

Bach squinted into the bright day and the dogs in the field. "Sammy really wants to lie low. If I'm found anywhere near that filming, his reaction isn't going to be good. You said Artemis is going with you?"

"She never lost that hunting spirit."

"Good. Watch each other's backs." He flipped his sunglasses out to cover his eyes. "And if something really bad happens, let me know. Sam wants to lie low, but he also wants to keep other firestarters out of this town. If you're in trouble, I can help, and we'll deal with him later."

9

Sadie had a habit of falling asleep at nine thirty on the dot, but only if she was at home. If she was already out, she became a creature of the night, hyperaware and strung out, the way she'd once been in high school with the Birdies. She'd been an insomniac then; only since becoming an adult, with the exhaustion of a full workday, did she find the release of sleep. She said sleep was possible at home because the bluffs were so peaceful and quiet. There were no cars driving by, but *peaceful* was an interesting description for howling wind and the constant grinding of the generator.

That night she fell asleep watching *Cheers* with me and Grim, with the generator still chugging out back. When she started snoring, Grim looked at his watch, said, "Oh," and carefully rearranged her so he could crawl out from beneath her sleeping form. We'd moved the TV out of the kitchen nook and onto a box of Dad's clothes for nighttime viewing, and Grim had to be careful not to knock it off its perch with his gangly limbs. Instead of leaving Sadie where she was, drooling into a pillow with one leg hanging off the cushion, Grim wedged his arms underneath her and picked her up. He was a brave man, lifting her. Sadie hated it when people tried to pick her up. He carried her back to her room, a snoring princess.

Grim and Sadie had begun going out in high school. Back then Sadie still wore ripped jeans and combat boots, and Grim was a sweet gloomy string bean with too much hair. Sadie was the kind of girl who got the nickname "Grand Slam Sadie" from the irony that she allowed no human to touch her, and from leading the Birdies on an all-night rampage smashing mailboxes with baseball bats. Grim was the kind of boy who would pick a handful of dandelions and hold them under Sadie's chin to see her smile when her throat glowed yellow. She said he made everything quieter; she rarely went out without him.

I liked Grim a lot, but sometimes the sight of them together was painful. Like someone jabbing me in the chest, over and over. It had taken me a long time to figure out why. I was alone. They weren't. I didn't have someone who believed me unconditionally. I didn't have someone who would pick me over everyone else. I had thought once that that person was Mom, but even she picked the firestarters over me, in the end.

"You staying over again?" I asked when Grim emerged from the bedroom a few minutes later.

He shook his head and smiled a little, then scooped hair out of his eyes. "No, not tonight. I will this weekend, though, if that's okay."

"You buy me cereal. Of course it's okay."

He picked up his door-stopper fantasy book and his shoes and said, "Don't forget, we need to get some funnel cakes at the homecoming parade. My treat."

"You're the best, Grimmie."

He bent his head to get out the front door. I waited for his car to start and gravel to crunch beneath the tires before getting up to peer through the blinds. He disappeared down the road that led back to town.

The trailer had two bedrooms stuffed into its back end, one a little larger than the other. The bathroom and a short hallway separated them from the tiny living room and kitchen. I crept back to Sadie's room to make sure she was really asleep. The room had once been Mom and Dad's, so her bed was a double with a solid wooden frame. She was a big, softly snoring lump under the crocheted blanket and comforter.

Not even the Chevelle's engine would wake her. I ducked back into my own room, where the mattress sat on the floor, and dug through my mounds of clothes for my mine-tromping boots and my flashlight. I would have hidden everything better, but Sadie didn't come in this room since she stopped sleeping there. She now referred to it as "Zora's dumpster." It was messy, there was no denying that, but I resented the implication that it smelled bad. I was very careful with my hygiene.

Once in the Chevelle, I started down the winding path into town. Out here, where there were only hills, the coal mine, the junkyard, and the trailer park, the streets remained empty and quiet. On the bluffs there were no ghosts—one of the reasons Mom moved the trailer there—but because they didn't make sound, even those around the trailer park kept the night peaceful. When I turned down the Goldmine, people came out of nowhere on late-night runs, dog walks, and tourist group outings. The ghosts here watched them pass by, sometimes drifting after a runner or a group for a little while, as if to catch their attention. When I passed, they fixed on me, but they never tried to follow me.

The Goldmine, the southernmost street in town, had once belonged to the founding families of Addamsville. The houses loomed at sharp angles above the treetops, all imposing Victorian Gothics with huge porches, windows that stared at passersby. They had front gates, and the gates were marked by metal signs decorated with each original family's name. Horwill House. Grimshaw House. Banforth House. Farow House. On and on, all the way down the street.

Artemis was lucky enough to belong to one of these: her mother had married a Wake. But they didn't even live in Wake House anymore. In the past month or so, they'd moved into Hillcroft House, the oldest of the old, perched on a rise at the very end of the Goldmine. It had been my last stop of the night when Artemis had found me hiding in her trash.

Sylvester Hillcroft had been the owner of the coal mine where his son, Salem, had died. Stories said Hillcroft House was haunted by the father, who had wasted away after losing his eldest child. It wasn't the most *famous* house in town—that honor belonged to Grimshaw House, with its long-lost buried treasure—but it *was* the most visible.

I parked at the corner at 9:40 p.m. Artemis was already waiting for me behind a tall walnut tree near the end of the driveway, carrying a backpack stuffed so full it threatened to tip her over. Hillcroft House rose behind her like a watchful Victorian toad.

"Took you long enough," she huffed as she tried to crunch herself into the passenger seat.

"*Long enough?* I told you I'd be here at nine forty-five. I'm five minutes early. If you were so worried about punctuality, why couldn't you drive yourself?"

"I would have, but it's in the shop. I've been waiting out here for ten minutes and it's so *cold.*"

"What'd you tell your mom?"

"That I was helping you, obviously. She knows there's a firestarter in town."

"What the hell?" I threw my hands up. "Then why has she been treating me like I'm a horrible person?"

"I don't know; she doesn't tell me everything. Come over and ask her yourself."

I wouldn't set foot in Hillcroft House until someone forced me. "What's all this?" I motioned to the backpack.

"Flashlights, some granola bars and trail mix, camera, EMF meter, voice recorders, extra clothes, matches, rope . . ." She stopped when she saw the expression on my face. "What did you bring?"

I motioned to my flashlight on the dashboard.

"You're *very* underprepared. You don't even have your axe."

"We're messing with some people, not robbing a bank. And if you want to go at a fully mobile firestarter with just an axe, be my guest."

"I've never investigated the mines before. Didn't want to go by myself. I want to see if I can learn more before the film crew gets there." She managed to buckle her seat belt, somehow. "I was doing research earlier today on the mine and I found some new stuff; it was really interesting. . . ."

I threw the car in gear and turned down the street. "Not the first place I'd spend time investigating when we know there's a firestarter inside. Don't you have better places to snoop around? Your brand-new spooky scary house, for example?"

"My mom didn't buy Hillcroft House for its history; she bought it because it's the most extravagant house in town. She won't let me investigate it." She paused, then a sneaky smile slipped onto her face. "I still leave my recorders on at night, though, just in case. Imagine what we could learn if we could find another way for the dead to communicate."

I headed back the way I'd come. The few people on the sidewalks watched the Chevelle as it passed by.

"Have you ever *found* anything?" I asked. "I always imagine you sitting around and listening to hours of empty noise."

"I've gotten some orbs on camera, a few EVP recordings that could be interpreted one way or another . . . and I had some very interesting EMF readings when I went to Maple Hills!"

"Gnats, weird noises, flashing lights. Cool."

"It's not an exact science," Artemis snapped. "If it were, we'd already know what exactly the ghosts are made of, how they form, their routines, their purpose—and if we could communicate with them, imagine what we could *learn*—"

"You want to know the history of the place; I get it." I didn't need to have that conversation over again. We pulled onto Hampstead Road. "That's better than everyone else, at least."

Artemis shrugged. "People like to be scared. They like to be creeped out by things they don't understand. That's why they tune out when I talk about history. Once you know the truth of something, it loses its power over you. Well. Usually."

"Usually?"

"You know the story about Gilly Strefford?"

"The girl who was kidnapped and murdered in the house by the funeral home? Yeah, it's stupid. It's like someone thought of all the worst things that could happen to a person and put them in one story. It's tourist bait."

"That one isn't made up," Artemis said. I glanced at her, and she wasn't laughing. "Gilly Strefford lived in New Valley in the sixties, which got renamed Harrisburg a decade later. Her parents went out of town and left her with her aunt, Mary Hemmings, who lived on Bolt Cross Road near the funeral home. During the two months Gilly's parents were gone, her aunt and cousins tortured Gilly to within an inch of her life. She died of infection in her injuries. I can't even explain the details of what they did to her—it was the worst thing I've ever read. People play it off now as an overblown murder story, but Gilly was a real girl and she really died."

I'd seen a girl lurking around Bolt Cross Road, but I'd never been able to figure out who she was. Ghosts didn't show the signs of how they died, so I'd assumed it had been some disease, or a car accident.

"Oh," I said.

"Yeah."

"What other stories are real?" I knew a lot of them, but apparently not all.

"You'd be surpris—"

I slammed on the breaks. Artemis jerked forward, caught by the seat belt and her bag. A boy jogged across the street in front of us, arms out. A girl on the sidewalk screamed. A group of people materialized behind her, laughing. Noise. Not ghosts. The boy, who looked old enough to be a college student, came around and mimed rolling down my window.

I growled, already counting down from ten. "Let's see what these interlopers want."

The boy leaned into my window before I had it all the way down.

"Hey, we're trying to get to the *Dead Men Walking* location, where they're filming tonight. The, uh—"

"Hillcroft," one girl called.

"The Hillcroft coal mine," said the boy.

"Ah, okay," I said in my best congenial suburban Hoosier voice. "You're gonna wanna head west here. Straight through the field; don't take the streets or you'll miss it. If you reach the Royal Six, you've gone too far."

"Hey, thanks."

"No problem! Have a great night and stay safe!"

He jogged back to his friends. I rolled up the window and kept driving; in the rearview mirror, the college kids crossed the street and started into the ditch on the other side. Artemis watched them go, then said, "The Royal Six is on the other side of town."

"The *DMW* crew should pay me for crowd control."

"You aren't worried they'll get hurt or lost walking around the fields in the dark?"

"Better than them getting killed by a firestarter. Besides, I owe them nothing. If anything, they owe *me* for not running them over while they're stumbling around in the street."

"If you say so."

I felt judged, but I always felt judged around Artemis.

We passed the trailer park on our way back to the bluffs. Lights shone through some of the trailer windows. A dog on a chain barked at the Chevelle as it passed. Artemis watched as we went by.

"You know what's weird?" she said. "The Coalmine doesn't have any ghost stories."

"The Coalmine" was what most people called the trailer park. Even people who lived in the trailer park used the name, but when they said it, it was with a much different tone than the people who didn't live there.

"My place has stories," I said.

"Your place has stories because your trailer sits where Aberdeen House used to be. There aren't any *here*. For all the stories we have in the rest of the Addamsville, the Coalmine doesn't have any."

I frowned. "Are you sure about that?"

"I've looked at almost everything in town. I'm pretty positive—"

"You don't know about Daisy?"

She looked at me. "Who's Daisy?"

"Hold on." I put a hand up. "You don't know trailer park stories? Daisy is, like, *the* ghost on the east side." I'd never seen her, but that didn't mean the stories didn't exist. "She's a white pit bull with a brown spot over one eye and a notch out of her ear. She wanders the edges of the trailer park, or on the fringes of the trees. She keeps little kids from going places they shouldn't and leads them back home when they get lost."

"I have *never* heard that."

"How many people have you talked to who live in the trailer park?"

She went oddly quiet.

"Well, there's your answer," I said. "It's not that they don't have stories. It's that you don't talk to the people who know them."

The *DMW* crew would use the north entrance to the mine, which was close enough to see the junkyard's floodlights. They would come down the same road George Masrell's house was on. The entrance was in a clearing, fenced off, with signs warning about fines for trespassing and the danger of cave-ins. Plenty of room for their SUV and van, even with all the ghosts stuffed in there.

Artemis and I would go through the south entrance. I pulled the Chevelle off to the side of the dirt road up the bluffs, in the shadow of the trees. Evergreens covered the entire hill up to the bluffs, nowhere near as dense as Black Creek Woods, but dense enough to hide the Chevelle.

"You're not going to need any of that," I said as Artemis hoisted her backpack over her shoulder. "At *least* leave the clothes behind."

"I never go to a location unprepared."

"Fine, but if we're late, it's your fault. I'm assuming they're going to set up and do some shots outside before they go in, so we have maybe ten, fifteen minutes to get there. Follow me."

"How far is it?"

"Ten or fifteen minutes. Pay attention." My flashlight beam skimmed the underbrush. Tree roots bubbled from the ground. Plant skeletons loomed from the darkness, catching on my jacket and pants. Our breaths came out in clouds. "Watch your step. The ground is going to slope. Stay behind me, unless you start to fall, then fall to the side. I don't want to die from a broken neck."

"You are the most sensitive person I know," Artemis said.

"Like a bed of nails," I replied.

It's helpful to know ghosts exist and how they present themselves when you're walking through the woods at night. There are a thousand noises, all of them unexplained. Wings in the dark. The crunching of leaves. A cry that is probably an animal but sounds an awful lot like a person. Ghosts didn't make noise. When they loomed out of the darkness, their edges wavered, like a TV with a bad connection. It was still creepy, but at least I expected it, so I kept myself quiet. Artemis could feel them but not see them, which meant she was weaving out of their way every few minutes, stepping on my heels and nearly toppling me over. Once she startled at an owl hooting and grabbed my shoulders. My toe lodged in a tree root as I stumbled forward.

"*Fu*—dge meringue, Artemis!"

"Oh, sorry—"

"I think I twisted my ankle."

"Are you going to be okay?"

"Just stop jumping on me. If there's something coming for us out here, I'm going to save my own butt before I save yours."

I was limping by the time we reached the south entrance of the mine. I knew it by the neon yellow shoelaces I'd tied around a nearby tree branch. Ten paces straight past the branch, turn left after passing between two pine trees. The ground had leveled out and sloped upward again, and the top of a wooden frame came into view in the underbrush. It would have looked like part of a tree if I didn't know where to look for it. I handed Artemis my flashlight and began clearing away the brush and branches I'd stacked in front of the entrance to hide it almost a year ago.

"Are you sure this is safe?" Artemis asked.

"I've been in here plenty of times and I never got hurt."

"You're sure there won't be animals inside? And it's not going to collapse on us?"

"It's, like, a hundred and fifty years old. If it hasn't collapsed yet, it's not going to now. If you're so worried about it, don't touch anything while we're inside." I kicked the last of the leaves out of the way and motioned for my flashlight back. The mouth of the tunnel had been narrowed by a cave-in, but past that it became wide enough for three or four people to walk in side by side, standing up. An old mine cart track ran along the ground. The tunnel dipped slowly downward, and my flashlight beam couldn't see past the curve in the floor.

Inside was warmer than outside. I shook myself and scanned the space while Artemis followed me in. Remnants of my last visit still littered the floor. Matchboxes. A burn mark on the rock where I'd lit papers, sticks, shreds of clothing, and plastic spoons. Anything I could get my hands on. My hand began to itch. Then the right side of my head. It still smelled like fire here, even after all this time. The scent made my skin crawl. My heart began beating too fast.

I remembered these things, but they didn't feel like mine anymore. They belonged to the old Zora.

Artemis had zeroed in on the litter. "Did you use to—? You came here to set fires?"

"Good job, detective." I brushed past her.

"I thought you didn't like fire?"

"I don't. I was testing something."

"What?"

"Mom always said we couldn't be burned by firestarters. Like the Chevelle. I wondered if we could be burned by regular fire. Doesn't work." I'd come here plenty after Mom disappeared, testing matches on my hands and arms. Burning paper and plastic, trying to see if any of that had an effect. I always came away unblemished.

Artemis squinted into my flashlight beam. "Do you think—my mom never brought it up—do you think it would hurt me?"

"Let's hope there's no reason we need to find out," I said. "Come on—we still have a ways to go."

10

"This mine was built in 1870." Artemis's voice echoed softly in the dark as we followed the old cart track. Talking had calmed her, so I let her ramble. "Salem Hillcroft was around five years old then. There was a record of poor labor conditions and abuse among the miners. The mine made Salem's father very rich, and according to journals from the locals, it made Salem very entitled. As he got older, he went with his father to oversee mining operations, and when he was eighteen, he went by himself. He disappeared, and the stories say he fell into one of the caves inside the mine."

I'd seen the miners—adults and children—but not Salem Hillcroft.

"Why'd he go all the way to the caves?" I asked.

"That's not even the point," Artemis said. "Why did he go into the mine at all? Why did he go so far? And he *happened* to slip at a place where the miners often wouldn't even go? Into a cave where they couldn't find his body? A cave the miners would know the location of *very well?*"

"You're saying the abused miners kidnapped Salem and tossed him down a hole in the mines."

"I'm saying it's a *lot* more likely than Salem suddenly becoming a klutz at exactly the wrong spot."

"Haven't you ever heard of Occam's razor?"

Artemis paused. "I'm surprised you even know what Occam's razor is."

I gave her the middle finger over my shoulder. "I read books."

The uneven mine floor was doing nothing good for my ankle, but we were already here and we were probably late. The route through the mine to the north entrance was direct, though I'd figured out early on that whoever planned the mine, while smart enough to leave supports for the ceiling, had not bothered to leave any directions or signs to let you know which way you were going. You'd think it would be easy to navigate a big grid, but when every tunnel looks exactly the same and you're not great at remembering how many left turns you took, you start running in circles pretty fast. I had explored this part of the mine before, but after I got lost the second time, I stuck to the south entrance.

"Okay, be quiet," I whispered. "I heard something."

We came around a bend in the tunnel. Several routes led to the north entrance, and most were still crowded with rubble, old supplies, or broken equipment, as if the day the mine closed down, all the miners dropped everything where they stood and left. A little boy in a dirty shirt huddled next to a broken crate, unblinking eyes tracking us as we moved past him. No sign of any firestarter yet, thankfully. A trickle of voices echoed off the walls. I waved a hand for Artemis to stay behind me and kneel down. We huddled behind a stack of rotted crates.

"No wonder people think this place is haunted," a man said. A flashlight swept across the wall farther up the tunnel. "It feels like there are still people here."

"Seriously, Mike?" Tad Thompson. What a dick.

"I didn't mean ghosts; I meant—look at this." Wood skidded on stone, then clattered to the floor. "Everything's still here."

"Can we hurry?" A feminine voice. Leila. "It's cold out, and I'm already on so much Sudafed I can't walk straight."

"Eric, you have the infrared?" Tad.

"Yeah, hold on." Probably the tech guy.

"Grant?"

"We're ready to go whenever you guys are." That had to be the producer. His voice was farther away, maybe still outside.

The voices faded, replaced by scuffling feet and the

flickering of lights. Artemis tapped my arm.

"Shouldn't we move?" she said. "What if they come this way?"

I didn't think they would. Flashlights threw shadows on the walls and highlights in the wrong places. The tunnel we were in was camouflaged. The tunnel directly ahead of them was the one that would take them deeper inside.

"It won't hurt to get ahead of them," I whispered back. "Get up, go."

As quietly as possible, we turned and headed back the way we'd come. After a few minutes, I pulled Artemis to a stop and redirected her down another tunnel that went deeper into the mine. It smelled of damp earth, and our flashlights made the shadows hard-edged and intense. Artemis scraped and stumbled over the uneven floor, her backpack rattling softly.

Voices echoed again down the tunnels. It sounded like Tad, but I couldn't make out his words.

"They must have started filming," I said. We reached a larger passageway. Two miners stood there, looking lost. I pulled Artemis past them, heading back to the north. She was huffing a little bit now. "I told you not to bring that backpack."

She grunted at me.

Footsteps echoed. My ankle throbbed as I kneeled at the mouth of the tunnel. We waited a few minutes, until a flashlight beam came around a bend up ahead.

"... get the KII and the EVP recorders out and see if we can capture anything in here while Leila and Eric head south." Tad, with his TV voice now. He and Mike stopped. Mike, the sidekick, who had his hair neatly dreadlocked and tied into a ponytail, stood pointing a camera down the tunnel. Tad, beside him in a black beanie and sweatshirt, stared at a KII meter. Behind them was another cameraman with a larger, bulky TV camera mounted on his shoulder.

"Is there anyone here who would like to communicate with us?" Tad's voice faded. It was quiet for a few moments. "If you are here, we would like to speak with you." Another pause.

In the long stretch of silence, I cupped my hands around my mouth and hissed nonsense. Tad's head whipped up; Mike straightened and focused the camera down the tunnel.

"You heard that, right?" Mike said.

"Is someone here with us?" Tad repeated, still in TV voice. I had to hand it to the guy; he did not break character.

I nudged Artemis. We got up and started back again, into the long tunnel parallel to Tad and Mike's, that ran deeper into the mine. We passed two cross tunnels this time, ghosts flickering in my peripheral, trying to follow the echoing shuffle of footsteps, then stepped carefully down the third cross tunnel to intercept Tad and Mike once again.

I let out another loud whisper.

"There it is again!"

"We're following it. Or chasing it."

Both Tad and Mike stared down the tunnel, frozen. Their lights didn't reach this far.

"Can you give us some sign?" Tad called. "A noise? Anything?"

I was about to whisper again when Artemis grabbed a rock beside my foot and tossed it out the tunnel mouth. It clattered into the darkness. I gave Artemis a surprised thumbs-up.

"I thought we told the assistants not to bother in here," Mike said. "Did Grant send them in?"

"Who cares. Keep the cameras on." Tad held out the KII meter and went back into TV voice. "I have in my hand a device with lights on it. If you come near, you can make these lights change."

We must have been lucky, because not a second after he said it, two lights along the top of the meter came on, flickering, then went down. The nearest ghost stood several feet behind him, impervious to the darkness of the tunnel. Tad looked back at the camera. Either he thought this was real, or he was damn good at playing off coincidences like supernatural fact.

"We're going to ask you a series of yes or no questions," he said. "If the answer is—oh—" The device had lit up again. All the lights this time. The hairs on my arms stood up, and I had to grip my forearms to make them go back down. More ghosts came to the ends of their tunnels, casting no shadows. They all looked at me.

I turned, expecting a sheet-white Artemis, and found her instead looking through the viewfinder of her own camera. She had the night vision turned on.

"What are you doing?" I whispered.

"There are so many dead down here!" She barely made noise.

Her voice carried. Too loud. Tad and Mike were looking down the tunnel again.

"Did you hear what it said that time?" Tad asked.

"Yeah," Mike said. "Sounded like 'dead down here.'"

I was already herding Artemis in the opposite direction when Tad said, "They're trying to tell us there *is* something down here? Do you think they're trying to lead us to it? Salem Hillcroft—"

Artemis and I made it to the other end of the cross tunnel.

"We should leave," Artemis whispered. "They're going to find us."

"Not yet. We only gave them good evidence. We need to make it obvious the evidence is teenagers messing with them; otherwise we did the exact opposite of what we meant to do. And we can't let them wander when there might be a firestarter around."

Artemis was already shaking her head and heading the other way. "No, nope—"

"Are you seriously ditching your duty right now?"

As Artemis turned the corner, a flashlight swept up the tunnel, followed by a new set of voices. ". . . it isn't as cold in here, anyway; that's nice!"

"Maybe you could strip and show some skin. The miners would like that."

"You're disgusting, Eric. Shine a light down these other tunnels. I feel like we're missing things."

"Oh, eff," Artemis whispered.

I grabbed her and pulled her deeper into the mine. The air got wetter and warmer, and the tunnel began to slope downward. Deeper into the hills. This was officially farther than I'd gone before, farther than I'd ever wanted to go. I had no idea if it was safe here. There might've been dangerous gasses or holes in the floor. The dead lined up so we had to charge through them, more of them than I'd expected. Adults and children. I wished I could stop, ask them what was down here, what could cause them turmoil, but they wouldn't answer. My ankle burned with every limping step, and we moved too fast to stay completely quiet. We escaped Leila's and Eric's lights, but their footsteps continued to follow us.

"Find a place," I whispered to Artemis as she overtook me, even with the heavy backpack on her shoulders, and I thanked god she couldn't see all the dead she sidestepped. "Find a place for us to hide."

My foot landed on a rock. My ankle bent hard. I yelped in

pain, clapped a hand over my mouth, and grabbed the back of Artemis's bag as I fell. She fell with me; we collapsed on the floor with a heavy thud and scraping, a rush of air and identical groans. Artemis's camera clattered against the rock.

"Wait," someone said behind us. "Did that sound like . . . ?"

I scrambled to my feet and yanked Artemis up by her arms. I'd ripped the backpack from her shoulders. She bent to grab it.

"No!" I pulled her jacket. She got her hands on her camera, the viewfinder still open. We started running before we realized we'd left the flashlights behind and were navigating by the camera's night vision. No ghosts appeared in it, though they loomed all around us.

"There's a backpack and flashlights. These aren't Tad's or Mike's."

Artemis ran with me holding her jacket, limping as fast as I could. The tunnel dove down and down and began to snake around, and footsteps followed us. Lights flashed. The dead pressed in. We turned down one passageway to the right, then another to the left. Anything to lose them. Voices echoed, and I couldn't tell whose they were or which direction they came from, though it seemed like they couldn't still be following us.

Artemis took another turn. The ghosts disappeared, and the floor dropped sharply out from under our feet. We landed with a huff several inches down, tumbling over each other.

"Are you okay?" Artemis whispered. Her breath stirred my hair. The air was warm all around here, muggy with humidity, and my hair stuck to my forehead.

"Fine, besides my ankle." I picked myself up. "Hey! This might have worked. They knew someone was down here, but they didn't find us. Now we just have to wait for them to leave."

Artemis was slowly panning around the room with her camera. It *looked* like a room, and not another tunnel. It was a large open space with a ceiling supported by six old beams. The mine tracks continued until they met a wooden bridge that spanned a deep crevice. I glanced up and around, shoulders prickling. The dead had left us.

"This is one of the caves, I think," Artemis said. "Look to the right—the crack in the floor goes farther that way, and it gets wider. Ten or fifteen feet. And how deep . . . ?" She moved toward it. I grabbed her arm.

"Uh-uh," I said. "Rule number one in old abandoned mines: do *not* step near the giant hole in the floor."

"Have you been here before?"

"No, which is why I'm saying don't touch anything. Let's wait for a while until they're gone, then we can get out of here and go home. Mission accomplished." As long as the *DMW* crew didn't come any deeper, we were probably safe. I could come back tomorrow night and investigate, but for now I needed to get Artemis out before she got herself killed.

"*No*, mission *not* accomplished," she said. "There is so much more to explore here."

"What happened to 'let's leave' Artemis?"

Artemis pointed the camera at her own face so I could see her look of annoyance. "We're here, and they didn't follow us. While we're in the clear, we should keep investigating—"

"*What is it?*" Tad's voice rattled down the tunnel. We both froze. The temperature ratcheted up several degrees.

A second later, Eric called back, "Some teenagers running around, we think. We found a bag and flashlights."

"These damn KII meters are still going off."

"Ignore them. We have to start over; this is useless."

"Start over? It's cold and late, why not play it as it is?"

"As locals fucking with us? I don't care if you're dying of Sudafed poisoning, Lei, I'm not putting that on TV."

"Tad, please."

"Zora." That was Artemis.

"Stay. Quiet," I hissed.

"No—Zora—Zora, look."

Artemis's hand found my shoulder and pushed me around. The room was quiet, yawning. On the opposite side of the wooden bridge was an impenetrable, gaping blackness, a hole in the world I knew well.

An entrance.

A hunched shape sat on the bridge. Even the night vision

couldn't make out the details, but it hadn't been there before because before I'd been able to see where the bridge connected with the rock. The shape moved. A limb slid out, a set of talons that scratched on the wood. It rose, unfurling, and lifted its head.

I looked up from the camera. A dark shape stood on the bridge, silhouetted by a soft red glow, like the corrupted ghosts. The dark shape had eyes. The eyes were red pinpricks.

"You're kidding," I said.

A blast of hot air whipped my hair back. The shape darted forward. Artemis grabbed me at the same time I grabbed her. A blaze of fire lit the room. *Fire.* Every fiber of my body jolted. I choked down a scream and yanked Artemis forward.

The tunnel entrance reappeared. I took Artemis by her collar and her belt and threw her up the short ledge before I scrambled up after her. A hot touch grazed my calf. The scream came out.

Then we were up and running, back the way we'd come, and the ghosts had fled, and my twisted ankle felt like a spike had been driven through it, and our flashlights and the backpack were gone but there were lights up ahead. We stumbled into a cross tunnel. Another blast of heat from behind. I looked back only once. There were the two red pricks of light, unblinking, chasing us. Burning, real, one hundred percent *godforsaken evil eyes.*

We turned another corner and hit something solid, tumbling again to the tunnel floor. Someone cursed. Limbs tangled. A flashlight blinked on and off. A hand grabbed my wrist, then my hair, then my neck. Artemis squeaked.

"Stop moving! Who the hell are you?"

A light burned into my eyes. "Get off! Get—*off*—"

"Mike, get over here! It's the two who were screwing with us!"

Tad Thompson had pinned me to the ground with his knees on my arms and his hand on my sternum. Artemis was rolling beside me, wheezing. Her camera was still on, several feet away. Mike scooped it up.

"They've been recording," he said.

"Take the memory card. I don't want them putting it up online."

"No!" Artemis struggled to her knees. Tad grabbed her ponytail and yanked her back down.

Tad grinned at her, at me. "Hey, it's ice cream goth and boring history girl. Thought you'd have some fun ruining our shoot?" The heel of his hand dug into my chest. "I wouldn't want to spoil it for you. Let's call the police and keep the party going."

I twisted my head to look past Tad, down the tunnel. There were no red eyes, no hot air. The firestarter was gone, as if it had never been. Sweat began to cool on my forehead. Someone was calling the police, the sound echoing back to us. Even with the alarms going off in my head—how royally screwed we were, especially me—I felt a rush of relief that the dark shape and its fire had disappeared.

"Hey, Tad," I grunted.

He looked down at me. "What?"

"I'm not goth, moron," I spat at him. "I'm grunge *at best.*"

Then I jabbed my prosthetics into his eyes.

11

I didn't poke Tad's eyes out. Unfortunately.

The *Dead Men Walking* crew pulled us out of the mine and dropped us by their van while we waited for Chief Rivera to arrive. They had Artemis's backpack, our flashlights, and the SD card from Artemis's camera, which Tad quickly stuffed into an equipment bag filled with other SD cards and tossed into their SUV. Eric guarded us while Tad, Mike, and Leila stood on the other side of the clearing, arguing.

The entrance to the mine sat silent and dark. Every time I glanced away from it, I expected to look back and find red eyes peering out, followed by a lick of fire.

Headlights swerved around the clearing. The cruiser came to a halt inside the chain-link fence. Chief Rivera climbed out.

"They took our memory card!" was the first thing I yelled to her.

She spared me a single look before finding Tad and the others. I twisted my arms together so hard my neck began to hurt. The *DMW* producer spoke to Rivera first; he'd been the one to put in the call. She got statements from him and every member of the crew, then went to look at their equipment. She searched through the bags in the SUV. Tad said something to her once she got to the bag with the memory cards in it. When she came to us, she wasn't carrying anything but her notebook.

"They stole the SD card out of Artemis's camera," I said.

"It's in with their other stuff," Artemis said, "with the other memory cards. We'll have to go through every one to find it."

"Mr. Thompson insists they took nothing from you," Rivera said, tight-lipped. "And I didn't see anything out of place, so we'll deal with that later. You girls are coming to the station with me. You can explain what you were doing when we get there."

She shepherded us into the backseat of her cruiser and closed the door. Tad watched. He was pale in the cruiser's headlights, everything except his eyes. I flipped him off.

Chief Rivera slammed the door and reversed out of the clearing. My heart thumped painfully; before we'd come here, I'd gone over the scenario of being caught, what I'd do, what I'd say, but my plan was gone now. Mom had gotten in her fair share of trouble, running around trying to solve the mysteries of Addamsville and the firestarters, but Aunt Greta had always gotten her out of the worst of it. And this wasn't good for more reasons than just that memory card: the *DMW* crew could still go back into the mine tonight, and now we knew the firestarter was in there.

Small crowds had gathered outside the fence. All living. A lot of them wore *Dead Men Walking* T-shirts or carried cameras, standing in grass up to their knees. Here to get a glimpse of the cast or a glimpse of the ghosts. They watched silently, faces obscured by the darkness, their red camera lights following us like eyes.

The Chief waited until we were well down the road before she glanced into the rearview mirror and said, "What the *hell* did you think you were doing? Zora, I expect something like this out of you—I don't *want* to expect it, but I do—but Artemis? I thought your mother raised you better than that. Much better. I cannot believe you two. And in the *mine?* Do you know how dangerous that place is? Do you know how easy it is to get lost or hurt in there?"

"No one was stopping the *DMW* crew from going in," I said.

"Because the *DMW* crew had trained professionals with them, and someone had gone to check the mine earlier today to make sure they were safe."

And *that* person could have been killed, too. Was there no end to the list of people I was supposed to save?

"So we weren't in any danger."

"You had no way of knowing you weren't in danger."

"Chief Rivera," Artemis said, leaning forward. "It's really, really important we get that footage back. If they keep it, they'll use it on their show."

Chief Rivera was quiet. She kept her stony, white-knuckled hold on the steering wheel. Of course she wasn't going to entertain this nonsense. "I'll look into it," she said finally. "But don't expect anything."

"Thank you!" Artemis almost bounced in her seat. "Oh, thank you, Chief Rivera, thank you so much."

The Chief wasn't looking at her. She was looking at me. We both knew why.

The police station sat on Handack Street a little north of where it intersected with Valleywine. It was a squat brown building with only one cruiser parked outside, a lone lamppost illuminating the parking lot, and an air of cleanliness and order. Inside, a front desk barred the way to another pair of desks and the chief's office.

Rivera took us down a hallway to the holding cells. There were only three. The chief ushered us both into one.

"Is this necessary?" I asked.

"For her?" The chief pointed to Artemis. "Probably not. For

you? I'm not taking chances. I told you to stay out of trouble and you do this. You're not a minor anymore, Zora. You were trespassing. If you'd damaged any of their equipment, you'd be charged with criminal mischief. You were lucky Mr. Thompson grabbed you before you stabbed him—if you'd hit him first, they could've gotten you for assault, too. These are all things that send you to prison. You understand that, don't you?"

I pretended to rub something out of the corner of my eye.

"Zora," she said again, stepping closer to the bars. "I know you want to prove you didn't set the fire at Masrell's house, but I can guarantee you this incident has already gotten out, and in the morning, your reputation will be *far* past saving. All you had to do was sit still, let me do my job, and wait for the storm to blow over. Now I'm not sure there's anything I can do to help you." She shook her head, then looked at Artemis. "I'm calling your mother."

Artemis's face drained of color. "Do you have to tell her what we did?"

Chief Rivera gave her a very pointed look.

"Don't worry," I said, dropping onto the cot. "She won't blame you for it. She'll think I poisoned you."

"As for you, Zora," the chief said, "I'm calling your sister."

"She won't be awake. Her alarm goes off at five in the morning. Try her then."

"You're going to stay here overnight?" Artemis said.

"No one else is going to pick me up."

"I have to decide what I'm going to do with you first, anyway," the chief said. "A ticket, at the very least. Trespassing. I imagine it's not the first time you've been there, either, so count yourself lucky that this is the first time I *know* about, and don't let me catch you doing anything like it ever again."

And she disappeared.

Artemis sank against the wall, boneless. I rested my elbows on my knees and bent over until my hair shielded my face, then took several long, deep breaths. I wasn't going to jail. It was a possibility, but I'd avoided it this time.

"Do you think this is going to go on my record?" Artemis asked.

"I dunno. Why?"

"I've never had anything on my record. I don't *have* a record."

"Congratulations, cherry popped."

"That's disgusting."

"I'm not surprised to hear you say that."

"Why, because I have a decent sense of humor?"

"No, because you look like you got thrown up by a teen Christianity magazine."

"At least I don't look like a raccoon that crawled out of Joey Ramone's garbage can."

"I do love 'Blitzkrieg Bop.'"

Artemis let out an irritated scream and threw her hands up. "How can you be so flippant about this? If that footage gets out, Addamsville will be flooded with tourists. And it'll be worse than them just tearing up our buildings and our stories— they'll go to the mine. The *DMW* crew might be going back in there *right now*. We're supposed to be protecting them!"

"No," I snarled, "*I'm* supposed to be protecting them. Don't talk to me like I don't know my own job. When was the last time you ran someone over with a car or chopped off their head? You can't even *see* ghosts. Your mom made you think you're so damn important. You're *not*. If the *DMW* crew or anyone else dies, it's my fault, and you'll get off free, like you always do."

"That's not true. I'm here to help. I want to help—"

"Shut *up*." I flopped over and rolled away from her. "Why do you think I fought that firestarter alone last time? You're a liability; you've never fought them before. You'll just get in the way and get yourself killed. Go play with your EMF meter and leave me alone."

There was a beat of silence that stretched, and stretched, and stretched, until I realized Artemis didn't plan to reply.

Greta arrived half an hour later in a contemptuous fury. Her hair was up in a curled Hallmark-movie ponytail, her makeup perfect even at this time of night, and her shoes made ringing clacks on the floor. Most of that anger was for me. Something about delinquency, poisoning her daughter, and not doing the memory of my mother justice.

I did catch the last thing she said.

"If you don't start doing something about yourself, you're going to send the whole town up in flames."

I refused to move out of spite.

"You were right," Chief Rivera said after they'd gone. "I got Sadie's voice mail. Is there anyone else who can come get you?"

I sat up. Grim probably would, but I didn't want to bother him; he had enough problems in his life. The Happy Hal's gang might come, but I didn't want them to know about this sooner than absolutely necessary. They'd trust me less than they already did. And that was the end of my list of people I could call.

"No, it's fine," I said.

"Then you're here till morning. I left Sadie a message, but we'll try her again after five."

I scooted back into the corner and curled up. "Thanks, Chief."

She didn't leave right away. Her eyebrows creased very slowly. She looked worried, not angry, and the way she stood made her seem tired. She wasn't freaking out, though, which I took to mean the firestarter hadn't made a reappearance at the mine.

"You're not a bad kid, Zora," she said, "but you do make bad decisions. I'm sure the reasons sound good or feel right, but it has to stop before you do something you end up regretting. I don't want to see you waste years of your life in prison."

"Like my dad, right?"

She shook her head. "Lazarus Novak isn't a bad guy, either, but like you, he tends to let his emotions get the better of him. I've known him for a long time, and after your mom died, he wasn't the same—"

He wouldn't have left us alone if he wasn't a bad guy, I thought, but said, "My mom's not dead."

Rivera tilted her head. "She's not?"

"No one ever found her body," I pointed out. "I get it— lost in the woods, never came back, been five years—she's probably dead. But she's not *for sure* dead. People go missing in the woods all the time. Some *trees* wouldn't be enough to kill my mom. She knows how to survive out there."

The Chief's frown deepened. "Zora, I investigated your mother's disappearance myself. If she wanted to leave town, she could have taken Valleywine to the interstate. She wouldn't stage a disappearance in the woods."

I didn't say anything.

"All right, well—after your mom went missing, your dad didn't deal with it in the most constructive ways. I can't say I blame him. Grief does things to you, especially when you don't have the resources to deal with it. All I wanted to say was that I think you're a smart girl and that you could make something of yourself, despite what everyone else thinks or says. If you're up for it, in the future, if you're thinking about doing something that might get you in trouble, you can come tell me about it, and we'll decide together if you should do it or not. You don't *have* to, but it's an option if you want it."

Unfortunately a lot of things relating to firestarters could get me into trouble, and I couldn't mention any of them to Rivera. "Sure."

"Get some sleep, Zora."

She left. A heater kicked on behind the walls. I stretched my legs across the muddy mess of the sheets. I kicked the boots off so hard they clanged against the cell bars. There was no fire here. I took a deep breath and repeated it several times in my head, once out loud for good measure.

We'd found the firestarter standing in front of its entrance. That round black nothingness past the wooden bridge was its gateway from wherever it had come, and I had to get it back through. Mom would have already had it done by now. It may not have even killed Masrell; she would have found it before that. She never stopped hunting. She was never scared of anything. Not firestarters. Not the town. She'd spent thirteen years teaching me everything she knew, but she'd never taught me how not to be scared.

I curled my right hand tight to my chest, the prosthetics stiff against my sternum, and turned on my side to draw my knees up. I had until morning to get myself back in order and figure out what to do about this firestarter. I knew where its entrance was, but it wouldn't stick around the mines now that we'd seen it.

I had time. Time to think. Time to breathe.

There was no fire here.

12

I didn't sleep. I couldn't. After the lights went out, I stayed awake, listening to all the little creaks and groans in the building and staring at the dark corner of the hallway. No matter how many times I told myself the mine firestarter wasn't coming after me, I waited for those eyes to appear in the shadows. If I hadn't been stuck in a cell, I could have at least run from it; Rivera had given me ice for my ankle, and it felt well enough now for me to flee, at least.

I spent all night worrying about the firestarter when I should have worried about Sadie.

I had thought Greta's fury would be worse than Sadie's. I had forgotten my sister's long-standing, if partially buried, reputation. I had forgotten she had once sent half the

Addamsville High baseball team running after a pop fly dented the roof of her car, and the bat she'd stolen to chase them with that day was the one that later became her weapon of choice.

Livid was too soft a word for her face. Her hair was up in a ratty bun, and she wore a bright pink sweatshirt with the words LIVIN' LIFE across her chest in bubble letters.

"What the fuck," she hissed, which was impressive for a sentence with no sibilant sounds.

Chief Rivera opened the cell door. "There'll be a ticket to pay," she said, "but it's better than what could have happened. Make sure she gets to school, too."

Sadie didn't say anything. By the muscle jumping in her jaw, I wasn't sure she was capable of speech. The chief spared me any more lectures and let me leave with Sadie, and only once we were heading home did I open my mouth.

"You can't tell Dad about this."

Sadie's grip made the leather on the steering wheel creak.

"Oh no," she said, voice much softer than I anticipated. "I won't tell him anything. *You* will."

"It was—"

"Chief Rivera told me what happened," Sadie snapped. "Trying to stop tourists from ruining the town? I hate to tell you, but we're already there! It's done! No ghost-hunting crew is going to make it worse than it already is. What did you think was going to happen? You'd make them look like assholes? Good job, you did that to yourself."

"No one's *wrong* about the tourists. They walk all over everything we have, and—"

"Oh, come *on*." Sadie rolled her whole head. "I hate the tourists, too, but Aunt Greta is right. This town sucks without its ghost stories. We don't have anything else to keep us afloat anymore. No coal mine. Just tourism. And yeah, maybe there should be some stricter guidelines about what the tourists are allowed to touch and where they can go, but there's nothing we can do about it. I know you don't like her, but Addamsville was dying before Aunt Greta turned it into a giant tourist trap."

I crossed my arms and looked out the window as the Goldmine passed by. Sadie didn't say anything else until we were back on the path up the bluffs.

"And you left the Chevelle out here in the open." She pulled to a stop so I could get out. She handed over the car keys, flashlight, and my phone. "You better tell Dad about this part, too, so he can be properly upset."

I raised my arms. "Mom left the Chevelle by the woods overnight, too!" If it was impervious to fire, some bugs and dirt weren't going to hurt it.

Sadie had already rolled up her window and started toward the trailer. I was glad she hadn't heard me; bringing up Mom's disappearance was too harsh, and I regretted it as soon as I said it. I should have brought up Dad, instead. That he didn't deserve to be upset about this. He didn't deserve to scold me for this when he had no idea what was going on in our lives, and what he'd done. But Sadie wouldn't listen to it. She always sided with Dad.

I found the Chevelle in the foliage, cleared some leaves off the hood, and climbed inside. My phone clung to the last of its battery, and there was one unread message from early this morning. From Artemis.

I'm sorry. You're right, I don't understand. But we need to get that footage back.

She still thought we were on speaking terms? She was so naive sometimes, like she thought she could get whatever she wanted as long as she was polite.

But Artemis knew what was going on. One of the few who did, and the only one willing to help me.

I replied:

Yeah, we do.

Let that be an acceptance of her apology. I started up the Chevelle, said sorry to the dashboard for leaving it outside in the woods all night, and drove back up to the trailer. By the time I got there, Sadie had thrown my backpack and coffee thermos out the trailer door, and Artemis had sent me another message.

Also, Tad Thompson can suck eggs.

I laughed.

13

I kept my head down at school and walked through the soreness of my ankle until it faded. No getting to class late, no extra-long bathroom breaks to calm down, no trampling freshmen in the hallway, even when they made passing jokes about me getting caught by the *Dead Men Walking* crew and I had to breathe through my nose and count down from ten until the red in my vision went away. There'd been no other fires, no injuries, no deaths; the firestarter had either been temporarily spooked by all the people in the mine or it was smart enough to bide its time.

Rivera had been right; the story *had* gotten out quickly. It was worse for Artemis than it was for me, ironically, because people expected me to do something like that, but from

Artemis it was shocking. She avoided me at school, either because Greta had told her to, or because she didn't want to prolong her misery.

The rising excitement about the homecoming parade came as a bit of a blessing, since it took at least a little of the attention off me. I liked homecoming okay. It meant more people out in the streets, but at least they were the residents of Addamsville and not tourists, and it was one of the few days of the year they didn't seem to mind if there were Novaks among them. This year it was a relief. To be forgotten would be better than being feared.

And to be forgotten would be especially nice this year, because Dad was coming home.

He'd been sentenced to seven years but had only served three and a half thanks to Indiana's good-time credit. Probably he'd schmoozed someone. My memories of him before he got arrested—when he took Sadie and me to Hal's to get ice cream, when he taught me to drive, when he sat with us and Mom on the bluffs and looked out across Addams Lake—were overshadowed by the new memories of visits to a concrete room with a table and plastic chairs, us explaining what we'd been doing for the last month and trying not to bring up how much the town hated us. Sadie had eagerly awaited those visits. I had dreaded them, because there was always a chance I would get angry and say something to Dad that would hurt him, and the guilt would weigh me down even more than before. It seemed like cruel irony that he could cause us so much harm and I could still feel horrible for feeding even a little bit of it back to him.

When the seventh-period bell rang, I bolted for the Chevelle, keeping an eye out, always, for any of the eyeless dead, and escaped the parking lot before the three o'clock rush. The drive took longer than usual, and when I got there, Sadie's car was parked in its normal spot, by the raspberry bushes along the treeline.

The trailer sat on the lot where Aberdeen House had once been, our plumbing jerry-rigged to the Aberdeen well and septic tank. The generator out back was already grumbling away, and a light was on in the kitchen window at one end of the trailer. My heart beat hard. I wanted to scream obscenities. I wanted to cry.

Instead I got out of the car and yelled, "PAPA BIRD SAYS WHAT?"

A heartbeat later, the front door of the trailer crashed open and Dad yelled back, "COME HOME, BABY BIRDS!"

I met him halfway to the door. He had to lean back to lift my feet off the ground, and he swung me around once before setting me back down and squeezing me hard enough to make breathing difficult. It was the first hug I'd gotten from anyone since the last time he'd hugged me, and I held on tighter, and I hated him, and I loved him.

"You weren't so heavy last time," he said.

He let me go and held my face. He smelled like shampoo and aftershave. His hair had been recently cut, probably by Sadie. There was gray at his temples where there hadn't been before, and more lines on his face than I remembered from the last time we visited him. He was a handsome guy, my dad, not especially tall or bulky, because you don't need to be when you're as charming as he is. But there was something different now in his eyes and his shoulders; where there once had been a glint of Novak mischief, now there was only weariness. *Good*, I thought, and reveled in that weariness. *Good.*

He took my hands in his and pulled them up, raising an eyebrow at my gloves.

"It's just so people don't ask questions."

"We talked about the gloves before."

"I don't want people to stare."

Both eyebrows went up. "You can't bullshit the bullshitter, Zoo." He held my hands tight. "You are a Novak," he said slowly, "and Novaks don't hide from their shame. They accept what they've done and the decisions they've made, they take their punishment, and they move on."

A snarl threatened to form on my lips; I quickly looked down. He didn't have any right to tell me what to do. *I'd* been the one taking *his* punishment for three years while he sat in prison.

I pulled my hands out of his. He cleared his throat. Wiped his hands on his jacket.

"I'm so glad to be home," he said.

"Can you guys hug over dinner?" Sadie came out the front door, locking it behind herself. The lights were off, the generator killed. "I'm starving."

"Shut up, Sadie!"

"You shut up, skunkface!"

"So glad to be home!" Dad crowed, dancing to the driver's door of the Chevelle. The change in him from hesitant to buoyant was instant, as if nothing strange had passed between us.

Sadie stopped with her car keys in hand. "Oh. Are we not taking my car?"

Dad looked stricken. I bit my lip to keep from laughing.

"Sadie. My darling." Dad held his hand out for the Chevelle's keys, and I tossed them over. "I have been away from *all* my children for almost four years, and you expect me to leave my eldest at home?"

Sadie rolled her eyes. "Fine, but I get shotgun."

"Oh, come on—"

Dad cackled as he climbed in the car.

"Home!"

Fool's Gold was a local restaurant that served great biscuits and gravy, good pizza, and mediocre everything else. A couple of pool tables and a dartboard were clustered at the south end of the room so players could watch the TV behind the bar, usually set to whatever seasonal sport was on. Today it was the news. We arrived before the dinner rush and got our table near the north window, where Piper Mountain made a purple shadow against the darkening horizon. A few bikers lounged by the pool table in the back, not stirring even when a living man walked right through them carrying beers to his table. There were fewer of them than normal. Fewer ghosts in the parking lot and on the streets, too. They'd been dwindling since Masrell's fire, like a classroom with too many empty seats.

We ordered, not on purpose, the same meal we'd ordered the last time we'd been here. Dad: a Coke, a Pyrite (a cheeseburger with jalapeños), and an order of onion rings. Sadie: sweet tea and a chicken Caesar wrap (which sounds healthy but is actually the fixings of a Caesar salad spread on a small pepperoni pizza and rolled up). Me: water, french fries, and the hottest hot wings they can possibly make (lovingly nicknamed "Eyeblisters").

When I pointed out it was the same meal from almost four years ago, Sadie said, "How the hell do you remember that?" and Dad said, "Yeah, sounds like us."

I remembered because it was the last meal all three of us ate together before Dad got arrested.

"So, who wants to go first?" Dad asked, twirling an onion ring around his finger.

"First for what?" I said.

"Telling me what's been going on recently. With you two."

Dad was already looking at me. Sadie's head turned slowly, as if she was giving me time to start talking. I bit down on my straw until my teeth ground together. This wasn't fair.

"Nothing," I said. "Everything's peachy." I stuffed a chicken wing in my mouth. Sadie bared her teeth.

"Zora has something she wants to tell you about, Dad."

I shook my head.

"Oh? What kind of something?"

My eyes began watering. Damn Eyeblisters.

"Did you hear about the *Dead Men Walking* crew filming here?" Sadie said.

"Sure, it's all anyone's talking about."

"Zora paid them a visit when they were shooting at the coal mine."

I swallowed, chased it with a handful of fries for the heat, and, still crying, said, "Wait, wait, wait. He needs to hear the whole thing. You're making it sound like I just arbitrarily decided to go do that."

"Do *what?*" Dad's voice dropped.

I cleared my throat. "Sneak into the mine and fake paranormal evidence."

"And then get caught on your way out and *get arrested*," Sadie finished. "Her and Artemis. They snuck in to mess with this film crew and got themselves arrested. I had to pick her up from the police station this morning."

Dad ran a hand over his face. "Why would you do that, Zo?"

He called me *Zo* and not *Zoo* when he was *really* disappointed. I'd already given him my answer. What else was I supposed to say? I knew what I'd done wrong.

"Tourists," Sadie said. "They did it because they're tired of tourists."

"That seems a little reductive," I said.

"Who isn't tired of tourists?" Dad sat back. "But that's not a reason to go into the mine—that makes me worry about you, you know? You could have been hurt, or gotten lost. The mine isn't safe."

"I *know.*"

I maybe said it a little too enthusiastically, because he paused. I'd never known him to pause when he was lecturing us. Granted, he didn't lecture us often. He lowered his eyes and said, "That's the first time you've gone there, right? There hasn't been more going on before that I didn't hear about?"

"I would have made sure you heard about it." Sadie cut a chunk off her pizza wrap. "Don't worry, I yelled at her this morning, too. She's probably heard enough of it."

If I agreed, Sadie would say I had *not* heard enough of it, so I kept my mouth shut. They wouldn't be tearing into me if they knew the real reason we'd gone into the mine. They wouldn't be acting like I'd actually done all the things the town thought I did. But that had been one of Mom's first rules: Dad and Sadie can't know about the firestarters. That just meant that now Sadie was on Dad's side for everything, even though she knew as well as I did that our reputation in town was mostly because of him.

"Anyway," Sadie went on, "I have some news, too."

"Did you also go late-night spelunking?" Dad asked.

"Hah, no. I don't have a ring or anything, but uh—Grim proposed."

I choked on my water. Dad's face lit up. He almost knocked over his drink reaching across the table to grab Sadie's hand.

"What? Really?"

"When did *that* happen?"

Sadie beamed at Dad and scowled at me. "A couple of days ago. I didn't say anything because I wanted to announce it when Dad got home."

"Grimmie proposed to you and you didn't tell me?" I said. "I'm surprised he didn't use a Fruit Loop as a ring."

"We thought about it. The hole is too small."

"Well, details," Dad said. "You're getting the Fool to cater, right?"

"We still have to figure out how we're paying for it."

He shrugged. "Just do what me and your mom did and have the ceremony at town hall."

"Or elope," I said.

Sadie threw a piece of lettuce at me. I flicked water back.

Dad caught sight of something at the bar. "Hey, your ghost hunters are on TV."

Across the bar, the Harrisburg news crew stood outside the entrance to the Hillcroft Coal Mine. The No Trespassing sign took up most of the shot.

"Great," I said.

The TV was muted, but a black band of captions scrolled across the bottom of the screen.

"*. . . and last night the crew was disturbed by two Addamsville teenagers playing a prank. No one was injured, but the teenagers were taken into the custody of the Addamsville Police Department.* Dead Men Walking *leader Tad Thompson has stated they will not press charges. . . .*"

"Of course they won't press charges!" I said. "They stole our footage and they don't want anyone to find out!"

The captions went on. "*. . . the show has delayed its official investigations in order to allow this weekend's homecoming festivities to take place without interruption, but this evening they plan to do additional filming of another famous haunted location: Grimshaw House, located on Addamsville's south side. The crew will be* *accompanied by a police escort to ensure no incidents occur."*

"Oh." Sadie's face fell. "Grim's not gonna be happy about that."

I already had my phone out to text Artemis. There would be plenty of witnesses around the house, not to mention at least one of the police officers, and if we hounded the police about getting the footage back, the *DMW* crew might hand it over. Hopefully Chief Rivera had a warrant or something to search their equipment more thoroughly.

A shot of Grimshaw House, paint chipped and weeds overgrowing its lawn, appeared for a moment on the TV. A haunted house if there ever was one, though of course no ghosts showed on screen. It should have belonged to Grim, but the will that passed the property down to the next Grimshaw had been lost years ago, and the town had sold it to Hermit Forester. That alone was enough to make me think there was something funky about it, though I'd never figured out what.

"They found the treasure in that place yet?" Dad asked. There was a theory that the Grimshaws had hidden their railroad fortune somewhere in their house. No one had found it yet, but not for lack of trying: it had been a favorite break-in spot for teenagers when my mom was young, but none of them had ever escaped without being horribly injured. Falling down stairs, tripping on things that weren't there, getting electrocuted by bad wiring. Even the Birdies didn't go near it now.

"Nope," I said, "the definitely-totally-real treasure remains hidden."

"Is Grim still trying to find the will?"

"He's looked," Sadie said. "We both have. There's nothing in the library about it, just old articles about the family. If the town council knew where it was, you'd think they'd have told him about it."

"I wouldn't be so sure," Dad said. "The Foresters have owned that place a long time. Imagine the town council prying a Goldmine house out of the hands of one of the old families, especially after all these years. And even if they did, and Grim got the will back and found out he was the heir to the house, he'd have to take Forester to court."

And if there was anyone in town who didn't have the money to take an old family to court, it was Grim. Grim, the oldest living Grimshaw, surely the heir to the house. Grim, who had never hurt a single living creature in his whole life.

The door to the Fool chimed. A large group of men shuffled into the restaurant. Their cheeks were chapped rosy red, their shoulders huddled up around their ears. Most wore junkyard jumpsuits under their coats, some the jeans and blue shirts from the auto shop. Buster Gates's wrecking crew.

Buster Gates looked like a bulldog that got stung in the face by a hornet. He shared no resemblance to Lorelei, his daughter, and he was the actual polar opposite of Grim, his nephew. How he ever got on the town council is beyond me, though it was probably money. He cheated people out of their junk and their car repairs, treated Grim like an indentured servant, and occasionally tried to run over teenage girls with his stupid ogre truck.

Buster said hi to Ecky Sanders, the bartender, and he and his group made their way toward the pool tables. I shrank into my seat to hide. Dad noticed my reaction and turned.

"Hey!" Dad raised a hand. "Buster boy! Long time no see!"

"No, Dad, *no*," Sadie said, but Dad was already standing.

Buster and his group stopped a table away and sized Dad up like a bull with a matador. Buster snorted and lifted his chin.

"They let you out already?" Buster said. "Thought you had another couple decades."

Dad laughed; either he didn't see the looks on their faces, or he didn't care. "No, three and a half years and I'm done! How's everything been? Junk business doing okay?"

Buster narrowed his eyes. He wasn't the smartest pig in town, but even I couldn't tell if Dad was messing with Buster, or if Dad honestly didn't realize he and Buster weren't friends anymore. I grabbed Dad's sleeve and tugged on it.

"Did you know your girl's been attacking people?" Buster said, nodding to me. "Trespassing on private property, putting her nose where she shouldn't, and now setting fire to houses, not just herself. George Masrell's dead, and she's still the prime suspect."

Dad's smile faltered. "Come on, Buster, you know Zora wouldn't do something like that." He took my hand off his sleeve and put his on my shoulder. "She's made some bad choices in the past, but we all have. She's trying to make up for it now, and that's all we can ask."

I rolled my eyes. Did he *really* think flimsy appeals like that would sway a town like Addamsville?

"You call robbing this town a *bad choice*?" The faces in the crowd behind Buster grew darker. A lot of people had been touched by Dad's scheme. A *lot*. "You robbed Masrell, too, and he helped send you to prison. How do we know you didn't do this?"

"That's not—"

"Some of us think it's time you and your *litter*"—Buster gave me and Sadie a sideways look—"find a new town to trash. Get that eyesore of a trailer off the bluffs."

Dad cooled. "You can say whatever you want about me, Buster, but I'm not gonna let you talk about my girls that way."

"What girls?" Buster said. "I only see dogs. At least your bitch wife had the decency to go die in the woods."

I grabbed Dad's hands at the same time Sadie shoved herself between him and Buster. I had never seen my dad angry, and I had never—*never*—seen him angry enough to hit something, but the moment the words left Buster's mouth, white rage flashed across Dad's face.

"We're going." Sadie shoved her way around the tables,

pulling me and Dad behind her. "We're going, we're going right now. Ecky, here's a couple of twenties, keep the change. Going, going."

Only when we were outside did Dad pull his hands out of mine. A furrow deepened between his eyebrows; with his new gray hair, he looked years older.

"I didn't think it'd be that bad," he said.

"People never liked us," Sadie replied.

I didn't say anything. Dad wandered toward the Chevelle, looking lost. It was good for him to hear that. Maybe he thought time in prison had been enough of a punishment, maybe he'd never gotten the full story of what had happened after he'd left. What people thought of us. How they treated us. It was his fault, and there was no point in sugarcoating it.

Dad gave me the Chevelle keys. "Maybe you should drive home, Zoo."

I watched him get in the backseat. He needed to see the ramifications of what he'd done, but that didn't mean I had to let Buster Gates get away with calling my mom a bitch.

I marched back to the Fool and got as far as the sidewalk before Sadie yelled at me from the car. I didn't hear what she said, but the sound was enough. I stopped.

Threatening Buster—even yelling something at Buster that could be vaguely construed as a threat—was one of those things that wouldn't help anyone. It wouldn't even make me feel better. All it would do was reinforce the idea that the Novaks were quick to anger and couldn't control themselves. I balled my fists, squeezing the Chevelle's keys so hard my fingers burned.

Ten. Nine. Eight. Seven. Six. Five. Four. Three. Two. One.

A deep breath.

I walked back to the Chevelle.

14

Dad went to bed early that night. He didn't want to stay in the bedroom he used to share with Mom, and we refused to let him sleep on the broken-down couch, so I took the couch and he was in my room. He was exhausted, he said, and just wanted to sleep. Sadie moved from the kitchen nook to the bathroom and back again, wearing paths in the floor, while I went over my excuse for leaving.

"I have to go to work." I shut off the TV.

Sadie stopped by a big box of Mom's old clothes and gave me a blank look. "No, you don't," she said. "You don't work again until tomorrow, after the homecoming parade."

I should have figured she'd been keeping track of my work schedule.

Her eyes narrowed to slits. "You're going out somewhere, aren't you? And you don't want me to know where."

"No."

"I can see your face, you liar. You're going to sneak out. Is this about the *DMW* crew again? What are you doing, going to Grimshaw House?"

"No."

"Is Artemis going to be there? Are you getting her in more trouble, too?"

"Christ, Sadie, shut up."

"You are not going. I forbid you to go. You're asking for a shitstorm of epic proportions, and we've already got a big one on our hands."

"And you're going to stop me . . . how?" I already had the keys to the Chevelle. I was faster than Sadie, and I was banking on the odds I could get to the car before she could grab me. "I don't want to start anything. Artemis and I are going to get her footage back. *Not* steal it. There are going to be other people around, and at least one cop. Nothing illegal is going to happen, I promise."

"You also said nothing was going to happen the day you went out and set fire to the Denfords' cornfield, and now you only have eight fingers."

My cheek twitched.

"If you're so worried about it," I said, "come with me. At

least then you can do recon and tell Grim what's happening with his house."

Sadie opened her mouth to argue, then closed it. She looked toward the bedrooms.

"Do you think Dad will be okay?"

"Here by himself? Why wouldn't he be? You leave me here alone all the time."

"Yeah, but people are scared of you."

And they weren't scared of Dad. They just hated him.

"Fine," Sadie said, and followed me out.

Grimshaw House had exactly thirteen ghosts.

A conveniently spooky number. It made a cute tourist story. Thirteen ghosts, all of them Grimshaws or servants of Grimshaws:

Edward Grimshaw, the one who built the house, who sometimes sat in the rocking chair on the front porch;

Lillian, his wife, who could be seen falling from the upstairs window with her white dress billowing;

Edward Jr., stumbling down the upstairs hallway with a bloody wound in his gut from an intruder;

Edward Jr.'s five children, four of whom died of horrible diseases and one of drowning in the lake;

Hattie, Edward Jr.'s sister-in-law, who committed suicide at the age of fifty-three after her husband died in a railroad accident;

Malcolm, Hattie's grandson, looking out the back window over Addams Lake;

Gerald Mosker, the cook;

Martha Lansing, the maid, and a distant relative of Officer Jack Lansing;

And a nameless gardener who could sometimes be glimpsed around the corner of the house.

These were the stories. I had never seen these ghosts; the house itself had a faint twinge of the supernatural about it, and Mom had guessed it was because the Foresters had lived there for a short time after Forester House burned down in the eighties. She'd checked inside, though, and hadn't found any firestarter entrance. The residual feeling was enough for all the ghosts in the Goldmine to give the house a wide berth, never coming within the confines of the yard.

When we arrived, the sun was setting and the sky behind Grimshaw House was deep orange, and the front windows were dark. The *Dead Men Walking* van was parked out front, and Eric the tech guy and Mike the sidekick stood nearby with the producer. The front door of the house was open to a gloomy hallway, giving the face of the house the impression of a distressed old man trying to throw up something he shouldn't have eaten. A police car sat in the driveway, and Norm stood on the crumbling porch with his arms crossed over his chest. He kept a sharp eye on the small crowd of people across the street, many dressed in *DMW* memorabilia and taking video with their phones. A lot of them had set up shop on the lawns of the houses there, spreading out with their coolers and their lawn chairs. I recognized the college kids I'd pointed in the wrong direction on our way to the mine. One person even had an umbrella. I wanted to ask if they knew they were camping on someone's private property, and that the interesting thing going on across the street didn't give them license to hang out wherever they wanted. A few ghosts stood over them, and though they had no expressions on their faces, their presence felt very purposeful. Disapproving.

Grim sat on the hood of his car a little ways down the street. I parked the Chevelle behind him. He wasn't looking at the house; he faced northwest, toward Black Creek Woods and Piper Mountain.

Sadie touched his arm so we didn't startle him. I wasn't sure it was possible to startle Grim. He swung his head around like an owl and smiled sadly at us.

"What's the matter, Grimmie?" I asked, though we all already knew.

"Nothing, really," he said. "My problems aren't that big when compared to others'."

Being forced to live with your abusive uncle who made you work at his stupid, dangerous junkyard because you had no money to live anywhere else or get a better education, and having to watch people tromp around your family's home when you weren't even allowed inside, and knowing that some jerk in the town hall lost the papers that might make your life five billion times better didn't seem like a small problem to me, but Grim was fundamentally a better person than I was.

Grim turned toward the house and the rest of us followed his gaze. Tad Thompson appeared at the front door, trailed by Leila, who held two cups of coffee and looked like she was going to dump one of them over Tad's head if he didn't stop talking.

"I feel bad for her," I said. "If I had to spend all day with that guy, I'd end up murdering him."

"Maybe don't say that out loud," Sadie said.

"Oh, right, I'm a cold-blooded killer."

"What are you doing here?" Grim asked.

Sadie sighed. "Zora wanted to get back some footage these guys stole from her and Artemis at the mine. These jokers pretended they didn't have it when Rivera asked."

"But she said she'd look into it," I added. The fact that Norm was here and not the chief didn't reassure me, but I still had to try.

Artemis showed up a few minutes later. She came speed walking down the street from the direction of Hillcroft House, wearing a thick cable-knit scarf and cute little ankle boots. She huffed like she'd just finished the Indy Mini. A quick glance at the fans and a wary look at the *DMW* van was enough reassurance for her to hop across the street and join us.

"Hey," she said. "Are you ready?"

"I figured you'd drive down here," I said.

"Mom grounded me for, like, three months. No car."

I doubted that extended to hunting firestarters, unless Aunt Greta was trying to take Artemis's help away from me to keep her safe. "How'd you get out of the house?"

"I told her I was going to a friend's to study for the physics midterm."

"That worked?"

"Why wouldn't it?"

I glanced at Sadie and Grim, then back at Artemis. "Your mom *believes* the excuses you give her?"

"Of course she does. I don't lie to her. I'm only doing it now because she's afraid I'm going to get arrested again." She paused for a deep breath. "I feel kind of bad about it, actually."

Sadie elbowed me in the ribs. "Learn something."

I swatted her away and motioned to the *DMW* van. "Let's go disturb these moles digging around inside Grimmie's house."

Artemis trailed after me, but so did Sadie and Grim. I wasn't super pumped about marching up to this house with the whole Scooby gang in tow, but their presence might mellow Norm a bit. It was only me he had a problem with; a firestarter had once scorched his mailbox and half his front yard, and he still thought I'd done it.

He had his eyes on us as we came up the sidewalk. When we entered the yard, he stormed down the front porch steps.

"You kids need to get on," he said. "Nothing here for you to see."

"We don't want to see anything," I said. "Did Chief Rivera tell you about our footage?"

"She told me not to let you two near these people while they were in town." He jabbed a finger at me and Artemis. "I don't know what made you girls think it was okay to go running around a mine at night, but you're not getting in this house."

"No." I held my hands up. "We're here for justice. They stole some footage from us last night and lied about it. Chief Rivera said she'd look into getting it back."

Norm looked from me to Artemis, and Artemis nodded her head quickly. Norm glanced at Sadie and Grim. Then back at me, hard, like he was trying to read my mind.

"You're telling the truth?"

"Yes, sir."

Norm leaned back and puffed up his chest. In my dealings with the Addamsville Police Department, I had learned many things about Norman Newall, but perhaps the three most important were these:

1. He was a cop of Addamsville, not Harrisburg or Indianapolis or anywhere else, and his loyalty was to the people who lived here,

2. He had a righteous and endearingly pure need to bring justice to those who have been wronged,

And

3. He likes you a lot better when you call him "sir."

"Wait here," he said, heading toward the *DMW* van. Then he stopped and looked at us again. "And when I say 'here,' I mean *right here*. Do not move, you understand me?"

"Yessir, Officer Newall."

He marched off.

"That was promising!" Artemis bounced on the balls of her feet. "They won't turn down a police officer."

"They already turned down a *chief*," I said, but she ignored me.

Voices came from behind us. "Screw the show; I would never film here, much less *live* here. Not after that stuff upstairs. Who knows how often they come here?"

"Shut up for, like, five seconds, Lei—oh! Well, speak of the devil."

You know that feeling when a bug crawls on your shoulder and you can't see it but you can feel the hairy legs tickling your nerve endings and it makes you want to peel your skin off? That is the feeling I got whenever Tad Thompson began to speak.

He appeared in the doorway, all smug smirks and stupid hipster clothes, holding a photograph. Leila floated behind him with their coffee, looking interested but not nearly so ready to bite someone. She also dressed like a hipster, but I didn't mind it as much. Probably because she didn't wear it like it made her better than me.

"We're here for our card, thief," I snapped, then remembered I'd meant to be polite. "Please."

Tad snorted. "What card? All the equipment is ours. We don't need to steal footage from a bunch of rednecks. Besides, shouldn't you be coming here to apologize? A lot of our fans are upset that we were attacked." He nodded across the street, where attentions and cameras had now been turned on us. "We're going to put that in our episode, of course. We're *Dead Men Walking!* We seek out danger as only the bravest can. A town where the ghosts *and* the inhabitants are hostile is so on-brand it hurts."

Leila made a noise. Tad's expression slipped into annoyance. "Not now, okay?" he said. "None of that feminist shit when we're not on the camera. I literally cannot take another second of it."

Leila rolled her eyes and walked away.

Tad turned back to us. "You're not getting your footage back. Drop it. You're a bunch of small-town hicks and you wouldn't know what to do with that footage if you had it."

"You watched it?" Artemis said.

His lip curled. "Of course I watched it. Watched it, saved it, made copies of it. I wanted to see what kind of damage it'd do to us if it got back to you. We don't look great on it, that's for sure, but you didn't only shoot us, did you?" He smiled then, showing all his teeth. "I don't know what that thing was in the mines, but I'm going to make it huge. Angry townspeople, creatures in the mines, old mansions burning down—this place really was the gold mine everyone said it would be."

Now Grim was the one making noises; he sounded like a wounded deer when Tad said "old mansions." Tad gave him a strange look and said, "Do I know you?"

Grim clamped his mouth shut and receded into his hair. Recognition dawned across Tad's face. He snapped his fingers on both hands.

"Oh! You're the guy! The—" He motioned to the house. "The Grimshaw guy! They told me about you. They said someone still lived in town, and that he looked like a scarecrow with a dead cat for hair."

Grim recoiled. The whites showed all the way around Sadie's eyes.

"I'm thinking about investigating here," Tad said. "The stories are amazing. Thirteen ghosts and treasure inside? I know you all have been using this rathole as your hideout, but we could make a documentary about it. Then, who knows, maybe that old creep in the woods will let us use it as a lake house."

"You don't belong here," Sadie said. "This house belongs to Grim."

Tad laughed. "I don't see his name on it. Well, *legally*, anyway." He looked Grim up and down. "Maybe you could buy it off Forester. Doesn't look like you have the money on you, though—or is it in your other jumpsuit?"

I felt the shift in the air by my left shoulder. Sadie blurred past me. Her hands were an inch from Tad's face when Grim caught her arms and yanked her back. Grim was deceptively strong, but not strong enough to hold back two hundred and thirty pounds of Sadie in a building rage, so I threw my back into her, hissing, "First Dad, now you—I thought *I* was supposed to be the one who had to be stopped from doing stupid things!"

Tad, gathering himself against the house's doorframe, stared at us with disbelief on his face and his eyebrows nearly in his hair. "I don't know why I'm surprised," he said. "You've seen one, you've seen them all."

"Hey!" Artemis stepped in front of me. "You're being a real jerk right now, you know that? Why do you have to go around insulting people all the time?"

I shoved Sadie off the porch. Grim towed her back to the street. Then I nudged Artemis behind me and stared Tad down. "What are you talking about, it's our 'hideout'?"

Tad held up the picture he was carrying. "Your mom? It's cute."

In the picture, two girls, probably around eight or nine, sat on a porch step with a dog. One girl had dark hair, one had light, but they were clearly sisters. Their eyes were a washed-out sepia, almost the same light color as their skin. They looked like me, like Sadie, like Artemis. I snatched the picture out of Tad's hands. He let me. On the back, in scrawled handwriting, was the year 1983.

"There were more photos all over, but I didn't have time to look through the rest of your junk upstairs," Tad went on. "I'm sure it's just as sentimental."

I stared at the picture. I had never seen pictures of Mom so young. I had never really seen pictures of *Mom*.

Norm's disgruntled bark flew across the yard. He appeared next to us a moment later, worked up and puffing. "What's going on here? Are they bothering you, Mr. Thompson?"

"No, not at all," Tad said. "They were about to go."

Norm glanced back to the street, where Sadie and Grim stood, calmer now, then gave Artemis and me a long, hard glare. I tucked the photo into my pocket, held up my hands, and said, "Swear to God, Officer Newall, we aren't here to start trouble."

Norm waited another moment before jerking his head toward the street. "Get out of here. They don't have your memory card. Producer confirmed they went through everything they had, twice, and didn't find anything out of the ordinary."

"You can't believe that."

"*Go!*" Norm jabbed a finger at the street. Artemis dragged me away. I looked back only once to see Tad standing behind Norm's shoulder. He winked.

When we were back at Grim's car, I took the photo out of my pocket and showed it to Sadie. "Tad found this inside the house. He thought it was my hideout. He said there were other things inside. Who would have a picture of Mom inside Grimshaw House?"

Sadie's eyes widened, her eyebrows pressing down hard over them. "It could be coincidence. Whatever else is in there—"

"But this was the one Tad found. It was easy to find. He thinks everything up there is mine. What if there are more? What if—" There was so much about her I didn't know. "What if there's more about her in there? *Who would put a picture of Mom inside Grimshaw House?*"

"Anyone," Sadie said, but a cloud had passed over her expression. Doubt. "It doesn't matter. We can't get in."

"We *can* get in," I said, "People used to get in here all the time."

Sadie and Artemis reacted at the same time.

"You want to trespass *again*—"

"—and got *horribly injured*!"

Sadie took me by the arm and pulled me aside, but I got words out before she did. "I get it. Whatever you're going to say to me, I know. And you're right. We shouldn't do it."

Her lips pressed tight together, eyebrows furrowing. "So why'd you suggest it?"

"Because it's Mom."

Because the harder I tried to ignore the mysteries of this town, the heavier they weighed, and there was one that weighed more than any other.

Sadie didn't speak right away, either, and that told me enough. I held up the photo. "Did you ever see a picture of her? Do we have any pictures of her?"

Her gaze flicked from me to the photo.

I pushed again. "She went into the woods that night for a reason. You know it's not teenagers keeping weird old pictures in Grimshaw House. Tad said there were more."

Her eyebrows tilted up.

"I'm not stupid," I said. "It wasn't lack of common sense that got me caught in the mines, or anywhere else. I know the risks. I think the risks are worth this. To see."

If I'd had my way, I would have gone without her, but if she was going to start monitoring my coming and going, then she was going to have to come with me. Her hand finally slid off my arm. She scraped her fingers through her hair, then turned back to Artemis and Grim. "Grimmie. It's your house. You decide if we go in."

Grim gave her a bewildered blink, apparently as surprised as I was that I'd actually managed to convince her. "I'd rather *we* break into it than anyone else."

"Oh god, this is a terrible idea." Artemis dropped her arms

to her sides and gave me a look. A *there's a firestarter on the loose and you want to waste time with Grimshaw House* look.

"You don't have to come," I said.

She scoffed. "I have a chance to go into Grimshaw House. I can't pass that up. Besides, if there are documents about the Aberdeen girls in there, there might be something about other stories from around town. Look at the photo—that already tells us something. That story about Daisy makes a lot more sense."

I looked again. Pit bull. Brown spot over one eye. Notch out of the ear.

"Daisy was Mom's dog?" Sadie said.

"That's probably where the story about Daisy leading children to safety came from. Our moms were found in the park when they reappeared, on the edge of the woods. Supposedly it was their dog that found them."

I looked again at the picture. Both Mom and Aunt Greta had light-colored eyes in it, maybe hazel or light brown. Mom's eyes had always been black. So had Aunt Greta's. That meant this picture was before. Before knowing. Before hunting.

"Tonight," Sadie said, jaw set. "We're going inside tonight."

"We can't stay late," Artemis said. "I have to get up early for the homecoming parade tomorrow."

"Seriously? For a *parade?*" I threw up my hands.

"Grim." Sadie reached out to smooth his hair. "Are you

sure you want to do this? You don't have to come, either."

Grim didn't answer for a moment. He was looking across town, where the woods hid the base of Piper Mountain, and the radio tower blinked red in the growing dark. Only when he focused faraway like this did he seem sharp and completely alert, like a dog honed in on a distant scent. "Do you ever feel," he said, "like there's something wrong with the world, but you don't know what it is?"

"Sure we do, Grimmie," I said, patting his arm, "but existential dread is just another part of life."

Grim laughed and said, "Yes, I'm sure. I'll go."

I looked to Artemis. "Going to lie to get out of the house this time? Momma Wake is going to find out eventually."

"No. She'll be asleep by the time I leave. I *do* have ways to get sneak out that she doesn't know about, but more importantly, even if I do lie, my mom doesn't snoop around. I know you think she's the worst person on the planet, but she can be really cool. She trusts me."

That must be nice, I thought, *to have someone who knows why you do the things you do.*

I sniffed at Artemis. "Tell her to stop calling me a criminal and maybe I'll believe it."

"Stop behaving like a criminal and maybe she will."

"Damn." I spun back toward the Chevelle, hands up in surrender. "Touché."

15

When I was thirteen, the Chevelle was found on the northern edge of Black Creek Woods, near the abandoned train cars. The driver's door hung open, as if Mom had gotten out in a hurry. She'd left a trail into the woods at almost the exact location where she and Aunt Greta had been found as girls, but there were no signs of a struggle.

The police followed that trail into the trees until it went cold. No dogs could catch her scent. No amount of canvassing revealed any clues. I had never known Mom to be particularly fond of Black Creek Woods, and being one of the Aberdeen girls, it was no wonder why. But the second disappearance had been willing. She had been hunting, I knew, because there was no other reason she would have left us like that. I thought she would have at least left clues for *me*, but the photo from Grimshaw House was the first I'd ever seen.

Staring up at the flaking back of Grimshaw House, I felt a wealth of secrets hiding inside the walls, waiting. The backyard was a dead jungle right down to the shore of Addams Lake, the house barely fending off the wilds with the remains of an old back porch. A few tourists and *DMW* fans still camped out front, but Rivera had kept Norm parked by the curb, so they hadn't come any closer.

Sadie kneeled on one side of me, Artemis on the other. Grim's lanky form folded into the shadows behind us. We'd crept along the lakeshore from the foot of the bluffs, behind the long row of Goldmine houses, avoiding homeowners and security lights. Artemis cupped a hand over her phone to block the light as she checked the time. 12:34 a.m. When we were sure there was no movement nearby, Sadie let out a long sigh and began making her way toward the door.

She'd been the one to answer the question of how to get in. Her time with the Birdies had not been forgotten after all, and she still knew where that experience was when she needed to bring it out and dust it off. She crept silently up the porch and kneeled by the lock of the vine-covered door, barely a shadow on the moonless night. Several quiet moments passed. The *click* of the lock opening was barely audible, and Sadie held the handle with one hand while she pried back some of the vines with the other. Then she pushed the door open slowly enough that its rust-stuck groaning could be mistaken for the old house settling.

Another several seconds. No movement. I tapped Artemis and Grim on the shoulders and led the way to the door.

We slipped inside. Sadie closed it behind us. Artemis's phone flashlight, pointed at the floor, gave us enough light to see one another. We stood in the kitchen, and from the animal droppings and dead flies at our feet, I was glad I couldn't see the rest of it. The air was thick with must and the smell of something dead.

Sadie was already tense. Not only was she three hours past her bedtime, she was in the creepiest house in Addamsville. Sadie did not do creepy. She hadn't even worn her combat boots, which might have helped a little; she'd once told me she never felt afraid when she wore those boots, because wearing those boots meant *she* was the thing to be feared.

"Ugh," she said now, huddled tight between me and Grim. "It's too quiet in here."

"There'll be some light from the street," I said, "but if you have to use yours, no pointing it at the windows. Tad said he found the picture upstairs, so that's where we should go first. Grim, is there anything else you want to look at while we're here?"

Grim took a moment to answer; he was frowning past me, into one of the front rooms.

"I can look around down here," he said. "You all go upstairs. I'll meet you."

Sadie squeezed his arm. Artemis turned off her light.

The Goldmine houses all followed the same Victorian Gothic layout, so Artemis led the way down a narrow hallway off the kitchen, past a dark doorway that led down to what I assumed was the basement, and through a living room to the steep staircase to the second floor. The upstairs rooms were mostly empty save for a few old armchairs, a bed frame without a mattress, and a vanity whose mirror was crusted over with age. In the master bedroom, Artemis almost stepped on a decomposing raccoon, and I had to clap a hand over her mouth to keep her from screaming.

Another staircase went up to the third floor. At the top was only one room, empty except for a dirty, unkempt bed. Artemis went straight to the dusty curtains and peeked through. The windows faced west, not out toward the street, and the western strip of the Goldmine, all the way to Hillcroft House, was visible.

Artemis turned on her light, and dozens of photos scattered across the floor were caught in it.

The photos were clustered to the left of the bed, trailing toward the door. Artemis kneeled, sweeping her light over each one, examining them without touching them. Sadie kneeled beside her and pointed to a spot on the floor. Artemis swung her light back. A rectangular area free of dust sat among the other pictures.

"Tad got the one of Mom from here," Sadie said. "And look—his footprints."

I kneeled. The photos ranged from Polaroids to drugstore-developed prints. A partially torn CVS envelope poked out from underneath the bed. Some were of people, some of places around Addamsville. The bridge. The church. The old town hall. The coal mine entrance. The crowds at the homecoming parade. Bach's black Mustang, parked by the graveyard. Aunt Greta as a teenager with the old town council members.

Artemis started flipping them over. All had years scrawled on the back in the same handwriting. She started lining them up by year. "Maybe someone was trying to tell a story."

I reached for the CVS envelope and any other photos still scattered under the bed, shining my own small flashlight through the cobwebs and dust, and found a section of one of the floorboards resting beside the hole it should have covered. Had Tad pulled it up earlier and not put it back, or had whoever left the photos cleared out in a hurry and Tad hadn't looked under the bed? Frowning, I spread out on my stomach, swiped the cobwebs out of the way, and crawled beneath the bed frame.

Inside the hole was an open shoebox, and in the shoebox was an old map, a mouse skeleton, more photos, and a small tan notebook.

I grabbed the box and wriggled out from under the bed. Artemis glanced inside and uttered a soft, "Effing dead animals." Sadie took out the map.

"It's old," she said, spreading it out on the floor. "From a few decades ago. See, the old town hall is still there. What do these mean, though?" She motioned to scrawled pen lines all across the map, areas of town that had been circled in red, lines drawn from one place to another in black. The most obvious marks were several fat black *X*s.

"Those were the locations of the Firestarter Murders," I said, and my spine knotted up. I handed the new photos to Artemis to look at while I skimmed through the notebook. There was no clue as to who owned it. The handwriting inside matched the writing on the photos, scrawled and loopy, like the person writing couldn't be bothered to restrain the strokes of the pen. Some of the writing wasn't legible. There were lists of names, first or last but never both; truncated sentences like *in the trees?* and *been here too long;* and occasionally pages headed by a location and filled in with small observations.

Old Town Hall Lot 10 12 12

5

Little movement

All red

My glove groaned as my hand tightened around the spine of the notebook. Each one of these pages listed the location of one of the Firestarter Murders. Each page named the number of ghosts at that location and their behavior. The writing was so vague, no one except the writer would understand what was being recorded.

One marking on the map, in the woods just a little north of where Mom had disappeared, was labeled with *Pg. 53.* Just to see, I flipped the notebook to page fifty-three and found an entry there that was dated and said, *Fnd Chvy.*

"Is there anything else in there besides dead rodents?" Sadie asked, peering into the box. "I was hoping—I thought maybe we could find something for Grim. Something about the will."

I shook my head, numb. "I don't think we're going to find the will here. Look at this. Do you . . . do you recognize this handwriting?"

Sadie glanced over the entries in the notebook. Her eyebrows furrowed. "That's Mom's. That's exactly hers."

I looked around at the mess. The photos. The map. The little notebook crammed from cover to cover with the strangest notes. "This was hers," I said. "When she went out at night, this must have been where she came. Or at least where she stopped before she went out to find . . . all of this." I motioned to the pictures, the notebook.

Sadie sat back, looking lost. "I thought she just went out to clear her head. She was trying to solve the Firestarter Murders?

But why? And what do these notes mean?"

Artemis and I glanced at each other. She'd been trying to find Bach's entrance, and she'd hidden all her notes here. The *Fnd Chvy* page was dated shortly before Mom and Dad got married, and had to mean "Found Chevy"—so Mom had *found* the Chevelle, not made it into what it was. There were pages in the notebook dedicated to Grimshaw House specifically, but I couldn't make out what she'd been trying to say—she'd been investigating this place, too, and maybe that was why she'd used it as a base of operations. But Sadie couldn't be allowed to know that.

"Look at these." Sadie plucked two photos from the floor. The first was Bach's black Mustang at the graveyard. "This is dated 1996. Bach is a senior at Harrisburg, right? He wouldn't have even been born." Before we could reply, she held up the second picture. "1973."

It was a fuzzy Polaroid of a manor house nearing completion in a clearing surrounded by trees. Construction workers moved in the background, and in the foreground stood a woman holding the hands of three children. All three kids looked like the woman, but the older boy and the girl were smiling, and the littler boy just looked scared.

"Hermit Forester's wife and kids?" I asked.

"No," Artemis said. "Hermit Forester is the little boy, with the darker hair and eyes. He would have been our age during the Firestarter Murders. He's in his forties now. The girl is Valerie, who haunts the Now Leaving Addamsville sign on Valleywine. The older boy is Brandon, who's supposed to be in the woods. Their mom is Lenore."

Forester's human mother. Not the firestarter mother.

"No, but *look*." Sadie pointed to a figure in black watching the construction crew work. Black hair. Sunglasses. Pale skin. The picture quality wasn't great, but I knew Bach at a glance. "He'd have to be fifty, sixty years old."

"Maybe the Foresters have a biased hiring process," I said. "You know. 'Only pale-skinned, black-haired teenagers need apply.'"

"Or he's an actual vampire." Sadie's voice had started to wobble. "Why did Mom have all of this? Why was it hidden here? I don't understand. What was she doing?"

I shrugged half-heartedly. I couldn't tell her. It would only make her life harder. "She was weird," I said, and it felt like a betrayal.

"I don't understand," Sadie said softly.

I dumped the mouse skeleton out of the box, then reached past Artemis and began scooping up the photos. "We're taking them with us. They belonged to Mom; they're ours now."

Artemis would be as eager to look over all of it as I was, but Sadie kept her distance like I held live snakes. We found Grim kneeling by one of the front windows, gazing to the northwest. Sadie grabbed him, and we left the house the way we'd come in. Down to the lakeshore, east to the bluffs. I clutched Mom's shoebox the whole way home.

Mom had always said it was her job to protect the town and its ghosts by solving the mysteries no one else could see. I understood why—not to atone for anything wrong you'd done, just because it was the right thing to do—but what we'd found in Grimshaw House made infinitely more sense to me.

She'd thought the firestarters were linked to the Aberdeen disappearances. Maybe specifically the Firestarter Murders. She'd gone back into the woods because that was where she'd disappeared, but it was also where Hermit Forester lived. So what had happened? Had she entered the woods and hadn't come back yet because she hadn't found what she was looking for?

Or had something else found her first?

16

On the morning of the homecoming parade, town center bloomed with mums and falling leaves, and streamers striped the lampposts lining the parade route. Locals and tourists alike filled the streets. The day was a sunny sixty-five degrees; smells of hot dogs, tacos, kebabs, and funnel cakes wafted down the street. Parents brought folding chairs, and games for their children to play while they waited; others found seats on the curb or the stoops of the shops along Valleywine. Even the ghosts had their spots, as if the people who had come to watch had subconsciously made space for the dead they couldn't see. There were far fewer ghosts than in previous years, and they hung around the buildings as if they meant to flee at a moment's notice.

I'd only come to be seen. It was way more suspicious if someone *didn't* come to the parade, no matter who they were. Better to stay out in the open so everyone could keep an eye on me. I planted myself on a picnic bench outside town hall. Above me four American flags hung along the face of town hall, framing the town seal showing a covered bridge adorned with the words ADDAMSVILLE, IN; EST. 1865.

Mom's shoebox was tucked underneath Sadie's bed, where Dad wouldn't go looking for it. I'd spent the rest of last night, long after Sadie claimed a headache and finally turned in, sorting through her photos and her notes, unable to put them down. The notes were a mess of code, even knowing that she was writing about ghosts and firestarters. She had kept track of routines and habits, likely spots for entrances to appear, the best ways to lay traps for firestarters that had already possessed humans, to get rid of them without anyone thinking she was a murderer.

Her pictures at least had an order to them. A sense of what she was looking for. Bach and Forester were part of it. She'd been looking for Bach's entrance for a long time, but her map drew so many lines between the spot where she'd disappeared, Grimshaw House, Forester House, and the Firestarter Murder sites, she must have also thought it had something to do with her and Aunt Greta.

The only evidence I took out of the house was the photo

of Mom and Aunt Greta. It rested snugly in the inner pocket of my jacket. They had been normal girls once, and something had changed them.

Artemis found me twenty minutes before the parade began, carrying two funnel cakes and a cherry slushy.

"Here." She handed over one funnel cake and took a seat beside me. I scooted over to give her more room. "What's that stare for?"

"How did you know I like funnel cakes?"

"You always walk around with one at the parade."

"I didn't know you paid attention to me."

"You're kind of hard to miss."

That was fair. And maybe also insulting. But fair.

"I didn't figure anything else out from the box," I said. "Still trying to decipher it."

"It was a huge find," Artemis said quietly. "We could have spent the night better. The firestarter from the mine will get stronger every day. We have to stop it before it kills someone else."

"Sadie never would have let me out of the house. Even if she had to sit outside so she didn't fall asleep."

Artemis made a noise. "Can I look through the box soon? She took so many photos around Addamsville. I'll definitely be able to learn more about all the things that happened here."

"Why are you so concerned with the town's history?"

Artemis took a long slurp of slushy, thinking. "When you understand the town's ghost stories, you understand the town. Tragic events and dark times are part of our psyche. Take the lake, for example. It's been haunted since it was created."

"Created? The lake hasn't always been there?"

Artemis shook her head and took another slurp. "It used to be a quarry. They started strip mining the coal so they didn't have to make more mine shafts. Part of it collapsed in the late eighteen hundreds, and a lot of people died. They filled it up after that. The origins of a lot of the lake stories can be traced back to terrible things that happened in the strip mine. Dynamite blowing arms and legs off, accidental burials, flooding."

"Huh. So it's like a middle finger to people like the *DMW* crew, who do it for the views."

Artemis held out a hand in acknowledgment. "The people we tell stories about were real once. They had lives, you know? We shouldn't let stupid stories bury the truth." She stopped, sliding the slushy straw around. "Think about your mom. We don't know what really happened the day she went missing. There are plenty of stories, but there's a truth there, and I'm sure you want to know it. Right?"

I kneaded my hand. "Right."

"With what we found last night, you're a little closer to that. Those pictures, that notebook—those are Dasree Novak's history. A piece of it."

"I think all of this is her history," I said, looking down the road at Addamsville gathered for the parade. "The ghosts, the fires, the disappearances. Figure out one and you figure out the rest."

"Too bad it couldn't clear your name," Artemis said.

I snorted. "All we have to do is make the town believe the supernatural exists. 'Yes, Chief Rivera, Bach is actually a very youthful septuagenarian! I have an old picture to prove it!'"

Artemis laughed.

Sadie and Grim appeared before the parade began, Dad corralled between them. He'd bounced back from last night and looked like the sun had risen inside his face. They stopped at one food truck for a walking taco, at another for a vegetable kebab, and at a third for an ice cream cone. Dad double-fisted the kebab and the ice cream while Sadie cradled the walking taco for him. I reminded myself to breathe evenly; they didn't know what was going on in town. They had no reason not to be at least kind of happy.

"You look like a smiling terror," I said. Dad finished a bite of zucchini with a satisfied sigh.

"It's a bright day, Zoo! Everyone's here, the parade's going to start—hey there, Artemis! Wow, it's been so long since I've seen you. What've you been up to?"

"Hi, Uncle Lazarus. I've been fine, focusing on school. My

mom should be around here somewhere, if you want to talk to her. She's been all over the place this morning."

"Hopefully she's a little more welcoming than Buster, eh?" Dad beamed.

"Everyone's more welcoming than Buster," Artemis said.

Dad laughed. Honestly laughed. Apparently one of the town council members hating you to your face because of something *you did* was super funny. I wanted to punch Buster as much as the next person, but if someone stole a bunch of my money for something I thought was a worthy cause, I'd be pretty pissed, too. I'd be furious.

I pressed my lips together and picked at my funnel cake.

Something caught Dad's eye down the street and he jumped like an excited dog. "Oh! There's Abby Rivera. I have to go say hi. See you girls later. Don't get into trouble, okay?"

Sadie gave me an exhausted look as she and Grim trailed after him. She wasn't used to getting up before noon on weekends, definitely not when she'd stayed awake so late, and definitely not when she had to babysit someone with as much energy as Dad, outside, around a lot of people.

The distant thump of the drums and high keening of the brass floated over the buildings. The parade began at the high school, marched down Handack Street, turned east at Walton, then southwest along the diagonal of Valleywine, where it would pass through town center and make the jackknife to go north up Handack again and end at the high school. The marching band led the way, followed by the four class homecoming floats and the color guard. The mascot, Morty the Dead Miner, ran up and down the parade line, high-fiving little kids and throwing candy.

Sidebar: the mascot was really called Marty the Miner, but ghost miners are more intimidating. Kind of insensitive about all the real miners who died in this town—some of whom had appeared today to watch the parade—but there were bigger fish to fry.

Artemis grew still as the marching band turned down Valleywine. I nudged her. "Why do you look so nervous? Do you have a crush on someone in the marching band? Who?"

I'd been joking, but she seized up like a rabbit in a flashlight beam.

"Nobody."

"Yeah, okay, that sounds legit."

Now *she* was picking at her funnel cake. I kept an eye on her, and not a moment after I'd turned away, she looked up again and became very focused on the band. At the head of their column was Mads. When she wasn't working at Hal's, Mads was in one club or another, or acting as drum major for the marching band. Today her long dark braid was gathered up at the back of her head, and she smiled and marched like a Miss America contestant. I wasn't a smiley Miss America sort of person, but if I was, I would have wanted to pull it off like Mads.

Artemis paused with a piece of funnel cake halfway to her mouth.

"Is it Mads?" I said.

She dropped the funnel cake. "No."

"Oh, it is."

Her cheeks flamed. "Oh my god, shut up."

"That's super cute. You should ask her out."

"She doesn't know who I am."

"*What?* Yes, she does! Everyone knows who you are. You're a town council kid, and on top of that you've been on TV."

Her blush deepened. "Yeah, for weird things like investigating ghosts."

"So? You're still popular. You have tons of friends."

"No, I don't."

"If you have at least two friends, that's 'tons of friends' to me."

"You can have people who call themselves your friends and you can still be alone. It's not about hanging out or liking the same things. It's about understanding each other. When you understand someone, you care about them, for good or for bad. You have a bond. *That's* friendship."

"Maybe you don't have friends because your definition of friendship is kind of lofty."

"Don't pretend like you're too cool for a meaningful examination of one of the most basic human experiences."

"Too many big words today."

Artemis rolled her eyes.

"You talk about how *I* deflect all the time," I said. "None of this had anything to do with whether Mads knows you. Mads definitely knows you. She was talking about you at work last week."

"She was?"

"She was wondering what you use on your hair to make it so shiny."

Artemis yanked her scarf over her face. "Ohhhh. Oh no."

"'Oh no' what? Isn't this a good thing?"

"She's *too* cute! I don't know what to do with my body when she's around!"

"You were talking to her the other night, at Hal's!"

"Yes, but I wasn't *looking* at her. When you want to date someone, you have to *look* at them."

"Ugh. I'm too asexual for this."

The marching band passed us. Artemis did look. Mads glanced our way. I waved. Mads pointed her baton and waved back. Artemis buried herself in her scarf and squeaked in defeat.

"Mads is going to be at Hal's tonight, by the way," I said. "You should come ask her—"

Artemis jabbed a finger across the street. *"Bach."*

My mouth snapped shut. I followed her finger to where Bach stood on the sidewalk outside the library, surrounded by empty space, no townspeople, dead or alive. Sunglasses hid his eyes, the breeze ruffled his hair. Except for the sunlight, he looked appropriately vampirish. Tall, dark, ageless. He never came to public outings. One of the hazards of having an immortal body was people noticing that you never aged.

He wasn't watching the parade. His head roved slowly back and forth, like he was scanning the street and the sidewalks. Looking for something, or someone. I tried to catch his gaze, but he didn't look my way. His eyebrows furrowed. Worried. The ghosts nearby had scattered. The ghosts all the way down the street had scattered. The ghosts in town were used to Bach by now; they wouldn't have left because of him. I grabbed Artemis's wrist.

"What is it?" she said.

"The firestarter is here," I said.

The floats turned down Valleywine. Four of them, one for each grade, all depicting the Addamsville football team crushing Harrisburg. The freshmen had made a giant game of Mousetrap with the Harrisburg's Eagle Pete as the mouse; the sophomore float was Morty the Dead Miner jumping out of a grave in a mini end zone to scare Eagle Pete to death; and the juniors had carved a giant Eagle Pete headstone out of foam and half the JV football team sat on it, singing the Addamsville High fight song.

The senior float rolled past to uproarious applause. On their trailer, another mound of foam had been carved and painted to look like the straining bodies of Harrisburg football players, all of them holding up a throne occupied by none other than Hal Haynes III, the hero who made a sixty-yard Hail Mary pass to win the 2011 homecoming grudge match against Harrisburg in the rain and mud, with a sprained ankle to boot. Up on that float he looked every inch the all-American boy: bright eyes and a white smile, apple pie and fireworks.

His blue and gold jersey and his glittering homecoming crown were set off by his dark-brown skin, and he wielded a golden scepter that flashed in the sunlight. He nodded and gestured to his subjects as he passed, and at one point stood up and yelled, "ALL HAIL ADDAMSVILLE! MAY THIS GAME BE BLESSED!"

The crowd cheered again. I scanned faces, looking for one out of place. But the only person not entertained by Hal's theatrics, it seemed, was Bach; he'd straightened, now focused on my side of the street. I tried to follow his line of sight, past the float, past the oncoming color guard, but there was only Tad "Ratface" Thompson and his crew of goons. No cameramen or producer, no dead nearby. Tad saw me, smiled, and winked.

The senior float exploded.

Screams shattered the air as the crowd fled. The color guard scattered. The band screeched to a halt. Artemis had a death grip on my arm.

The senior float was in flames taller than the bank, hot enough to feel from our perch. I stared, frozen. Blood pounded in my ears. Fire spun. So fast. It had gone up so fast. The light and the size of the flames and the smoke. Twisting, curling. Foam blackening. Throne melting. Ghosts were gone. Hal lay sprawled next to the float, and someone ran up to grab him and haul him to the sidewalk. Dad.

Through the flames, Bach appeared.

He hadn't moved. He met my gaze and held it; it felt as if hundreds of seconds passed while we stared at each other. Then he bolted. With the rest of the crowd, toward his sleek black Mustang parked in front of the auto shop.

I pried Artemis's hand off my arm. "Go see if Hal's okay!" I told her, and leaped off the bench before she could stop me. I sprinted away from the fire, away from the screaming, to the Chevelle in the town hall parking lot.

I gunned the engine and peeled onto Elmwood Lane. Bach couldn't use Walton Street because of the parade route block off, so he'd have to turn down Cherry Hill where it intersected with Elmwood. I was right; I reached the intersection in time to see the Mustang roar past, heading south. I whipped out behind him and followed.

The Chevelle rumbled like a panther after its prey. We curved down the strip of the Goldmine, out past the Denford farmland, over the long wooden bridge that spanned Black Creek. Black Creek Church, surrounded by the cemetery, stood stark and uninviting against the pale blue of the sky. Bach sped down the dirt road, hardly pulling back even on the rough terrain, even when he slipped into the forest.

Black Creek Woods was a different kind of haunted than the rest of Addamsville. The rest of Addamsville was tourist haunted. Postcard haunted. Haunted in a regulated way, so you were always safe. Even though Forester House and Maple Hills were *in* the woods, they, too, were policed carefully by the living, used as tour locations and hot spots.

The woods were like the coal mine. Unregulated territory. Feral hauntings happened here, and you were always being watched. The trees grew tall and close together, a phalanx armed with shields and spears of underbrush. The canopy blocked out the sky, plunging the world below into an gloom. Two cars could barely pass on the dirt road. Bach's taillights swung right at a fork in the road, heading west.

The west road dead-ended deep in the woods, in enemy territory. The one place Mom had told me never to go. The most dangerous place in Addamsville.

Forester House.

The woods swallowed the wings of the house so only the

arched front entrance could be seen from the roundabout driveway. The gable roof pierced the gray sky, shadowing the long steps up to the front porch and a shuttered entryway. The wind rustled the trees to a slow rhythm, as if the house itself was breathing.

I braked at the edge of the roundabout. Bach had stopped his Mustang by the porch. Now he stood at the base of the steps, watching me.

"Get out of the car, Zora."

I tightened my grip on the steering wheel. Bach was alone, and the house was still.

I unbuckled my seat belt and got out.

"Why'd you run?" I called from behind the Chevelle's open door.

Bach didn't try to come any closer. "I ran because it would have looked suspicious if I hadn't, and because I needed to get back to Sammy right away. This firestarter is showing itself in the open now. It *wants* to be known. It could have burned Hal if it wanted to, but it didn't. It burned the float instead."

"Why? They've attacked in crowds before"—*Bach* had, actually, when he killed Hermit Forester's Aunt Yvette in the grocery store parking lot—"but that was to *kill*. Not to injure."

"To send a message," he said. "To you. Think, Zora. Who was attacked? Where? And what did you do immediately afterward?"

Hal, my friend. In public, where everyone could see. I ran.

I ran from the scene of the crime.

"It's trying to *frame* me?"

"And send you a warning."

The wind howled through the trees now. Raindrops darkened the pavement. Shadows hid Bach's expression.

"Why didn't you stop when you noticed I was chasing you?" I asked slowly.

"Because I needed you here. To show you something."

Bach pointed to the front of Forester House. On the double wooden front doors was burned a large and crude *L*. The stumps of my fingers itched horribly, and my chest felt too tight.

"When we first came here, Hildegard and I, we weren't alone," Bach said. "Hildegard brought another of her offspring. He called himself Ludwig. She banished him once for threatening Sam, and he's tried before to come back. He's back now, and he left this for us. He knows you."

"How do I know this is true, and you didn't make it up to cover yourself—burn your own door to make me believe?"

"Believe that I wouldn't hurt or lie to you unless Sammy ordered it, and he's not going to lie to you about a firestarter he wants removed." Bach's voice was a rumble of thunder. "Ludwig is very real. He knows who you are. He knows your friends. He knows your reputation in this town. Because he's fought you before. He's been here before."

I ran through the list of firestarters I'd gotten rid of myself and the ones I'd helped Mom with. It wasn't a long list, but none of them had named themselves the way Bach had. Or they all named themselves and I never waited around long enough to find out what their names *were*.

"When?" I asked. "When was the last time he was here?"

"Almost a year ago," Bach replied, and my heart sank before he finished his sentence. "He was the one who took your fingers."

17

I drove away from Forester House in a daze. Rain pelted the windshield.

Bach was going to talk to Hermit Forester; with such a public display of firestarter powers, even more attention would return to the murders thirty years ago, and he was sure that kind of pressure would make Forester agree to help me. I wasn't normally big on taking help from murderers, but I didn't have many other options.

Alone in the Chevelle, with the rain drowning out my voice, I said, "Hey, Mom, if you were thinking about coming back, now would be a great time."

Ludwig knew who I was. He'd been just another firestarter to me. Last year I'd found him almost by accident, patrolling around the Denfords' cornfield because Artemis had mentioned to me in passing that she'd felt a little weird there the night before. Ludwig's entrance had been inside one of the Denfords' barns, and he'd been camped out near it, probably just come through. He hadn't even had time to kill anyone or possess a body. I'd gone after him with only my axe, because he seemed so small and weak, and I was so angry all the time I never stopped to think.

He found out pretty fast he couldn't burn me, so instead he caught my hand and ripped my fingers off.

I still had my left hand to hold the axe, and adrenaline or fear or some combination helped me get his head off and throw it through his entrance, but not before the field caught on fire. They saved the barn. I went back only once, six months later, to retrieve Dad's wood axe where it had fallen in the weeds by the barn door. I ran away that night and hid behind Happy Hal's, curled up on myself and close to tears.

Now he was back. He'd already killed once. He'd taken a host, if he was at the parade today. He'd threatened Hal, and by extension, everyone I cared about. Mom had not prepared me for this.

Dad and Sadie were already there when I got home. Dad yanked me inside, pulled off my hood, and snapped, "Where have you been?"

My legs quivered. "I—I followed Bach—he ran from the

scene and I thought he might—he didn't do anything, but I thought I'd check."

Dad ran a hand over his face. Behind him, Sadie crossed her arms. "People saw you running. They think you had something to do with it. You and Bach both."

"Is Hal okay?"

"He's in the hospital. He got some nasty burns, but he'll live."

I put my head in my hands. I almost poked myself in the eye with my thick plastic pinkie, so I tore my gloves off and then my prosthetics. Sweat coated my hands. My finger stumps ached. I pressed the heels of my palms into my closed eyes and gritted my teeth to keep from making any sound.

"You'll have to stay home until this blows over," Dad said. "You can't just go running off like that, after everything that's happened, the way this town thinks about us now. It's too dangerous, and you're only giving them more ammunition."

My molars squeaked. He was telling *me* this? He was telling *me* how the town would react to this, as if he'd been the one who had to live with the ramifications of what he did instead of us? As if he'd been here for the past three years?

"I'm fine," I said, not caring that no one had asked. I shucked my boots off and stomped to the bathroom.

Twenty minutes later, I was sitting in the shower, hugging my knees to my chest. The water was already turned off, and two long wet strings of hair dripped between my feet. I wished I could have kept the water running so no one would hear the sounds I made and come knocking at the door, but wasting anything was a sin in this house.

The only knock came after ten minutes, and Dad said from the other side, "You okay?"

"Yes," I replied. "Just want to be alone."

"Chief Rivera is here. She wants to speak to you."

I toweled dry and put on my sweatpants and my ratty Apocalyptic Seagulls Midwest Tour T-shirt, then crept out to meet the chief in the living room, dripping on our doormat. She had me recount everything I did up to the parade, during, and where I'd gone afterward. I didn't detail my conversation with Bach, just said that he denied doing it. When I was finished, she put a hand on my arm and said, "Thank you, Zora. Hang in there. We'll find who's doing this."

She left, and I slipped back to the bedroom before Dad or Sadie could lay into me again. I curled up at the head of the bed, which now smelled a bit like Dad, and opened my phone.

Artemis had already texted me.

Where'd you go?

What happened?

people think you set the fire and fled the scene

I told them you didn't but I don't think they believe me

Where are you?? are you okay?

did you go to the woods???

I started mashing out a response, then gave up and called her instead. It rang once before she picked up.

"Oh my god, what happened?"

I told her what Bach had said. Ludwig's name, that he knew me. Artemis listened carefully. It felt better, talking about it. Like while I was talking about firestarters, they couldn't hurt me. Ludwig couldn't be sitting right behind me now, or lurking outside my window.

When I finished, Artemis was quiet, then said, "Bach might be able to help now. That's good."

"Yeah."

"Are you okay? If he's the one from last year—"

"I'll be fine."

"I can—I can do it, if you want. I could take the Chevelle and try to—"

"*No*. It's my responsibility." *Why*. Why did it have to be mine?

A knock came at the door.

"Can I call you back?" I hung up as the door pushed open. Sadie stuck her head in. "What is it?" I said.

"Jesus, I didn't even say anything yet." She slipped into the room.

"Sure, you can come in," I said.

She shut the door and planted herself at the end of the bed. She wore an old Addamsville High sweatshirt, a scarf, and a pair of mittens she'd made during her knitting phase, and her hair was half up in a ponytail. The other half had fallen out. Dark bags ringed her eyes.

"I didn't sleep last night." Her hands hung loose at her sides. Her lips pressed together. "I need to talk to you."

"I'm sorry about running away. I know it looked bad."

"That's not why we need to talk. What do you know that I don't know?"

I stopped and blinked at her. "About what? The float? I didn't—"

"I know you didn't do it, but you know something about it that I don't. Mom's notes, her pictures. What it all meant. You and Artemis both knew something." Sadie's face grew paler as she talked, her eyes shadowed by the lamplight. "Mom always spent more time with you. She was always taking you places, showing you things."

"She loved us both."

"I know that," Sadie snapped, "but there was something—you know something about her that I don't. You always have, and I always knew that, but I didn't say anything because I figured some parents just have favorite children."

"I wasn't her favorite—" I stopped myself. Was that even true? Had I been Mom's favorite? I'd never thought about Sadie being the outsider—Sadie had Dad—but I'd also never thought about Mom not spending as much time with her as she did with me. "I—" I sighed. "It's worse, knowing it. She said never to tell you and Dad, because it would be worse."

Tears rimmed her eyes and anger sharpened her voice. "Nothing is worse than not knowing. What's going on? Is it the reason she went missing?" She swallowed, hard. "I'm her daughter, too. I deserve to know."

She was right. What was the point of keeping it from her now? She'd seen the notes and the pictures. Maybe Mom would want her to know, at this point. Maybe knowing would keep her safer.

"You know the stories about Mom talking to ghosts?"

She nodded.

"They're true."

Sadie stared at me, black eyes swallowing the light.

"Mom could see them. So can I. Artemis and Aunt Greta can feel them." I told her about the firestarters and the corrupted ghosts, about Forester and Bach, and what it meant that we'd found Mom's notes in Grimshaw House. "She disappeared while hunting. So now it's just me, and I'm not very good at it, and I was hoping she'd left something for me with all her stuff, but there's nothing. I'm sorry I didn't tell you before. I wasn't supposed to."

Sadie said nothing for a long, breathless minute. Her lips turned white. The tears spilled over onto her cheeks.

Then her lips curled back from her teeth.

"Asshole," she spat. "If you're going to lie to me, at least come up with a better story."

She turned and stalked from the room, slamming the door behind her.

18

Not only did Sadie always have to take Dad's side, but when I let her in on *my* side, she didn't even believe me.

Rain beat down hard. Hal's dad called to let me know the shop would be closed. He was brief and to the point. He didn't give me time to ask how Hal was doing. I texted Mads to ask, and after an hour-long silence, she sent a short text back to say Hal was drugged up, but okay.

I didn't bother asking Lorelei for details. She'd probably be too scared to answer.

I ventured out of my room around eleven to find Sadie watching *Cheers* and knitting while Grim read a fantasy book with a spine as wide as his forearm. Sadie still awake at this time of night meant nothing good, and we didn't look at each other as I passed. I had expected all my life that if I told Sadie about Mom's ghosts, she wouldn't believe me, but after this—after today and this afternoon and what we'd found at Grimshaw House—the reality of it felt like being kneed in the gut. I made myself a bowl of Fruity Pebbles and stood by the TV, and neither of them said anything.

Finally I asked, "Where's Dad?"

"In town," Grim replied after several seconds of silence from Sadie. "He said he was going to talk to Chief Rivera again."

He arrived home an hour later. The Chevelle's engine growled louder than the storm, and he came in soaking wet. I'd peeked back out of the bedroom in time to see him hold his hands out, as if to show they were empty.

"I scoped out the Fool and town center," he said. "Then I went to talk to your Aunt Greta. That's all, I promise."

"Why'd you talk to Aunt Greta?" I said.

"To make sure she doesn't believe you did it." He took off his coat and hung it by the door, where it dripped on the linoleum. "Which she doesn't, by the way. Count yourself lucky."

Of course she didn't believe I'd done it, because she knew the truth. But that wasn't what he'd gone out to find. He was surveying the damage, and from the slump of his shoulders and the way he nearly pulled his hair out by the roots, the damage was bad.

Aunt Greta didn't believe I'd done it, but the rest of Addamsville did.

❧❧❧

The next day, Sunday, I went to the hospital to see Hal. I knew what happened to him wasn't my fault, but it felt like it. I had known about Ludwig. I'd wasted a whole night I could have used hunting to go look through Grimshaw House for hints about Mom. I should have acted sooner when I saw Bach at the parade, when I knew something bad was going to happen. I should have done *something*. Jumped in front of a parade float. Screamed my head off. Anything.

I knew something bad was going to happen and I could have stopped it. It was my responsibility to stop it, no matter what the consequences to myself.

The hospital was in Harrisburg, and had probably more ghosts than all the rest of the city combined. They loitered in hallways and doorways, stood at front desks waiting to check out, hovered around the emergency room doors. Ghosts were about the same everywhere, but ghosts in hospitals were especially chatty, and I'd always wondered if it wasn't because they didn't know they were dead. When I passed them, some tried to speak to me. There was no sound, just like always.

Visiting hours were short on Sundays, and when I arrived, Mads and Lorelei were there. They swung around when I stepped through the door, tipped off by the change in Hal's expression.

Bandages wrapped Hal's left arm and leg, both raised off the bed, and a smaller bandage covered the left side of his jaw. A bit of his hair had been singed, too, and he was bruised and cut up. He was awake, though, and nursing a little cup of orange juice.

"Hey guys," I said stupidly. I fiddled with the small Tupperware bowl I'd brought. "Hey, Hal. I made you some soup. It's probably terrible, but my mom used to make it for me when I was sick, and I thought you might—I know you're not sick. Sorry. I wanted to check and see how you were doing."

"Hey, Zora." Hal's eyes followed me as I sidled past Lorelei to put the Tupperware on the bedside table. Lorelei huddled her shoulders up around her ears. "I feel a little crispy, but otherwise fine."

I rubbed my knuckles on my right hand. "They don't know who did it yet," I said.

There was another long pause. Then Mads said, "Why'd you run?"

"I was chasing Bach." Lying about it wouldn't get me back in their good graces. "I saw him before it happened, acting sketchy. I thought he might have had something to do with it."

"And?" Hal said.

I shook my head. This I could lie about. "I lost him."

Hal made a noise. "I talked to my dad this morning. He said it was just like the Firestarter Murders. No chemicals, no pressurized air, no gasoline. Nothing that would make an explosion like that. And you need those to make an explosion like that, right?"

"Liquid gasoline doesn't explode," I said. "But you need something, yeah."

Hal waved his cup around. "Well, that's just it—my dad said that the cops checked the whole float. They even brought in the bomb unit from Harrisburg. No one found anything. No accelerants, no debris. And here's the other thing: those floats ride on metal trailer frames. The frame burned, too. All of it, up in flames, immediately. It's not right."

"Then it's like Mr. Masrell's house," Lorelei said.

Her voice was so soft I almost didn't hear her, and I was standing right next to her. Lorelei curled a length of her hair around her hand.

"My dad was complaining the other day because Chief Rivera hadn't found any accelerants at Mr. Masrell's house, or even what might have been the source of the fire." Lorelei twisted the hair tighter around her hand. "It may not mean anything, but he thinks they should have some kind of evidence by now."

I could imagine Buster raging around his house like an angry pig, but he wouldn't have only been angry that they couldn't find accelerants or a source. He would have been angry that they hadn't been able to find accelerants or a source that linked this all *to me*.

Hopefully the town knowing this much of the evidence

and linking it to the Firestarter Murders would be enough to convince Forester to let Bach help me.

"That's really weird," I said, my legs suddenly aching. "Anyway, I just wanted to stop by. If you need anything, seriously anything, let me know. Okay? I—" Denying I'd done it would only make me seem petty and scared. Like I needed to defend myself. The urge to raise shields was so strong, and none of the three of them had even accused me out loud yet. But I could see it on their faces. Wariness. Hesitance.

How could you convince people of the truth when they had already decided what version of the story they wanted to believe?

Hal, Mads, and Lorelei stared at me, and I stared back. I had nothing.

"What are you going to do?" Mads asked.

I realized none of them actually expected me to *say* anything. I knew what the question meant, and I had no answer. I had not made a reputation for myself as a person who *said* things. I was a doer. I always had been. Want something? Take it. Fear something? Fight it. Bored? Get the Chevelle. Annoyed? Yell at a janitor.

Angry? Hunt firestarters.

But doing had gotten me deeper and deeper into this mess until I couldn't tell right from left or up from down. A firestarter knew me, and was not only framing me for its fires, but threatening my family and friends if I didn't leave it alone. I knew how to struggle against the confines of the old Addamsville, but this new version had teeth.

"I don't know," I said. "I have to go. I'll see you guys later, okay? Get better, Hal."

Their mumbled good-byes told me everything I needed to know. We worked in the same building, but we came from very different places. It wasn't safe to be friends with me. It wasn't even safe to sympathize with me.

The hospital hallway was empty except for a few ghosts and a nurse who disappeared inside a room. I hid in the alcove by the bathrooms, fists pressed to my forehead, my prosthetic fingers bent to follow the slope of my nose.

When you feel alone, you don't admit it to anyone. If you do, they'll either use it against you or they'll pity you, and it's a toss-up which one is worse. You keep loneliness inside, squeezed so tight in your chest it hurts. If you're lucky, you can forget about it for a while. If you're unlucky, you are surrounded by things that make you think of it all day long: people who don't believe anything you say, people who make fun of you, people who blame you for things without regard for whether you actually could have done them.

And loneliness brings fear. Fear that there are things out there you don't understand and you'll have to face them by yourself. Fear that no one will be there to help you when you get lost. Fear that the truth will be more than you can handle.

I stood, straightened my clothes, and glanced in the reflective surface of a nearby door to make sure my face looked okay.

Get it together, Novak, I thought. *You're not alone yet.*

Artemis was on my side. And I always had Dad, as much of a hypocrite as he might be.

It wasn't time to give up.

19

Happy Hal's reopened Sunday afternoon, and Hal's dad, despite any of his suspicions, didn't say a thing about me not coming to work. I showed up for the afternoon shift, said hi to Mason, the manager picking up Hal's lost hours, and took my window.

Mads and Lorelei were both there. Neither of them brought up the fires or the hospital, and it was probably for the best; the shop was swarmed all afternoon and straight into the night. The *Dead Men Walking* crew was doing their Forester House investigation, which meant plenty of fans and thrill seekers were setting up at Hal's for the unobstructed view of Black Creek Woods. It wasn't as if you could *see* the Forester House from here—you couldn't see anything except trees and the red blinking lights of the radio tower farther north, toward Piper Mountain—but I guess they thought this was better than nothing, and the ice cream was a bonus. Officers Norm and Jack had parked themselves at the bridge and weren't letting anyone pass over Black Creek.

The tops of the trees rippled in the wind, making a roar loud enough to hear even from this far away. Somewhere in there was my mother, hunting for secrets, lost to the darkness and the snagging branches. If I thought hard enough, maybe I could pull her out. Pull her back here so I didn't have to go after Ludwig alone.

"Zora."

I jumped at Mads's hand on my arm and let go of the lever on the soft-serve machine. Ice cream trailed over my glove. I hissed through my teeth and took the napkins she offered me.

"Are you okay?" she asked.

"Yeah, fine." I said it too hard and too fast. "Sorry. Thinking."

"Okay, well, put your game face on. Bach just pulled in."

His Mustang was indeed parked in his usual spot, and he was visible behind the wheel. All the ghosts in the vicinity had fled, including the old town council members. The chief had questioned him about yesterday, too, and found nothing. I busied myself and kept Bach in my peripheral. He stopped and tilted his head up as if he was reading the menus nailed above the windows, but he always knew what he wanted.

There had been a time when, despite his history, I'd have been giddy that Bach was waiting for me. Most of the time I loved that I was only aesthetically attracted to people who fit the gothic vibes of your eighties' movie vampires, but when the person you like is an *actual* supernatural creature, it feels like there's something wrong with you. Like natural selection had determined *I* would be the easy kill.

I had long since decided that natural selection didn't own me or my sexuality. There was nothing wrong with me when *he* was the one lighting people on fire.

When he got to my window, he said nothing, just slid me a picture and walked back to his car. It was a photo that must have been taken around the same time, if not the exact same day, as the picture of the Foresters we'd found with Mom's notes. It was the Forester mansion again, with workers moving in the background and a tiny Sam Forester tottering through a gravel driveway. Behind him, in the same clothes as before, was Bach, standing with a woman and another man.

The man had short gray hair, light skin, and a brown suit. He looked like a bad lawyer, maybe. The woman was statuesque. I couldn't make out details of her face because of the fuzziness of the picture, but she had waves of dark hair, brown skin, and a black trench coat. Scrawled on the back in long-faded pen, not in my mother's handwriting, were three names and a year.

BACH

LUDWIG

HILDEGARD

1973

I turned it over and looked at the figures again. Ludwig, in an earlier body, before Hildegard banished him, and Hildegard, before she herself had disappeared. I couldn't even begin to fathom the reasons for that, but if she could create something like Sam Forester and control other firestarters, I wasn't begging for her to come back.

I stuffed the picture into my jacket. "Mason, I gave a customer wrong change. She's sitting outside; I'm gonna go correct it."

Mason didn't look up from the Oreo topping dispenser, which had gotten clogged again. "Okay, make it quick."

I hurried out the back door and jammed to a halt. Bach was already there, standing by the dumpster, and he wasn't alone. With him was a shorter man, who next to Bach looked positively delicate. Wire-framed glasses perched on his birdlike nose, red from the cold. He wore a button-down shirt and khakis, like any upper-middle-class suburban dad, and his dark hair was neatly trimmed. He turned glittering black eyes on me.

"Who's this?" I said.

"Zora" —Bach motioned to the man— "this is Sam Forester."

There was something not quite human about Sam Forester. Something writhed under his skin, a shadow that disappeared when I looked too closely. He smiled as he watched me.

"It's nice to meet you," he said.

I had to force words out. "You came out of the woods."

Forester clasped his small hands in front of him. "I hope I didn't startle you too badly. After Bach told me what happened, I thought it might help if I came with him to explain."

This was the man who had killed twelve people, including all the members of his own family. *This* was the man who now fed off their souls, corrupting their ghosts. He smiled as if there was nothing wrong in the world.

"Zora," Bach said. "The photo."

"Right." I handed it back to him. "Are you here to say you'll help me with Ludwig?"

"Let's not jump ahead of ourselves." Forester held up a hand, cheerful as a Sunday school teacher. "We should take a moment to get to know each other before we start talking about partnerships. I knew your mother, and Bach tells me that you have the same abilities she did and have taken up her mantle. Is that right?"

"To a degree," I replied, jaw tight. I had the entirety of the parking lot behind me, and somehow Forester still made me feel like I was backed against a wall.

"True or false: your mother told you the truth of the so-called 'Firestarter Murders.'"

I looked to Bach for any hint if this was a trap, but he stared at the ground, unmoving. "True," I said.

"I long suspected she spent a lot of her time searching for Bach's entrance. This, as you can probably guess, was not ideal for us, but we didn't worry that she would find it, and as long as she didn't try to out me to the town, I didn't mind what she did. Besides, she cleaned up others of our kind who came through here looking for a meal—firestarters, you call them?—and kept them from revealing us. This town is like a beacon for them, because of the mark my mother left, so there were always more that threatened us.

"I don't consider myself a dangerous person. I think it's important for you to know that. I love this town. It's the only home I know. I don't leave because my mother will come back one day, and I have to be here for her. I'm sure you understand that."

"If Ludwig is such a threat to you," I said, "why don't you just have Bach get rid of him? His entrance is in the mines; Bach can swing an axe probably better than I can."

"I would," Bach replied quietly, lifting his head, "but it's easier for you to find him."

His head yanked down again, as if there was a collar around his throat. My fingers brushed the handle of the door behind me.

"What do you mean?" I asked.

"We know you find firestarters by communicating with the ghosts of the people they kill," Forester said. "Unfortunately, as you've noticed, the dead don't come near us. And Ludwig is at least smart enough to keep his distance while we're around."

I swallowed. "So I find Ludwig and you help me get rid of him. What about your mother? Hildegard? I knew she had disappeared, but I didn't know you expected her back."

"You don't need to worry about that. If Hildegard does return," Forester said, "she won't be any trouble to you."

"How do you know?"

"Because she's my mother," he said simply. "And Bach's. And as long as nothing threatens us, she'll pay no attention to you. But if she does come back and this mess is still going on, I can't promise we can protect Addamsville."

I was smart enough to catch the warning in that. The murderers wanted me to find another murderer so a third murderer wouldn't show up and murder everyone, including me. Cool.

"What happens between us after I get rid of Ludwig?"

"We all go back to our lives," said Sam Forester, unruffled, "just as they were."

With him feeding on Addamsville's dead, and me trying to look at lit matches without panicking.

A spark of flame flashed behind Bach's sunglasses. He winced and said softly, "Sammy . . ."

My hands had balled into fists and my gloves were squeaking. "Fine."

Forester smiled. "Great. Bach." He nodded toward me.

Bach pulled a folded slip of notebook paper from his coat pocket and gave it to me. A phone number.

"Yours?"

Bach cleared his throat. "You're the only one who has it now, besides Sammy."

Forester had receded into the shadows, though I hadn't seen him move his feet.

"And, if I help, and Hildegard comes back . . ."

"Sammy's right," Bach said. "She'll only come back for him. If something threatens him, that's what she'll go after. You don't have to worry."

Coming from Bach, it didn't sound so dangerous.

"Fine," I said again. "I'll let you know when I have something." I glanced at Forester. "And uh, thanks." I didn't know for what. Not killing me?

Forester nodded. A small smile. Dark eyes. "Anytime, Zora Novak."

I straightened my visor and slipped inside Hal's, pressing the door shut behind me and working a violent shiver out of my shoulders. When I peered through the front window, Bach was climbing into his car again. Forester was nowhere to be seen.

Despite all the stories about Sam Forester, no one would believe the truth. Son of a firestarter. Actual serial arsonist. There was no remorse visible in him, and no apparent guilt for what he'd done.

Bach was something else entirely.

Despite knowing about Hildegard, I'd never thought of Bach having a mother. He fit into this town so well it was like he'd come included in the package. But I recognized the tone of his voice when he talked about Hildegard, the way he flattened his words and evened out his expression, like it didn't matter. Like it didn't hurt.

"That was a long time to correct change." Mason rolled up on me, his face right by my shoulder. "You already took your break tonight and I don't care if your boyfriend's here, you can't have another one."

"Mason," I snapped, rounding on him, "He is not my fudging boyfriend and you do not know what the flipping funsicle fudgecakes you're talking ab—"

A gasp rose from the crowd outside. Someone pointed toward the woods. Then two people. Then ten. People stood from tables and chairs, raising their phones to the darkness and the ocean of rustling trees. Mads and Lorelei were already at one window looking out; I ducked down to see better out of mine.

There was a light in the trees. A campfire would not have been visible from so far away, even at night. It would not have risen over the treetops, flickering, growing.

Someone yelled, "That's where the house is!"

And someone else, at exactly the same time, "The crew!"

For the second time in thirty years, the Forester mansion was on fire.

20

No one from the *Dead Men Walking* crew was seriously injured. Addamsville's single fire engine raced past Hal's on the way to the woods, and the next morning, the story was plastered over the news.

The *Dead Men Walking* cast and crew had all been inside when the arsonist struck. No accelerants. No explosives. The investigators, the only ones inside at the time, had escaped by jumping out a window. Emergency vehicles came and went throughout the morning. Chief Rivera called in the Harrisburg Police Department to help with crowd control; even with the bridge blocked, ghost hunters and *DMW* fans were wading across Black Creek to get into the woods.

Forester and Bach hadn't been there, of course; they'd

been with me, at Hal's. Ludwig had struck while they were away. Maybe when he knew they'd be talking to me, and he'd have a whole van load of people in one place, unattended. Bach had once done the same thing with the old town hall. Forester and Bach had remained at Hal's while the fire raged to solidify their alibi, but Forester looked ready to bare his teeth and scream.

I just stared. I couldn't have gotten the Chevelle past Jack and Norm at the bridge, and I would have been caught by the emergency vehicles on my way out of the woods. But more than that, I would have had to fight him. Ludwig. In the fire. Alone.

On the news, Tad Thompson stood by the *DMW* van outside the local clinic, waiting for the medical staff to clear the injured crewmembers for work. "It was terrifying, for sure," he said, "especially with how fast the flames went up, but this is the kind of work we do, you know? This is why we chose to come to Addamsville. Whoever is setting these fires is a criminal and has really hurt people, but we don't blame the town for this."

The reporter took her microphone back. "You told the police you saw someone lurking outside the house shortly before the fire began. Can you elaborate on that?"

"As we were setting up for filming, I saw someone in black creeping around. It's not strange, you know, we have a lot of fans following us and every once in a while they'll sneak onto the set. Just look at what happened in the mine. Our production assistants did a sweep around the house and didn't find anyone, so we started shooting. Then maybe a minute before we noticed the fire, I saw him again. Black jacket, kind of wavy black hair, black sunglasses. Had to be at least six feet tall, maybe more. I thought it was weird that he was wearing sunglasses when it was so dark outside, but I figured he didn't want anyone to see his face."

It couldn't have been Bach, because he'd had been at Hal's. Which meant Ludwig was impersonating Bach now, too.

Monday became an exercise in telling myself I had to do something, then looking over my shoulder, skin crawling. I went to school on autopilot and managed to be on time to all my classes for once. Unfortunately, that meant I had to hear every rumor about what might have happened.

In homeroom Nathan Riley claimed he saw Chief Rivera walking Bach into the police station, handcuffed. Ally Reed, in my history class, swore the fires had been started by the ghost of the arsonist who'd committed the Firestarter Murders. Then there was Joe Denford, in my physics class, who said to Will Harrison, ". . . and they teamed up so one person could have an alibi and one person could be doing the deed. Then they switch back and forth so no one can link the fires to either one of them. That's what my dad says. He didn't want me to come to school today because she's still here." He started looking around, and before he spotted me, I did him a favor and threw a pencil at the back of his head.

"I didn't set any fires or try to kill anyone, Joseph, thank you for asking." I said it loud enough for the whole class to hear. "And you can tell your dad to stop spreading stories he gets from Buster Gates."

Everyone talked, always. I heard a story that Bach and I were some kind of Bonnie and Clyde duo, into arson kink and killing old men. I heard another story that I'd given my amputated fingers to Bach as a declaration of undying love. Another that said we were in a cult.

At lunch I found a corner to myself, finally some peace and quiet, and put my hands around my hot cup of nacho cheese to warm them. Things like eating seemed trivial. I needed to hunt. Right now. But how do you hunt for something no one knows exists when everyone watches your every move during the day and Buster Gates is ready to chase you down with his monster truck at night?

I looked up from my cheese. Artemis leaned toward me, frowning.

"*Jesus!*"

"We have to get my memory card back," she said, as if she hadn't startled the daylights out of me. "We *have* to make sure it doesn't get out—people are going to want to know what happened. It's more important than ever. Before the *DMW* crew leaves town."

I settled into my seat, willing the goose bumps on my arms down and reaching for a breadstick. I was done with the stupid memory card. "Yeah, so?"

"So we have to go there and talk to them."

"You sound as stupid as your mom sometimes, you know that? Those people are probably going to have trauma for the rest of their lives. They already forgot about the memory card."

"You think at least one member of that crew won't see that footage and use it as publicity? And what about the fans? That footage will get out eventually, and someone is going to come here looking for the truth. It doesn't matter what you have to do to get it back—it *cannot* get out."

A cold chill slithered over me.

"What *I* have to do?" I frowned as I chewed. "I thought we were working on this together? Freudian slip? And yes, Artemis, I know what a Freudian slip is."

Artemis leaned back, some of her intensity fading. "I'm grounded. I'm not allowed out of the house except for school, and I have student council today, so by the time that gets done it'll be late."

"So you want me to go to the hotel where the *DMW* crew is staying and ask them for our memory card. Less than twenty-four hours after they almost get killed in a house fire. That a lot of people think I helped start. They aren't going to give me the time of day, much less that memory card."

Artemis sat in silence for a moment. She pushed her fingers together and apart on the table, spreading them flat. "You could also *not* talk to them."

She stared at the table when she spoke, only glancing up at the very end. My stomach had coiled in a rope, but I kept chewing. Then I swallowed and set my breadstick down on my tray. "Are you telling me," I said slowly, "to *steal* your memory card back?"

"They stole it from us!" she said. "And they're not shooting tonight, so all their equipment should be in their van or their rooms. I'm sure they'll go out for dinner or something. It's not that hard to break into a motel room, right?"

"Why would I know how to break into a motel, Artemis?"

Ten, nine, eight, seven . . .

Her ears turned red. "I thought—"

six, five, four, three, two . . .

"Why would I be *okay* with breaking into a motel, Artemis?"

She glared and puffed out her cheeks. "We did it at Grimshaw House—"

I shoved my tray sideways. It flew off the table and hit the wall, spraying yellow cheese and chocolate milk across the blue paint and sending breadsticks scattering onto the floor. Artemis jumped.

"Is it because my dad was in prison?" I said, standing. "Because I'm *poor*? Perfect Artemis is *grounded,* so she can't do it, but Garbage Human Zora is already accused of trespassing, destruction of property, arson, and *murder*, plus she's got no money and nothing to live for, so it's totally fine if *she* does it. And thievery is hereditary! Totally, totally. Sorry for doubting you, cuz; I see where you're coming from now."

I grabbed my bag and stalked away from the table, anger knotting my jaw and turning my vision red. I kept my gaze locked on the cafeteria doors, walking fast, ignoring the hundreds of eyes following me. Angry, delinquent Zora doing what she does. Getting angry. Probably going to set a fire. They didn't know me. None of them knew me, definitely not Artemis. They knew stories. They knew lies.

A few boys coming out of the lunch lines approached me, and the closest one said in a soft, mocking voice, *"Because I'm poor."*

I grabbed the bowl off his tray with one hand, took his belt in the other, and dumped hot cheese down the inside of his low-rise sold-ripped skinny jeans.

"I don't need to tell you how lucky you are it wasn't hot enough to burn." Dad glanced sideways at me as we drove away from the school. *He* drove. He'd had to walk to the high school from town center, where he was looking for a job, and then he'd insisted on driving the Chevelle home. "I heard what Principal Sutherland said. You want to tell me what actually went down?"

"People being stupid," I said.

"You don't shove hot cheese down someone's pants for being stupid," he said. "That's more of a Sadie move. They have to do something to upset you. So what happened?"

I breathed evenly through my nose. "I don't know. Artemis."

"'I don't know, Artemis.'" Dad nodded. "That's something. I thought you two were getting along. It was kind of nice."

"She's a spoiled rich kid," I said.

"Yes, but you knew that already."

I threw my hands in the air. "She thinks I know how to steal things because—because we're *us*." I could yell *poor* and *thievery* to the whole cafeteria, but I couldn't say it to Dad. He knew what I was saying without me actually having to say it. People thought I was a thief because Dad was a thief. They thought we stole because we didn't have much. They thought we were dirty people. They thought we were lazy. The more money someone had, the worse they thought of us, and Artemis's family had the most money in town. I don't know why I ever expected more out of her.

I don't know why, every time she said *we*, I didn't hear *you*.

"Well," Dad said after a few moments of silence, "it does make sense that Artemis would have a blind spot to certain things. Many things, probably. She's a smart girl, but smart people don't always see what's obvious to others."

"I get privilege," I said. "What I don't get is how you're supposed to put up with this *garbage* from everyone all the time. Even people you kind of like. You try to tell them that they're wrong, and why, and it goes in one ear and out the other."

Dad gave me a small, sad smile. "Sometimes it takes a little while. If you want them to understand, you have to keep trying. But you also have to realize the difference between someone who can understand with a little work, and someone who doesn't *want* to understand. I learned a long time ago not to spend too much time on people who didn't want to see things the way I see them. It isn't worth the energy." His expression brightened again. "Sometimes, though, it is. And those times can be very worth it. Those are the times you can learn from one another. That's what happened with me and your mom."

I started. "You and Mom? You had to explain something to Mom?"

He laughed. "Your mom grew up rich—she was an Aberdeen, after all. Even when their house burned down, they still had money. I had to explain a lot of things to her, like why anyone would ever think of splitting a roll of two-ply toilet paper into two one-ply rolls."

"Was this before or after you got married?"

"Way before. But after we started going out. She was so

naive, your mom—did I tell you how we became friends?"

"You hung out at the Fool at, like, one in the morning."

"Yes, but did I tell you *how?*"

"Drinking, I assumed."

"No, no. I tried to con her."

That shouldn't have surprised me, but it did. "And she didn't fall for it?"

He smiled ruefully. "Ah, but she did. She fell hard." He scratched his chin. "I knew who she was, but we'd never spoken. She struck me as one of those uppity types. Kind of floated around, like nothing could hurt her. A rich kid. Pampered. I wanted to knock her down a few pegs, so I scammed her and got away with all the money she had on her. It wasn't a lot, but you could tell she was going to use it for something or other. Maybe she'd been saving up, I don't remember."

"So you scammed her," I said. "That's super romantic."

"It is, isn't it? No, I gave her the money back. It was the first time I'd ever really felt bad about stealing from someone. She didn't fall for the scam because she was stupid, though I'm sure some people would call it that. She fell for it because she didn't expect anyone to try to steal from her. She still had that kind of trust in others. I saw it when she handed me the money. Then it became a choice between two evils. Keep her money and have cheated the trusting innocent, or give the money back, apologize, and ruin her trust forever. Not just trust in me, but trust in anyone. What kind of rotten person does something like that? No one ever loses their own innocence. They have it taken from them."

By people like us. He didn't say that, but I heard it. That was the Novaks, after all: rotten people.

"But you gave her the money back."

"I gave her the money back. In the end I figured if I didn't ruin that trust in her, someone else would, but at least I'd apologize for it. I expected her to hate me. I think she was more stunned than anything. Then confused, and she thought the apology was part of some bigger scam. After I convinced her it wasn't, she asked if I wanted a drink, and she went on and got me drunk and wheedled my entire life story out of me, along with about twenty-five bucks for the booze."

"So she stole back from you!"

"She was good like that. You girls got your quick learning skills from her, I'll tell you that. I woke up in my bedroom the next morning, hungover as hell, and found her in my kitchen making pancakes. She regaled me with my own embarrassing childhood stories, we called a truce, and we saw each other nearly every day for the next twenty-six years."

Twenty-six.

"That's all I was getting at," he went on. "Your mom and I didn't see eye-to-eye, but that doesn't mean she was a bad person. It meant she hadn't seen what I'd seen. She didn't have the same experiences, and the worlds we lived in were very different because of it. But she learned, and I learned some things, too, and we became better people together. I wouldn't have given her up for anything."

Twenty-six years. It seemed like an eternity.

"What's wrong?" he said. "Didn't like that story?"

"No. It's just—the end of the twenty-six years was when she went missing."

"Ah." He sniffed. "Yep."

"Do you ever think of where she might be?"

He gave me a strange look. "I'm not big on the heaven-hell dichotomy, but if I had to choose . . ."

"No, I mean, like, in the woods. How did her trail disappear? Where would she have gone?"

He turned his head to look at me full on then, his expression screwed up with confusion, and a sharp stab of shame hit me in the chest. His voice went flat. "What are you talking about?"

I turned away, focusing on the houses passing by outside. "They never found anything. Clothes, or anything."

"Zora."

"Do you think there was something else?"

"Stop it!"

I jumped. Dad's knuckles were white against the steering wheel; a muscle strained in his jaw.

"You're eighteen, not twelve." He sounded like he wanted

to say more, but closed his mouth. He flexed his hands until his jaw stopped twitching, then said, "I don't think we should talk about this right now. Let's get home."

If anyone was going to believe Mom was alive, it was him. For all his flaws, Dad always bet on Mom.

"No," I said, and he glanced over at me. "I want to talk about it. Right now." I swallowed hard. "You can't tell me what I can and can't think about Mom."

He laughed, a harsh sound. "You can't think she's still— still *alive*!"

"Like hell I can't!"

"Have you believed that this whole time? Have you been telling *other people* that?"

"Yeah, I have. What's wrong with that?"

"It's *wrong*—it's not *healthy*—"

"Oh, okay, now *you're* lecturing me on what's right and healthy? The guy who had a mental breakdown and committed a major crime? Whose main career is stealing things from other people?"

"And I've had a lot of time to think about the things I did and why they were wrong—"

"—and while you were thinking about it, the entire town was punishing *us*! You got to leave! Sadie and I had to stay here. I bet it was nice in prison, being away from everyone who hated you, being able to come back cheerful and happy like everything in the world can be fixed. Things weren't great for us before you did all that, but after was—was—" There were no words for it. Waiting in the trailer for someone to take everything we had. Fearing school because of the horrible things people said, learning how to skip. Hunting firestarters because it was the only thing that eased the anger, until I got sloppy. "First Mom leaves, and then you think it's totally okay to fly off the handle and rob the *whole town*? Did you even think about me and Sadie before you did it? I know you didn't do it for the money, so don't lie and say you did."

His lips were pressed in a thin line. His eyes were glazed. He said nothing.

"If Mom were here," I said, "she would never have done something to hurt us, not without good reason."

A pause. A tremble in his voice. "I never meant to hurt you girls."

"Save it," I snapped, leaning my forehead on the passenger door. "You taught us how to lie."

21

In my whole childhood I only saw my father cry once.

Lazarus Novak wasn't an especially stoic man. He wasn't hardened by bitterness, or cynical. He enjoyed having fun. He believed you won life by being happy, and he was always a winner. He never yelled when Sadie or I did something we shouldn't have, and he didn't have to—we understood our mistakes because he stopped smiling. He never, ever raised a hand against us.

He wasn't the kind of man who cried because he was sad. It wasn't that he'd learned to bottle it up in some show of masculinity. More like nothing dug so deep into him it struck sadness. He didn't seem to have any sadness inside him. Sad things passed right through.

Neither Sadie nor I received this mystical power. Sadie cried often and for anything, sometimes just because the box of Cinnamon Toast Crunch was empty. Once, because she'd accidentally bought wingless pads instead of winged ones, and decided maybe she should bite the bullet and wear tampons, even though she hated having something jammed inside her all day. I cried never and for nothing, but not because I didn't feel like it. I felt like crying sometimes. Doesn't everyone? I wanted to cry when I was angry, mostly, and I was angry a lot. It's hard not to be, when people look at you like you shouldn't be allowed to breathe. But I kept that bottled up, because I was apathetic delinquent Zora Novak, and I wasn't supposed to cry.

So I didn't cry when they told us Mom was gone. But Dad did.

Mom was a strange spirit, perching on top of the trailer, gliding around aloof and mysterious often enough that people called her a witch. They knew something was different about her. When she didn't come back after a night of hunting, I was the first one to get worried. Then Dad. No one had seen her. Her phone couldn't be reached. After a full twenty-four hours, Dad got Chief Rivera on the case. He tried to smile then, and I believed it, because he didn't know what I knew, that she might have run into something much worse in the woods than a wild animal.

Then the chief came to the trailer. The Chevelle had been

found by Black Creek Woods, abandoned. The windows were rolled down, the keys in the ignition, the driver's door open, as if Mom had meant to return. A trail of footprints led north into the woods, and they matched Mom's shoe size, but they disappeared near an offshoot of Black Creek. Her trail went cold. The chief tried to get a team together to comb the woods, but not many people offered to help.

Dad stayed out there longer than others. He only came back when the chief made him, and for days after he tried to form a group to go back and look. He would have gotten lost in the search if not for me and Sadie. I was thirteen. Sadie was twenty. The ghosts hadn't acted strangely, so I went on as normal. Sadie walked around in a daze.

It wasn't as if Mom had died, after all. She'd just gotten out of her car and walked into the woods. She was hunting, but she knew how to handle herself. She knew a lot more than me.

A week after she went missing, Dad was making macaroni for us in the microwave when he burst into tears. I'd never heard those noises out of him. They made my stomach turn and my eyes water, and when Sadie leaped up to cry with him, I wanted to crawl away and disappear.

I think Dad cried a lot after that, but I only ever saw it the one time. And that one time was enough. The look on his face, not any worry I had about Mom, was what made me shove my head under my pillow that night and sob silently until I fell asleep. It was the last time I ever did. I didn't shed a tear when Dad got arrested for turning the town upside down and shaking the money out. I didn't cry when Ludwig tore my fingers off and tried to kill me. I didn't cry now, when it felt like every movement was wrong, every option a trap.

I had found the secret to Dad's magic: crying was useless. A waste of time and energy better spent fixing the thing that upset you in the first place. Do menial outdoor chores for your neighbors to assuage your guilt. Scare off the tourists. Get rid of *Dead Men Walking*. Dad only cried about Mom because there was nothing to be fixed, nothing he could do. There was only pain building and building and building on itself, and with no release, he had been overwhelmed.

I wonder sometimes if he had felt it coming and knew, one day, he wouldn't be strong enough to stop it.

I wonder if he feared it.

22

After we got home, every one of Dad's words was tight-lipped, every sentence short. He rearranged the boxes crowding the trailer, making a slightly neater path from the kitchen to the bedrooms. He told me to start working on my homework. Wanted to know if Grim was coming over after Sadie got off work. Then, when it seemed like he didn't have anything left to say, he grabbed his axe and went out to chop down the saplings that had begun to creep up on the trailer. It was the first time he'd touched the axe since coming home; before prison, I only saw him clearing brush on quiet, overcast days when no birds sang in the trees.

I watched him until Sadie came home, and then a little after.

"How long's he been like that?" she asked, voice flat. She still didn't look at me when she spoke.

"Couple of hours," I said. Six. He had been out there for six hours, cutting anything he could find. I'd finished my homework. I'd cracked open one of the fantasy tomes Grim had left at our place and read some of that. Even silly fantasy jargon couldn't distract me today.

I made dinner for all of us, ravioli with some broccoli and a near-expired tray of watermelon Sadie had picked up on her way home. Dad acted like his usual bright-eyed self, and though Sadie appeared to play along with it, she frowned and watched him carefully every time he looked down at his plate.

Sadie retreated to her bedroom at 9:25, but I didn't know if she'd be able to conk out like she usually did. Dinner must have helped Dad find his groove again, because he smiled and kissed my head when he said he was tired, too, and asked me if I wanted my room back yet.

I didn't believe him. He was lying with that smile and that happiness. He didn't want to be around me; that's why he'd spent six hours outside, instead of talking to me. He thought I hated him. I didn't tell him otherwise.

"I'm good." I patted my blanket and pillow on the couch. "I'm going to sleep soon, too."

The shadow that swept across his expression told me everything. Yes, he had been lying. Yes, he knew I was lying.

No, he wouldn't say anything about it, because even though none of us could risk this family getting in deeper trouble than we already were, and he didn't trust me not to get in more, he knew I'd been right this afternoon.

But the shadow passed. After a moment he said, "Okay. Sleep well."

"I will."

Artemis was right. It didn't feel good.

Dad put his hand on my head, over the spot where he'd kissed me, then disappeared into the smaller bedroom. I waited a few minutes for another laugh out of *Cheers*, then flipped the TV off and grabbed the Chevelle's keys from the stack of boxes by the door. I paused there, where Dad's axe rested against the wall. I reached for it. Brushed the wooden handle.

A spike of fear drilled my chest. I whipped my hand back and hurried out the door.

A cold mist had settled along Valleywine Road. My butt went numb against the Chevelle's chilled seats long before I reached the outskirts of town. The streets were empty of the living and the dead, and lights shone in every window. I thought I saw Buster's truck turn a corner, so I crept along a little more carefully. Even the Chevelle's engine seemed to rumble a bit softer tonight, like it was afraid to draw attention.

The Cherry Motel was at the town limits, with a Marathon gas station on the opposite side of the road and long empty cornfields straight out to the horizon behind it. The motel's neon sign, with its big double cherries, looked like an advertisement for a strip joint. It was a squat brown building with a long line of rooms. There used to be a dead man holding an empty dog collar on the end of a leash near the motel check-in, but he wasn't there anymore. The *Dead Men Walking* van sat outside room ten, on the south end of the building, and next to it was the SUV. I parked a few doors down and cut the engine.

The *DMW* team and their crew would have rented more than one room. I couldn't walk up to the front office to get any information; even with a good lie, they would assume I was an obsessed fan. No telling how many of those they'd already had. I could knock on every door until I found them, but I didn't want to get someone who was going to automatically call the cops on me. Their stuffy producer probably would. The camera people had been following the producer around like puppies since they'd gotten here, so I doubted they'd listen to me without telling him. Eric would tell Tad. I wasn't sure about Mike or Leila, but they had gone along with everything else up to this point.

Tad's sheer narcissism was going to be the only thing that saved me. If I could get him talking, maybe he wouldn't call the police. And if, God help me, I begged, it might stroke his ego enough to show mercy.

I heard yelling. The door to seven swung open and banged against the wall, and Leila stalked out. Her clothes looked pristine but her hair was ruffled.

"*Christ*, Tad, you're such a pig! I am so tired of all your weird bullshit! We almost *died*!"

Tad appeared in the doorway, pulling his shirt back on. "At least I'm not a fucking iceberg!" he yelled back. "Yeah, go tell Mike, I'm sure he wants to hear *all* about your gross woman problems!"

Leila slipped into nine. Tad stood outside seven for another moment, sneering, then went back inside and slammed the door behind him.

I hopped out of the Chevelle and started down the sidewalk. The wind pinched at the tips of my ears and nose. Room seven was quiet. Eight was, too.

"Hey!"

I jumped and spun. Tad was leaning against the doorframe, arms folded.

"What are you doing? Here to screw with us some more?" he said.

I forced myself to straighten up and did my best to wash the look of disgust off my face. "No. I wanted to ask one more time for our memory card back. *Please.*"

"I already told you, you can't have it."

"What do I have to do for it? Seriously. For you to get rid of copies you made, not to air it, to give me the footage, what do I have to do?"

Tad rolled his shoulders and looked me over from head to toe. I had to clench my teeth to suppress the full-body shudder that came over me. I was glad Artemis hadn't come here; I could deal with people looking at me like I was something less than human, but I didn't think she had quite as much experience.

Tad motioned with his head. "Come in, I'll see what I can do."

"Is the card in your room? Because if it's not, I don't see the point of coming in."

"Do you want the card back or not?"

I'd dealt with firestarters this week. I could probably handle a blue-balled nerd. Probably.

I went inside, hands out of my pockets, every hair on my body standing on end. If he came within arm's reach of me, he was getting his nose relocated to his brain. He closed the door. The room had one bed with sheets the color of mustard, an old tube TV on the long dresser on the opposite side of the room, and a large window facing the cornfields, the curtains pulled closed. Both lamps on either side of the headboard were on, as well as the lamp on the desk by the dresser. A suitcase sat on the floor by the desk chair, overflowing with wrinkled shirts and balled-up socks, a toothbrush without a holder, and a collection of CDs in slim jewel cases, neatly slotted into the netting in the top. It was so much warmer than it was outside, sweat gathered on my neck immediately; he had to have the thermostat set to eighty. The whole room smelled like smoke.

"Are you cooking something in here? Why's it so hot?"

"Why's your damn town so cold?" he shot back. He walked around to my left, staying carefully out of arm's reach, like he'd read my mind. He circled around and sat on the very corner of the bed, more resting on the balls of his feet than anything, and looked me up and down again. He wore old jeans and a button-down short-sleeve T-shirt that made him look like his shoulders were too narrow and his neck was too long.

"I don't have any weapons on me," I said. "If you're thinking anything else, stop now; it's not happening."

He snorted. "You must think you're hot shit if you go around accusing people of wanting to have sex with you. You *do* know you look like you crawled out of a garbage can, right?"

I never accused people of wanting to have sex with me—I never even *thought* about it—and he wasn't going to gaslight me into submission.

"You literally hit on me the first time we met," I snapped. "Did you forget that?"

He blinked slowly and said, "Wait, you're into Bach, right?

Or is he into you? He *would* be into you; look at him, he looks like he climbed out of the garbage, too. So have you hit that yet? Or no?"

If my own head didn't explode first, I was going to pop his off his neck. "What do you want?" I said. "You brought me in here because you want something for that memory card. What is it?"

He leaned back and rapped his fingers on his chin. "Well now, let's see. What would that footage be worth to you? Five hundred dollars? A thousand?"

I held my arms up. "Does it look like I have any money?"

"Fair. Any property, family heirlooms? No? Hmm . . . and the sex thing is *completely* off the table?"

My nostrils flared. I would not break my hard swearing rules for this jerk. I wouldn't.

"Okay, okay." He thought for another moment. I wanted to punch him. I wanted to kick him in the crotch and go find someone reasonable to ask. "How about this?" He held his hands open and smiled. "You help me frame Sam and Bach for these fires."

I froze.

"It would be easy, with me backing you," he went on. "You could clear your name and get them out of town, just like you want. Then we could discuss more after that—like you helping me get into Grimshaw House."

A cold and unsettling feeling spread from my spine, out through my back, and down my arms and legs. There's a deep animal instinct that tells you when a person is no longer joking. It tells you the heat in the room isn't coming from a thermostat. It tells you those appraising looks were not the usual kind of inappropriate. The rational side of your brain wants to tell you these feelings are silly or stupid or insane. The rational side of your brain is wrong.

Tad's eyes snapped up to mine. Still, dark. Black. His thumb rubbed a slow circle on his knee. The room was quiet except for the low whistle of the wind outside. No ghosts watching in the window. No blasting heater set too high.

"So," I said, "your name is Ludwig?"

His lips split to reveal straight white teeth. His eyes lit with glee.

"Nice to see you again, Zora Novak."

23

"Do you know what a pain in the ass it was to get back here after you kicked me out the first time?" Ludwig stood up from the bed, his shirt wrinkled and bunched up around his belt, his jeans catching under his heels. "I need you to do something for me. Tell me I'm smart."

He waited. I said nothing.

"I'm *smart* because *this* time I found out who I could kill that would make problems for you. I couldn't have you running around trying to hit me with your car, right? I think I had pretty great self-control, waiting that long to set a fire.

"I was going to do a few more before I took a body, but then you and your cousin and these ghost chasers waltzed right into my mines! I tried to take you, first, but surprise—can't be hurt by fire, can't be possessed. Turned out fine, though." He patted his chest. "Did you know people let healthy young boys like this one get away with almost *anything?* I should have tried this much sooner—"

"Shut up." My stomach heaved. "You've killed people."

"Whatever. Bach has killed way more than me, and I don't see you cutting his head off." He stepped toward me. "He's always been the worst."

I spun and lunged for the door. Ludwig's hand came down on top of mine on the door handle, searingly hot; it felt like he was pressing a clothes iron to my knuckles. I ripped my hand away and tore my glove off. It had melted, but the skin underneath was unharmed.

Ludwig held the door handle until it melted into a lump of malformed metal in his fingers, then let go. "Who needs locks? That'll be hot to the touch for a while." He smiled again. I heard him, but my heart was beating in my throat, making sounds pulse in and out. "Now, are you going to sit down and listen? I like watching the expressions on your stupid human face."

I took a deep breath.

"No, no screaming for help, come on!" he said. "I'll have to melt you a muzzle. You don't want that, trust me, I've done it before, and people were not happy about it."

I let out a long, slow exhale. It was nearly a scream.

He loped back to the desk in the corner, where a laptop

and phone sat beneath the lamp. He scooped up the phone. "I can't wait to get out of this town. The sooner the better."

"Get out?" I said. "You could have left whenever you wanted."

He glanced up from the phone. "Bach hasn't told you? Hildegard, *our loving mother,* left us here. If I can find her entrance, I can find her.

"And I already know where it is. All these idiots thinking the treasure beneath Grimshaw House is jewelry or money, they're all wrong. It's Hildegard's entrance. She escaped Addamsville through Grimshaw House and hid it there by giving Sam ownership of it. If I can get rid of them, if that ownership passes to me, I'll be able to get back to her. She's out there somewhere."

"I thought she abandoned you."

He grinned as he raised the phone and tapped something on the screen. "Only because she thought Bach and Sam were more worthy of her time. Once they're out of the picture, it will just be me and her again. So what do you say? Partners?"

I tried to speak, but no words came out. I couldn't say no because he would kill me. I couldn't say yes because I couldn't help him kill anyone else. And I couldn't cry, because it would do no good.

"That's a shame." He tapped the screen again and put the phone up to his ear. When he spoke, his expression was flat but his voice shot up an octave, breathy and fast. "Oh god—please, come quickly—she's got—it's some kind of fire—please, my name is Tad Thompson, I'm in room seven of the Cherry Motel on Valleywine Road. Please, please come—it's this Novak girl, she's setting the room on fire—please!"

And then he melted the phone and tossed it on the floor.

"Five minutes, tops," he said.

The mustard-yellow comforter burst into flames, all at once, an even coat of orange fire that spread to the bedposts and down to the carpet. I stumbled back, catching myself on the dresser. With a hiss like a blowtorch, the dresser top went up, wood splintering. I whipped my hands away and scrambled for the desk. Smoke billowed toward the ceiling. Tad—Ludwig— shimmered in the sudden heat.

"Help!" he yelled. "Help, fire! Help!"

Fire sliced the curtains from their rods. The wallpaper cracked and curled. Smoke stung my eyes, my nose; acrid chemical smoke, things burning that shouldn't be. The alarm clock melted on the night stand. A painting of old Addamsville crashed to the floor. The building groaned. Fire crept along the carpet fibers. I dropped, my knees unable to hold me up, my head spinning.

"It's beautiful, isn't it?" he said. "Fleeting, bright, destructive. Fire's the only true way to go."

I was dying. I was going to die. I couldn't breathe. Couldn't see. The fire corralled me to an empty spot on the carpet and held me there, shaking, shivering, useless. I couldn't feel my arms or legs. If I moved, I would die. If I didn't move, I would die.

Ludwig paced around me. Sometimes he was Tad Thompson, sometimes a creature that swallowed the light, its eyes two little red pinpricks. "I don't feel like myself if I'm not setting something on fire. I don't know how Bach stands his abstinence. Maybe it's easier when you have someone else holding your leash?" He dug claws into the carpet. Smiled with human teeth. "I'm glad Hildegard didn't make me the pet of her spawn. I'm not sure I would've liked being leashed."

He leaned down. Brushed a lock of hair away from my face with a black talon. "It's probably been enough time now. They'll be wondering why I'm not dead yet."

Then he grabbed the desk chair, spun, and slammed it through the window. Glass shattered. He slithered through and started screaming. I had to move. I wouldn't burn, but I still had to breathe. There was sweet cold air outside. Outside. Outside was five feet away, and I wouldn't make it. *Go go go,* said one part of my brain. *Fire fire fire,* said another. That part was louder. I pressed my forehead to the hot, rough carpet.

"Get up, Zora." I could at least move my lips.

"Get *up,* Zora." A whisper this time. I curled my fingers, the ones that could be curled.

"Get up, Zora." Pushed my forehead off the floor. I was two breaths from screaming.

"Get up." On my knees. Looking at the window through the licking flames.

"Get up." Legs wobbling, feet shuffling.

"Get up. Get up. Get *up*." Forward. Hands on the windowsill. Eyes burning, lungs burning. An ungainly leap.

My sleeve caught and tore; my stomach grew hot. I kicked off the window ledge and crashed to the hard-packed dirt outside, coughing, sobbing, alive. Smoke billowed out the broken window, whipped into the air by the cold night wind. I scrambled to my feet as the world tilted beneath me and my vision blurred, and I sprinted toward the end of the building. Wood popped. Flickering light leaped into the windows I passed, the other rooms. Eight, nine, ten. The building groaned again. The night brightened as fire overtook the roof. I rounded the end of the building and stumbled into the parking lot.

The other motel patrons were already outside. The fire had reached the rooms closest to Tad's. Leila, Mike, and Eric stood in the parking lot, Leila without a coat, Mike without his shoes, Eric without a shirt. All of them clustered around Tad, who was sprawled on the ground. The cameramen were yelling about their equipment; the producer and the assistants were staring at the building, mouths open. The producer saw me come into the light.

"Hey!"

I tried to run. The first cameraman came around the van and hit me from the front. The second one knocked us both sideways. We crashed into dirt and grass, me wheezing, them cursing.

"I didn't do it!" My voice was barely strong enough to be heard over the fire and the wind. "I didn't do it—Ludwig—Tad—set me up—"

Sirens floated in from the distance. The guy who'd tackled me first grabbed me by the wrists and the scruff of my neck, hauled me to my feet, and dragged me back to their van. Something warm ran down my arm.

The producer got in my face. "Do you know how many thousands of dollars of equipment we had in there? Do you *know?* Even if you hadn't put all of us in danger, we're going to make sure you pay for every *cent.*"

"She's crazy!" Tad cried. "She—she barged in demanding the—the thing—and she set the bed on fire—she threatened me!"

"Liar!" I screamed. "I didn't do anything to you! I didn't do it! I didn't! Let me *go!*" The cameramen only held on tighter, one on either side of me now, so I couldn't aim a kick at their kneecaps or slam my head into their faces. The fire was only getting bigger.

The sirens were upon us. Addamsville's lone fire engine, followed by a police cruiser.

"*We're* the liars?" the producer said. "Try to lie your way out of this one, you stupid b—"

I spat in his face. He slapped me. I swung my body forward and drove my boot into his groin. He doubled over.

"DON'T EVER CALL ME THAT NAME! I DIDN'T DO THIS I DIDN'T SET ANY FIRES I DIDN'T DO ANY OF THIS LET ME GO LET ME GO *LET ME GO!*"

"Zora!"

The wind quavered beneath the whipcrack of Chief Rivera's voice.

24

My lack of burns baffled the paramedic. The fire had overtaken the room so quickly. Tad had gotten out right away, but I hadn't. My clothes were charred. My skin was fine. My only injuries were the cuts from the glass.

Jack and Norm stuffed me in the back of their cruiser and drove me to the station. My pulse throbbed where the broken window had sliced straight through my jacket and into my biceps. I still couldn't quite breathe right. None of these things were helped by the handcuffs.

Norm and Jack never said a word. Neither did I. There was no Ludwig, to them. No ghosts. There was just Tad Thompson and lies. I caught Jack giving me sympathetic looks in the rearview mirror, but only because he'd been a little rough as he put me in the car. There was no more *I don't think you did it.* The two people who knew I hadn't done it were me and Ludwig, and he was going lie all the way back to hell.

Police station. Same cell. I paced because I couldn't lay down. The other cells were empty. Norm and Jack stuck around. Norm answered phone calls while Jack stood near the door to the hallway my cell was in.

"Hey, Jackalope. What happened to Bach?"

Jack turned to me. His voice was subdued, and he kept his distance. "He was released. He didn' do nothin', had a clean alibi for the night of the Forester mansion fire."

I shivered. All of my organs felt like they were standing on the tips of their toes, ready to either explode or help me burst into a sprint. I shouldn't have been asking about Bach. "You know I didn't do this, right?"

Jack didn't say anything.

I stood close to the bars. "I need to talk to Chief Rivera. I have to explain this to her." I didn't want to be stuck in here. "Jack, come on."

"The chief is busy." He shifted as Norm said something from the main office; for a minute, I thought he was going to leave me in here.

"What about the Chevelle?" I said. "The Chevelle is at the motel."

"It'll be impounded for now," Jack said.

"Impounded? But—*Buster* holds the impounded cars. At the junkyard."

"Yeah," Jack said.

I swallowed.

"My dad could go get it. Has anyone called him? He was sleeping. He could run over there with my sister and get it. Please, Jack, you have to call him."

"They can pick it up from the junkyard later."

"No—no, Jack, please—Buster will destroy it—"

Norm said something else. Jack walked away to answer him, and the door slid smoothly shut. The lock clicked. I was alone.

Ludwig wants me dead, I thought. Now he had me somewhere I couldn't escape. Why not make it look like I'd killed myself by setting the police station on fire? That would be rebelliousness up my alley, right? Fire, fire everywhere. Fire for everyone, including me. That was the truth for Addamsville. I was a firestarter. I would go down in flames.

I didn't sleep that night. The phone rang off the hook for the first few hours, then stopped. I only knew it was morning when the light outside the small hallway window brightened. They'd taken my jacket, and my phone and the Chevelle's keys, the only two things I'd had on me, so I didn't know what time it was until Dad and Sadie arrived.

Chief Rivera was the one who let them in. The expressions on their faces were unreadable, and as soon as I saw them, fear clenched in my stomach. They could get trapped here as easily as I was, and they wouldn't know until it was too late.

Dad looked at my hand, my arm, my face. Sadie just stared at the floor.

"What happened?" Dad asked.

I opened my mouth to answer, then stopped. Even Dad had a limit to how much bullshit he was willing to listen to, and I had lied to him last night. I glanced at Chief Rivera. There was no way she would take this as anything other than me either losing my mind or building a fantasy world.

"I didn't do it" was all I could say. "He framed me; all I wanted was the memory card back. I didn't do it; I swear I didn't."

My insides had started shaking again. They wouldn't believe me this time. This was too much. I'd built this wall, and now I had to live on my side of it, alone.

But then Dad took my hands from the bars, both of them, carefully, and held them in his.

"Someone's been calling Harrisburg trying to get their police involved, too. Sadie has to go to work, but I'll see what I can find out, and later I'll go speak to them myself."

"You don't have to do that—the Harrisburg cops—the prison—"

He kissed the back of my right hand. "No one's gonna take my girl away. I'm so sorry I wasn't here for you before. I'm sorry I made such a mess and left you in it. I'm here for you now."

Sadie stepped up beside him. "Don't say anything more than you already have, okay? We're going to try to get a lawyer."

"We can't afford a lawyer."

"We're going to try!" she snapped. "This is serious, Zora!"

"I know it is!"

"Stop it, both of you!" Dad said. Both of us shut out mouths immediately. "This is not the time to argue. Zoo, we're not going to let you stay in here for long. I promise. I love you. Sadie, let's get going; you can't be late for work."

Dad let go of my hands. As they left, Sadie paused for a second to grab my fingertips. "I love you, too," she said quietly.

Then they were gone. The phone was ringing in the main office again, and I was alone.

I slept, finally, sometime around midmorning, and my dreams were filled with fire and little creatures poking me with pitchforks, the skin burning off my hands and leaving only prosthetics that didn't move, my hair falling out so blood could seep from my scalp as my friends watched, saying I deserved it.

In one dream, I came out in a clearing in the woods and

saw my own burned body staked in front of Forester House.

In another, Bach was kissing me, and my skin melted and sloughed away from every spot his lips touched.

In a third, I burst into flames and screamed, only to realize a moment later that I wasn't burning because my arms and legs were short, thin, and black as pitch, tipped with claws and talons.

Norm brought me a hamburger and fries from the Fool that afternoon. I ate, but I didn't taste it. The phone kept ringing. I stared at the ceiling and focused on my breathing. Worrying about the building catching on fire wouldn't do me any good while I was stuck in here. Where was Ludwig now? Still with the *DMW* crew or out patrolling the town? Was he going after Bach? Norm came again to bring me dinner, which I had even more trouble eating. When I asked what was going on, he gave me a closed-off look and said, "They ain't happy about it."

Shortly after dinner I fell into another restless sleep. No real dreams, not that I can remember, only a bad feeling deep in my chest every time I pulled myself back to consciousness. When I finally couldn't make myself sleep anymore, when the lights were out again in the hallway, I sat up on the cot and held my pounding head.

Then I realized it was too dark. It wasn't just the overhead lights that were off, but *every* light. The desk lamps in the main office. The soft illumination of the security light. The red eye of the camera by the exit. Only a little glow came through the small window on the door, and it must have been from the moonlight flooding into the main office. There was no hum of electronics.

I sat up, listening. Ludwig had cut the power to the building and he was coming for me, making sure there was no way for me to call for help, even if I did get out. Something moved outside my cell, and I stilled. There was breathing. Not my own.

"Zora."

Chief Rivera. I stayed pressed to the cinder-block wall at the back of the cell.

"Why is the power out?" I said.

"So I can speak to you."

"You don't have a flashlight or something?"

She ignored me and said, "I know who Sam Forester is. So did your mother. So do you."

I waited, breath held. My limbs felt like jelly, my urge to run overwhelming. "Are you . . . like us?"

"No. But twenty-eight years ago, I had two good friends." Her voice was soft in the dark. "They were ghost hunters, like your cousin. They wanted so badly to uncover the truth of this town, and they thought they would find something the first time Forester House burned down. They were excited because they thought big events like that always meant an uptick in paranormal activity.

"Then the Foresters moved into town. The fires continued. People kept dying. Your mother and your aunt almost died when the Aberdeen house went down. My friends thought all of the fire, all of the destruction, would reveal secrets no one else knew. They were down in Maple Hills one night when their cabin caught on fire. It went up so fast they didn't have a chance to get out. Can you imagine how fast it must have burned? For them not to have a chance to run? How hot it had to be?

"Sam went back to the woods. The fires stopped. The stories became myths, but I remember. I saw things that summer I've never told anyone, because I knew they wouldn't believe me."

I couldn't see her face, but I could feel her gaze.

"I know you and your mom have something to do with all this. I know Dasree wanted to stop Sam as much as I did." She paused. Keys rattled. "I can't stop these fires now, and I can't—I can't relive it. I'm sorry. But I can at least do this."

The key turned. The cell bars passed through the weak light as they slid open. "You'll get fired," I said. "You'll lose your job; everyone will think you're—"

I stopped. She knew I had no case against the *DMW* crew. Against Ludwig. I was the lunatic who had tried to kill Tad Thompson, and it was only my word against his.

"You need to find a place to hide," she said. "You need to run. Your dad and Sadie got held up in Harrisburg. It's about ten thirty now. Here's your jacket. Your phone and keys are in the pocket. Buster still has the Chevelle; I suggest you leave it where it is. Find somewhere safe to go. You understand?"

I nodded, mute, then realized she couldn't see me and choked out, "Yes."

"Good girl. I'll open up the back door."

25

Behind the police station was a sparse stand of mulberry trees and a swath of grass. Past the mulberries stretched the Denfords' cornfields. Grandpa Denford usually stood like a scarecrow out there, his flickering edges the only movement in the night. He wasn't there now. I slid down a short slope and kneeled beside a tree, making sure the tall grass hid me.

An Addamsville without its ghosts was a house without people. Abandoned.

I flipped my phone open. Hit the power button. An empty battery icon flashed. I'd charged it two nights ago; a flip phone this old couldn't hold a charge for two whole days, even when it wasn't being used.

I had to call Dad and Sadie to warn them to stay away, and

to do that, I had to get my phone charged. The fastest way to the bluffs meant a hard diagonal cut straight through town, crossing over both Handack Street and Valleywine Road. A lot of bright public parking lots, but no one would expect me to be walking in plain sight.

I crept back up to the road. Chief Rivera's cruiser was gone from the parking lot, if it had ever been there. The lights were still off. I pulled my hair back, put my hood up, and stuffed my hands in my pockets. I'd done plenty of sneaking around in my time; I wasn't going to let dyed hair and gloves give me away. Most people couldn't tell me from the next teenaged trash fire when they couldn't see my face or my hands.

Crossing Handack was the easy part. The Fool was far enough away from the police station that no one saw me, and the Family Dollar was already closed for the night. I slipped between the Family Dollar and the antique shop and slid into shadowed yards divided by chain-link fences. Trees hid them from the main roads; tourists cruising through town would never see this clutter. Old swing sets and plastic sandboxes stacked with coiled hoses, fraying lawn chairs, and sun umbrellas. I tripped over a rusted bike and almost speared myself on a fence. A round Sputnik grill with a maple tree sprouting through its grate. A playhouse, plastic door hanging open to reveal its empty insides, waited for occupants who would never return.

I grabbed the last fence to quiet its rattle as I climbed over, into the bank parking lot. Valleywine was lit up from the fire station to the post office, but there weren't nearly as many people out as I had feared. I jogged across the road, heading for the shadows of the trees near the library. As I hit the sidewalk, a girl came out of the gas station right next door, with a wave of swinging black hair and a Happy Hal's visor dangling from one hand. The other held her cell phone up to her ear. Mads.

I sucked in my breath, and the sound was enough for her to glance my way. The phone dropped from her ear. "Zora?"

I ditched calm and charged into the bushes behind the library, through another thicket of trees and out onto a long, rolling lawn. One lawn, two. I sprinted down a fence line, across a street, then dove behind the hedge between two houses.

Seconds later Mads appeared, barely winded. She scanned the empty street, then hissed into the night, "I'm in the marching band, Zora! We work out more than the football team! You can't outrun me!"

Except I had, just this one time, because Mads might have been in better shape, but I knew Addamsville at night. I hunkered down in the bushes until her expression turned to worry, and she pulled her phone out again. I crept away before the cops could show up.

I hurried on toward the bluffs, past the last of the houses and into the wide field that spanned the gap to Hampstead Road. On Hampstead, a fork split east to the bluffs and west to the trailer park and the rest of town. The trailer park's lights glowed to my right. As I neared Hampstead, the ground sloped upward.

Headlights turned onto Hampstead from the north, the direction of the junkyard. I dropped into the grass and waited for it to pass. An old truck, probably one of Buster's guys. Someone inside was hollering like the Colts had won the Super Bowl. My bones rattled as they swept past, but they hadn't seen me—were they celebrating? Or had they found someone else to chase down? I climbed onto the road and watched the truck go, and something tickled in the back of my mind, a little voice that said *don't turn left, don't turn left, don't turn left.*

The truck reached the fork and turned left. Up to the bluffs.

I ran. It was too far to run the whole way there, but I ran. The ground began to rise more steeply and my knees burned, my head pounded. There was shouting ahead, breaking the still night, rising above the trees. I tore up the path. Shouts and metal grinding, metal screeching. Someone was laughing like a hyena. I ran. Light up ahead, in our clearing. Headlights from four trucks, an SUV, and Buster Gates's own red juggernaut, the truck so big it could take a semi head-on. They all rumbled, spewing clouds of exhaust into the chill air. Figures of men and women stood silhouetted in the light, including Buster, next to the open door of his truck, which was poised at one end of the trailer. Four other guys moved the cinder blocks and potted plants we'd put around the base of the trailer to keep it in place and make it look nice.

"Hey!" I pushed on, realizing too late that my adrenaline was gone and my legs had turned to jelly. I stumbled toward Buster, wheezing. "Hey! Stop it! Stop!"

A few people near their cars turned and saw me, and one of the guys holding a cinder block motioned to Buster.

"How'd you get out of jail?" Buster said, leaning against the door of his truck. "Abby must be slipping."

He didn't move as I lurched forward, grabbed his collar, and took a drunken swing at his face. Surprise took over his expression until he grabbed my arm and tossed me onto my back. Laughter erupted.

"This is what happens when you grow up with a father who doesn't know how to fight," he said. "Stay down there and let the adults take care of business." He turned to climb into the truck.

Get up, Zora. "Stop it—leave my house alone—"

"House?" he snorted. "This is barely a sardine can!" He snapped the door shut. "Is it all out of the way, Bobby? Good, make sure she stays straight."

I grabbed hold of Buster's truck window and reached in for him. I got a fistful of sleeve before someone caught me from behind and lifted me, flailing, away from the truck. Buster revved the engine. The truck's massive grille guard bumped into the end of the trailer. Buster kept going.

Forward. To the gap in the trees. To the edge of the bluffs.

I reached back and dug my fingernails into the face of the man who held me. He let go with a yell. I scrabbled back to Buster's truck, but he'd rolled up the windows and locked the doors and made no move when I pounded on the glass and screamed.

The trailer lurched. Another guy tried to grab me. I used the side-view mirror and the huge wheel well to climb onto the truck's hood. Buster wouldn't look at me. I couldn't hear myself. I couldn't hear what I was saying, but I know I screamed it at the top of my lungs. Metal screeched; the pipes Mom had jerry rigged to the old Aberdeen plumbing tore open. The generator wires snapped.

I slid off the hood and hurried to climb the ragged remains of our front steps. I fumbled with the Chevelle's keys until I found the right one and unlocked the door. The trailer's walls swayed. The TV fell off the table in the living room and smashed on the floor. Cereal and canned food rained from the cabinets in the kitchen nook. The boxes of Mom's and Dad's things remained where they were, too heavy to be unsettled. Too heavy for me to carry out by myself.

Dad's wood axe fell from its spot by the door and hit the linoleum with a solid *thwack*.

I grabbed it and leaped outside.

Trying to hold an axe with one hand missing two fingers doesn't make for great swinging, but I managed. Buster's side-view mirror went first. The axe-head cleaved a fat line down the back on the first swing, and sliced it nearly off on the second.

Then I was on the hood again. I was no longer sure how I got from one place to the next, only that I was there, and my legs had found some of their strength, and my arms brought that blade down on Buster Gates's windshield like an executioner. The spider cracks made him jump, but the truck revved again, and the trailer shuddered. The trees were behind us, and now there was only night sky above the trailer. Night sky above, and the sound of water lapping against rock far below.

Buster reversed. I lost my footing and grabbed the windshield wipers to stay on top of the truck, which meant letting go of the axe. It slid sideways off the hood. The green glow of the dashboard lit Buster's furious face. The trailer groaned. The engine roared again, and the truck shot forward.

The trailer made a last soft whisper as it fell.

The force of the impact rattled through my hands, and the sudden stop pried them free. I slipped off the hood. I caught for a second at the grille guard, hands failing me. My toes clipped the ground, then that slid out from under me, too, and my torso hit the edge of the cliff, knocking the air out of me.

My arm caught on a lone root sticking from the ground, and my hand snagged a large tuft of grass. My feet kicked at open air.

Below me was the empty sound of something large falling. Then a crash and crunch of the trailer; a cacophony of furniture, cardboard, metal, and glass slamming; a creak and groan before one final crash; then only the hush of the wind.

Buster's truck reversed again.

"Help!" I couldn't breathe. "Help, I can't—" My hands weren't made for holding on to things.

They had to see me. They had to know I hadn't gone over the edge. I heard voices, but none of them came closer. My boots scraped the curving rock wall beneath me. My shoulders had already begun to protest. My arms drooped and my head dipped below the cliff edge.

Someone made a noise. Tires rumbled on dirt. Headlights began to move. Someone was yelling now, a woman, her voice carrying into the darkness.

"What have you done? I know all of you, I know all your faces and where you live, and when this gets reported—I can't believe this—this—this inhumanity!" Her voice came closer.

My arm slipped slowly and steadily from its nestled spot, and the grass in my grip started coming up by the roots.

The night sky above was so clear.

Just let go, I thought. *It'll be easier if you let go.*

You won't have to do this anymore if you let go.

A face appeared above me. Dark eyes and blond hair. Artemis. Then Mads, Lorelei, and Hal, piling on top of one another to reach down for me. They hooked my arms and pulled. Artemis grabbed my belt to haul me up the rest of the way, then dropped beside me, panting, as soon as I was out of danger.

"I saw some of Buster's guys heading this way, and I knew you were, too," Mads said, quiet and breathless. "So I called Mrs. Wake. I didn't think . . . I didn't know it would be like this. . . ."

"They ran once we got here," Hal said, voice rough. "Even Buster, like he thought we wouldn't know it was him."

Lorelei shook like a leaf.

Headlights still shone in the clearing, but in a different arrangement. The shouts and hollers and growls of engines had faded, and from between headlights came the silhouette of a woman blazing toward us.

"Are you okay?" Greta kneeled in the dirt in her pristine white pants to rest a hand against the side of my face. "Are you in one piece?"

I wriggled out from her touch, turned away from them all, and crawled to the edge of the bluffs. Hands latched onto my belt and my coat, but I stopped before going over, just enough to peer down at the rocks and sand far below.

The trailer was a crushed can in the moonlight. It lay on

its top, half on the shore and half in the water, glass sprinkled around it like glitter. Curtains fluttered from windows and both doors swung open. Seams had split in the walls.

Ringing filled my ears. Louder, louder, louder. It began to sound like screaming. Then like chanting, chanting to the fast, hard drum of my heartbeat, louder, until it was all I could hear, until it was a primal command that had lived inside me since Mom disappeared, stifled after losing my fingers, waiting for the moment it could return.

FIRE, FIRE, FIRE, FIRE

On aching arms and unsure legs, I pushed myself up and past Greta and Artemis, past Mads and Hal and Lorelei. I grabbed the axe from where it had fallen. There was nothing left in the clearing. A few scattered potted plants. Cinder blocks. The foundation where a house had once stood. I had firestarters after me, and Addamsville thought *this* would do me in?

"Zora!" Artemis yanked on my arm. "You almost fell off a cliff. You need to stop."

"Let go of me." With more than a little effort, I pushed her hand away. My hands shook. My legs ended in stumps.

Artemis grabbed at my sleeve again, then my hand. She held it so tight my bones ached. "Stop! Jesus, Zora. Where are you even going?"

"Let go of me!"

"No!"

"I'm going to set fires!" I rounded on her. We were almost the same height, but Artemis shrank back as I towered over her. "I'm *done!* I'm done with all of this! I'm done with firestarters threatening my family and assholes pushing my house off a *fucking cliff.* I'm done trying to help people who don't care about me! I'm done trying to figure out why I'll burn everything down myself, and then there'll be nothing left for Buster, nothing for Forester, nothing for Ludwig, nothing for *you.* Everything will be gone, and I'll be gone, and I won't have to deal with this *bullshit* anymore!"

"*Zora!*" Artemis screamed. We stared at each other in silence, me trying to get my breath back, her cheeks puffed up, looking scared. When she spoke again it was very soft, but not comforting. "You're not going to burn anything down," she said. "You aren't going to set any fires."

"What did I just say?"

"You *aren't*. You love this town."

"Like *fuck* I do."

"Shut up!"

I snapped my mouth shut. Artemis had actual tears in her eyes. The others stood behind her, looking just as stunned as I felt. "You *do* love this town! You wouldn't go around fixing porch lights and pruning mums in the middle of the night if you didn't! You care about what happened here, and you care whether tourists trash the place. You care about your mom and what she started. Your whole family came from here. You grew up here. I'm sorry about what I said before. I don't think you're a thief or a liar or a bad person, and I'm really sorry I was horrible to you. I *do* believe you. You don't need to set anything on fire. You need to sit down. You probably need sleep and real food, and you definitely need a shower and new clothes. You look terrible."

She paused, panting.

"You always say I look terrible," I muttered.

She finally released me. "No, normally I say you look like a raccoon that got into garbage. This time I mean . . . ugh, Zora, really. Look at yourself. You've got bruises and cuts all over the place, your clothes are torn, you're covered in soot and dirt. And Mads said you ran all the way here. You're a mess. Mom, can you—?"

She turned to Greta. Greta, who had been watching silently with that unforgiving look in her eye and that hard set of her lips.

"Who knows that you're here?" she said.

"Buster and the others," I replied. "And you all."

Now they'd heard my ranting. Did it matter anymore? Did it matter who knew and who didn't?

"Have you called your dad or your sister?" Greta asked.

"No. My phone's dead. I was coming back for the charger."

"Mom," Artemis said, "can they stay with us? Can she—"

Greta was nodding before she finished, fishing her phone out of her pocket. "The two of you get in the car; we're going home." She put the phone to her ear. After a moment, she said, "Lazarus, where are you now?"

Artemis towed me toward the car.

"Wait." It was Lorelei who grabbed my sleeve. A ghost of a touch. Mads and Hal flanked her. "We know you didn't set the fire at the motel," she said, voice quivering. "Did Tad do it?"

That question made everything seem so simple. But the truth was anything but simple. "You wouldn't believe the story if I told you."

"We're willing to listen, though." Mads stepped up. Her black hair was in tangles now, but she didn't stop to fix it. "Whatever's going on, we know you aren't doing it, and we want to help you prove it."

Lorelei nodded vigorously, the most determination I had ever seen in her.

"You sure you don't feel guilty because your dad pushed my house off a cliff?" I asked her.

"Of course I feel guilty," she said. "But I want to help because it's the right thing to do. The two aren't mutually exclusive."

I looked at Hal. He was still bandaged up and moving stiffly. "And you?" I said. "You were already in the crossfires of this thing one time. You really want to go again?"

"Are we going to take out the motherfucker who set me on fire?"

"Ideally."

Hal considered for a moment, then tipped his head back. "Then you have the services of Hal Haynes III, local legend."

"The story can wait," Artemis said. "It's too late tonight."

"And I almost fell off a cliff," I added.

"And it's, like, twenty-five degrees too cold," Hal finished.

"Tomorrow," I said. "I'll explain tomorrow."

They agreed and retreated to their own cars. Artemis opened the back door of Greta's Lexus. As I climbed in, I caught my foot on the doorframe and nearly collapsed on the seat. Sometimes you don't realize how badly you need to sit until you're crumpled on the cushions. I rested the axe carefully on the floor. My legs and arms shook hard, my muscles going haywire.

Artemis climbed in the back with me and leaned over to buckle me in. I mumbled, "Thanks, Mom," but she acted like she didn't hear. She buckled herself in, too. We waited while Greta stood outside and made her calls.

Finally Greta slid into the driver's seat, dropping her phone into the cup holder, and shifted the car into reverse. "Lazarus and Sadie are on their way," she said. "I got ahold of Chief Rivera. She says she doesn't know how you got out of the station, Zora, but she's going to find Buster now. Are we all buckled in? Good."

Her voice was neither gentle nor kind, and for once in my life I was happy for it. My home getting pushed off a cliff was not an occasion for kindness. It was a time for rage. Right now there was nothing for me to do. But Aunt Greta *could* do things. She could do a lot of things. And if she was angry for me, shit was going to get done.

Her eyes flashed up to meet mine in the rearview mirror. They looked just like ours—mine and Sadie's and Mom's—dark and furious. Intense. Those weren't from the Novak side of the family. Those were Aberdeen through and through.

I looked away. Aberdeen, Novak, what did it matter? Our homes had met their end on the bluffs because of the people in this town. Artemis was right: I didn't hate Addamsville enough to set it on fire. I didn't hate Addamsville at all.

But Addamsville sure hated me.

26

"What are you looking at there, Zoo?"

Dad's voice was soft, almost timid, as he came up behind the couch. I shoved the picture of Mom and Aunt Greta into my shirt. "Nothing."

He came around the couch and sat down, his knees by my shoulders. I stayed kneeling in front of Greta's glass-topped coffee table, my wet hair dripping on the carpet.

"Sadie's asleep," he said. "You should get to bed, too. Greta said you could stay with Artemis on the third floor."

"Of course they have a third floor," I said, but my heart wasn't in it. The living room was warm and quiet and smelled like fresh laundry. My limbs ached, and every inch of me felt like it had been bruised or cut. I held my arm against my stomach to keep the picture in place and stood. "Sure. Bed."

Dad reached out as if to grab me, then withdrew. "Zoo, wait." My skin prickled. "Was that a picture of your mom? Where'd you get it?"

A clock ticked in the other room. Aunt Greta was in the kitchen, and Artemis had gone upstairs to get her room ready for me. I cleared my throat. Dad took my wrist in his hand, very gently, as if he was checking for a pulse. "Zoo, sit down."

After a moment of hesitation, I did. Dad still wore his own clothes, and he hadn't taken a shower yet, so he looked rumpled and tired. His eyes were red and puffy. He put his other hand on the other side of my wrist and held me there.

"I'm sorry for what I said the other day," he said. "You were right on all counts. Pulling that scheme was irrational and selfish of me. I pride myself on thinking that I'm here to take care of you and your sister, but that just made things worse for both of you, and I'm still not sure what I can do to make up for it. And I shouldn't have told you what to believe. That's up to you and only you. It's hard sometimes not to confuse belief with fact."

I picked at the hem of Artemis's shirt.

"Can I ask you something?" he said. "I promise I'm not trying to interrogate you."

"What?"

"Why do you believe Mom's still alive?"

"Because," I said, "if I can believe she's alive, why would I believe otherwise? Why would I choose to believe something that upsets me?"

Dad smiled and reached up to smooth back my blond sheaf of hair. "Can I ask more questions?"

"I thought this wasn't an interrogation."

"You're allowed to say no."

"Fine. What?"

"How many years has it been since she went missing?"

I knew it was a trap. "Five."

"Five years. If she's alive, why haven't we heard from her in all that time? Why didn't she come home? Why didn't she tell us she was okay?"

Because she was hunting firestarters. Because there were secrets left out there for her to unravel.

I shrugged. "I don't know. She had more important things to do."

Dad squeezed my arm.

"I know you remember enough of her to know that she loved you and Sadie more than anything in the world," he said. "There was nothing more important to her than you. Absolutely nothing, you understand? If she was alive, she wouldn't have let *me* go on thinking she was dead, much less you two girls. I don't know the truth of what happened to her out there—Lord knows I wish I did—so I have nothing to convince you. But I know she wouldn't have left you this long on purpose."

One of his hands moved to my elbow, the other to my face. "Zora, look at me. I'm not trying to hurt you again, not after everything, but I don't think it's good for you to keep doing this. This kind of hope isn't the helpful kind. It eats at you. It makes you wait for something that won't come, when you should be looking forward. We have to move on. You can believe she's still alive because the alternative upsets you, but sometimes we *have* to be upset. It's okay to be sad, and scared, and angry. I was scared, after she was gone. I didn't know what to do without her. And that's okay. We can figure it out."

I pulled my face away from his hand. "Mom can't be dead."

His eyebrows furrowed. "Why not?"

"Because she—" A knot stuck in my throat.

"Because she what?"

I looked away.

"Zora."

"Because she's not here."

He went quiet. His grip on my elbow tightened. "What does that mean?"

"She's not *here*!"

I watched understanding light his eyes, swiftly overtaken by pity. "Zora . . ."

We never admit these things for a reason, but it was too late now.

"She's not *here*. Everyone comes back here. It's *Addamsville*; that's what they do. That's what they're supposed to do. You die; you're here. In the streets, in the high school, in the woods. If she was dead she'd be here, she'd be with us, and she's not, she's not *fucking here*, so she's *not fucking dead*—"

When you've trained yourself not to cry, there's nothing you can do to stop the release when the pressure becomes too great. Nothing to be done for the noise you make or the tears that pour from you like rain. Here is the overwhelming tide. Here it crashes down and carries you out to sea.

You have no choice but to let it, because you have been fighting it for so long you have no strength left to swim.

27

I was glad Dad was the one there for the release, because he was the one who understood it. He let me cry myself out without judgment. When I was done, I wanted to sleep. Just curl up on the carpet and sleep for days, knowing he'd be watching over me, keeping me safe. I thought maybe that was why Sadie had kept taking his side: even when she knew he'd done wrong, she didn't stop seeing the parts of him that were good.

Dad tucked my hair behind my ears and pushed me up the long, curving staircase of Hillcroft House. The place really was beautiful on the inside. Small chandeliers hung from soaring ceilings, rich oak and mahogany paneled the walls, an actual rug covered the stairs instead of carpet. Aunt Greta had made sure everything was restored as it should be. A few ghosts—

Hillcroft family servants, according to Artemis—stood in doorways or rocked in chairs, their faces turned away from me for once, used to Aberdeens living under their roof. At the top of the stairs, Dad took me down the second-floor hallway to another staircase at the end. The stairs creaked horribly.

At the top was the third floor. A crow's nest of a bedroom, with windows on two sides, curtains closed over all but one of them. There was a tidy desk next to a bookshelf, a yoga mat rolled up in the corner, a large trunk at the end of a queen-sized bed, and a nightstand holding a tube of lip balm, a retainer case, and a picture of Artemis and her mother on a boat on Addams Lake. At the foot of the nightstand was a row of Artemis's shoes, neatly lined up and standing at attention.

Artemis sat on the edge of the bed, pretending to look through something on her phone.

"Knock knock," Dad said. "Have space for one more?"

Artemis sprang up, throwing the phone onto the nightstand. "Yeah, of course. Zora, I didn't know which side of the bed you prefer, so you can make yourself comfortable. Mom washed your clothes." She motioned to where my clothes were neatly folded and stacked on the trunk at the end of the bed, my boots balanced on top. "Mom said I could take off school tomorrow, too, until all this gets figured out, and then you don't have to stay here alone."

"I'm good," I said to Dad, who hesitated at the door for a moment before kissing me on the temple.

"Night, Zoo. Night, Artemis."

"Good night, Uncle Lazarus."

He disappeared back down the stairs. Artemis said, "You can close the door if you want."

I did.

She scooted aside to give me room on the bed. I took it. My right hand ached. I pulled my remaining glove off and dropped it on the trunk next to my boots. Next came the prosthetics. Artemis watched as I flexed my hand and massaged the stumps, and I found I was too tired to care what she thought.

"Do they hurt?" she asked.

"Sometimes," I said. "It's kind of a dull pain. The prosthetics are cheap, so they don't fit very well. You get used to it."

She hugged her legs to her chest and stared at me over her knees.

"What?" I snapped.

"I don't think I've ever seen you without makeup on before."

"So?"

She shrugged. "I didn't mean anything by it. It's just interesting."

I sniffed. "Whatever. I know I have acne."

"You're pretty both ways."

"Thanks. I guess."

"Do you want to talk about it?"

"The fact that I'm pretty?"

Artemis gave me a withering look.

"Come on," I said, "you have to give me *one* bad joke."

"Not even one."

"No, I don't want to talk about it." Mom's pictures and notes might right at this moment be washing into Addams Lake, and I could have saved them when I went into the trailer that last time, but I chose Dad's axe instead. I hugged my legs to my chest, too, and we faced each other on the bed, our toes almost touching.

"What happened at the motel?" she said.

I told her. I could still smell the smoke, still feel the fire. I remembered exactly how disorienting it was to watch Ludwig's form flicker in the heat haze, worse than the flickering edges of the ghosts. When I finished, she didn't ask what we were going to do. I couldn't think about hunting.

"I didn't know you had a thing about neat shoes." I motioned to the neat row of footwear.

"I don't," she said. "Salem does."

I narrowed my eyes.

"Well, I don't know that it's Salem for certain," she went on; talking had brought a little color back to her cheeks. "If I leave my shoes scattered around at night, when I wake up they're neat like that. Same order, same place."

"So your mom is doing it."

Artemis shakes her head. "I've tested it. It happens even if I'm barely asleep, or for only a few minutes. It happens if I hide shoes where Mom wouldn't know to look for them or wouldn't be able to get them without making enough noise to wake me up. And did you hear those stairs? Anyone coming up here makes enough noise to wake me up."

"You think Salem Hillcroft is rearranging your shoes." I'd never seen an Addamsville ghost affect a physical object, but I was far from knowing all of Addamsville's secrets.

"I think something is rearranging my shoes."

"Have you tried asking?"

"Six times."

"Cool, so I have to stay in the haunted room tonight." It would make me feel better, to have at least one ghost around.

"You *get* to stay in the haunted room tonight. This is the best room in the house. You remember the third floor at Grimshaw House?" Artemis crawled to the edge of the bed and got up to push back the curtains on the other windows. Then she moved around to turn off her lights.

The entire basin of Addamsville was visible. The long line of Valleywine Road glittered in the night, stretching to the northeast until it disappeared on the horizon. There was Black Creek Woods. The radio tower with its red lights blinking.

The looming shadow of Piper Mountain. The high school and its football stadium, town center, a bursting wealth of houses and streets. The sweep of the Goldmine, the trailer park, the junkyard in the distance. A partial cover of trees that trailed south to hide the mine and then, eventually, the bluffs. The shore of Addams Lake was visible. There was a straight line of sight into the third-floor room of Grimshaw House.

"Oh wow."

"This was what Sylvester Hillcroft saw after he founded this place," Artemis said, standing next to me. "From here he could survey the whole town as it grew."

"Maybe he's the one messing with your shoes."

She shoved me with her elbow, then went to close the curtains again. She was smiling. "It's really late."

"Can we leave the curtains open?"

"Sure."

I pulled back four layers of blankets and sheets on the bed and slid in. It was a firmer mattress than I was used to, but most mattresses would've felt firmer than the broken-down thing I'd slept on my whole life. Artemis got in on the other side and busied herself putting in her retainer.

"Don't drool on me, okay?" I said.

"I won't as long as you don't snore," she replied.

"I *don't* snore."

"I guess we'll find out."

She was asleep in minutes. I knew because she slept like Sadie; heavily, on her back, arms sprawling everywhere and mouth slightly open. I ran a finger down the bridge of her nose and she didn't so much as twitch. Her stories about not waking up for the boots or footsteps on the stairs seemed dubious.

I laid back, pulled the covers up, and stared out at Addamsville.

Sometimes you have so many thoughts and feelings that your brain decides to ignore every single one of them. It hangs a Closed for Business sign and walks out. No more worrying whether you did right or wrong. No more flashes of the only home you've ever had reduced to beach wreckage. No more fear. No more anger. No more tears. You can't look inward anymore, so you look out and see what's left, and you're happy to take it, no matter what it is. And if you're lucky, you find exactly what you need.

You find lights in the darkness and a place to rest your head.

In the night, I woke.

My mouth was bone-dry, and the alarm clock was blurry. Artemis was a lump under the covers. The stairs creaked as I descended, though not as loudly as they'd seemed to on the way up. Hillcroft House was still awake.

I couldn't remember where the bathroom was on the

second floor, so I went all the way down to the first floor. I followed the path of moonlight on the hardwood, and after the bathroom took another couple of turns into the kitchen.

Of the whole house, the kitchen had been remodeled the most. Granite countertops. Refinished cabinets. Stainless-steel appliances. A big window over the sink looked to the northwest of town, over the woods at the mountain. A dark form obscured the view, her hip leaning on the edge of the sink, a mug in her hands. I stopped in the doorway, squinting. Her edges were solid. Aunt Greta glanced at me over her shoulder. Her hair was up in a messy bun and haloed by the moonlight coming through the window, her face shadowed.

"Sorry," I said. My voice came out hoarse.

Without saying anything, she took a cup from a cabinet, filled it with water from the refrigerator, then held it out for me. The stark smell of black coffee wafted from her mug. We stood together by the window, watching the red lights of the radio tower blink on and off, a Piper Mountain lighthouse.

I cleared my throat and said, "Why did you show up at the bluffs? You never cared about us before. A week ago you were accusing me of killing George Masrell and telling Chief Rivera to arrest me."

"I never accused you of killing him," she said. "I knew exactly what you were doing there, and I knew you were going to cause more trouble for yourself and our family by showing up. Dasree was the same way when she was younger. Couldn't resist going to the ghosts, even if it got her in trouble. She eventually learned to hunt at night, when no one was watching, but even then people noticed."

I stared at her, my brain blinking awake. "If you knew what I was doing, why didn't you try to help?"

"I was," she replied. "The day after Masrell, most of the town council wanted a witch hunt. I've spent all my time over the last week keeping the living in Addamsville from completely impeding your ability to track this firestarter down, and you can tell tonight I didn't do a very good job."

"You tried to keep Artemis from helping."

"Artemis is . . ." She paused. Sipped. "She wanted to do it herself. Hunt this one. I knew if I grounded her, she would understand why that wasn't a good idea, and she would go back to you. God forbid she listen to me when I say it in plain terms. Neither of you should be doing this alone. Artemis wants too much, and without someone there to pull her back, she goes too far. It was the same with Dasree."

"Goes too far?"

"She wants to know the truth. So did Dasree. She wanted to solve every mystery, especially about what happened to us.

"Did she ever tell you that we had no memories from before the disappearance? We knew our names, and we knew we were sisters. To this day, no amount of therapy or medicine or meditation has helped me remember my childhood or the months we were gone. I still don't know what happened to us. All I know is we came back different, and Dasree was furious about it.

"She thought she'd find the answers in Black Creek Woods. I didn't; the woods still scare me. I only wanted to stop what happened to us from happening to anyone else. The older we got, the more concerned I became with keeping this town alive. Dasree convinced me that solving the mysteries would do that. So we agreed—she'd take care of the dead, and I'd take care of the living. It worked out well, because she didn't care about her reputation, and I cared too much about mine. We didn't spend much time together, in the last few years."

"Do you really think she's gone?"

"She would have sent word." It wasn't really an answer, and she looked back out the window when she said it. Steam clouded her expression. "Answer a question for me: do you still believe Addamsville is only a cute little tourist town?"

I frowned at her. "*You* believe Addamsville is only a cute little tourist town."

Her lips curled on the rim of her mug. "Your mom would have a fit if she saw you acting like this."

"Like what?"

"Passive. The one thing I always saw when I looked at you, no matter what the circumstances, was her unflinching refusal to be or to think the way anyone else wanted her to. She got on my nerves more often than not, but I envied her for that. I was so concerned with the hows and whys of becoming my own person that for a long time I let this town tell me who I was. Just one of those poor girls, lost in the woods. Dasree didn't care about the hows or the whys of learning to be herself again. She didn't wallow. She didn't rest. We weren't the same after we were kidnapped, and she had to *know* what had changed us. Those mysteries would have killed her, if she'd let them. But she didn't; she went out and hunted them down. I think she found the truth, in the end.

"She taught you to hunt firestarters because she hoped one day you might find the answers she couldn't. She hoped you would go at life with your teeth bared, instead of getting beaten down by bad things that happen to you. Like I did."

She looked at me again. Dark and furious.

"What's going on now isn't right. These fires. This unrest. I can deal with the living in this town, but that's as far as my reach goes. I don't know any more about firestarters than you. We both know there are answers here, and you're one of the few people who can find them. So what's it going to be? Death or hunting?"

She watched me for a heartbeat, then returned to sipping coffee in the night.

I took my water and stumbled back to the third floor.

Artemis hadn't moved even to swat a corner of the blanket off her face. I stopped at the end of the bed and stared at my boots on the trunk, both standing up. I tipped one over with a finger.

I fell asleep a second time to a soft pounding in my head, like words spoken over and over, a chanted question that chased me into my dreams.

Doubt or belief.

Ignorance or truth.

Death or hunting.

28

No one knew where I was.

Aunt Greta told Chief Rivera I had disappeared after the incident at the bluffs. Rivera had relayed the news to the Harrisburg police. Officers Jack and Norm were out looking for me, but Rivera herself was busy dealing with the *Dead Men Walking* crew and Tad Thompson, still shaken over their ordeal, and now Buster Gates, who refused to admit he'd pushed the trailer off a cliff despite the deep tracks in the ground, the damage to his truck, and the fact that several of the people who had accompanied him there had already confessed.

Early the next morning, Dad paced around the house for a while, speaking to Aunt Greta alone in the kitchen, then talking to someone over the phone. After he hung up, he said, "I've found a few people who are going to help me with the trailer. We're going to see what we can get out of it, and hopefully the water didn't destroy too much. This could take a while."

"We'll be okay," I told him, patting his arm. I sat on the couch and he leaned over me. "Go get our stuff; I don't want all my things washing into the lake."

Someone stopped by in a white pickup to get him. Not even a week back from jail and he already had friends again. One trailer over the bluffs was enough to win us back some sympathy.

Sadie watched him leave, then marched to the couch and loomed over me while she pinned her hair up. "Lorelei told Grim that you're meeting up with her, Hal, and Mads today, and they're helping you clear your name."

"It was their idea," I said immediately.

"I'm not accusing you," she sniped back. "I'm telling you Grim and I are coming, too. I've got appointments this morning, but I can leave this afternoon. Grim's getting off work early. When your friends get out of school, we'll come meet wherever you are."

"You're helping now? Are you actually going to believe what I say?"

Sadie shoved the last pin into her bun and dropped her arms. She glanced at the kitchen door; Aunt Greta had gone outside to take the trash cans down the driveway. Artemis's blow dryer hissed from upstairs. "Do you know how sometimes you think you hear someone say something when they didn't? Or you hear a voice call your name, but there's no one there?"

"Sure."

"I've been hearing things like that my whole life. *All* the time. At school, in town. The only place it stopped was at home. It's really annoying, you know, when people are whispering in your ears all day long, especially when they say things about death and sadness and grief—" She shuddered and wrapped her arms around her middle. "I thought something was wrong for a really long time, but I could ignore it, so I did. But when you told me what Mom and you could do, I started thinking maybe all these distant voices I hear when I walk through town, the half sentences, the weird mumbling, maybe it's not my ears going haywire."

"You can hear them?" I said.

"Can't you?"

"No. I can only see them. I didn't think they could speak."

"At least you knew they were there. I thought something was wrong with me. I always thought people were talking behind my back. Tricking me. I used to get so angry about it, but after high school it just got exhausting to be so angry all the time. It was—it *is*—distracting." She flattened the hem of her shirt. "I don't think Mom ever knew."

"She didn't," I said. "If she had, she would have explained to you what it was."

Sadie looked down at her fingers now, nodding.

"After all this is over, I could help you," I went on. "Like, we could do some tests. Find a ghost, talk to it. If you want to. Maybe if you know who and where they are, hearing them won't be so distracting."

"I'd like that." She looked up. "Dad doesn't know about any of this, does he?"

"I . . . I think he might. At least part. The ghost-seeing part."

"And he's okay with it?"

"We didn't talk about that."

"Do you think we should tell him?"

"Maybe. Maybe . . . after the dangerous part is over."

Ask for forgiveness, not permission. Grand Slam Sadie's old motto.

Sadie left for work. Artemis came down after finishing with her hair and joined me on the couch.

Aunt Greta swept around the corner from the kitchen. Her hair bounced in ringlets of Hallmark glory, her shoes clip-clipping on the hardwood floors. She had her purse over one arm and her car keys in her hand. "I have to go into town to speak to Chief Rivera about what happened last night."

"I thought you already gave her your story?" Artemis said.

"I told her what happened," said Greta. "I didn't give an official statement. After that I have errands to run. I'll be out for most of the day. You'll be safe by yourselves. Don't open the door for anyone." She clip-clipped past the couch and out the front door, only pausing to look back at us, look back at *me*, for a second. Then she locked the door behind her and disappeared down the front walk.

Artemis turned to me. "Where are we meeting the others?"

"Wherever Bach is going to be."

"And how will we know that?"

I held up her phone. "Already texted him. Your passcode is really easy to guess, by the way. Two-four-six-eight? We're going to meet him at the cemetery."

She swiped the phone back, sullen. "The cemetery? In the middle of the day?"

"When was the last time you saw someone in that cemetery? Even Pastor Keller?"

"Well, I don't go there that often, so—"

"Exactly. No one goes over there anymore; it's creepy as hell."

Artemis held her phone to her chest, the sullenness giving way to worry. "Are you really sure it's safe to involve Bach in this? You're sure he's on our side?"

"Bach will help us. Forester won't. And as long as Forester's in the picture, Bach's not safe, either. But I have a plan for that."

"That sounds promising." Artemis leaned her head back on the couch, stretched her legs in front of her, and let out a long, weary sigh. "I'm missing a calculus exam for this."

"You're fucking welcome," I replied.

Black Creek Church looked especially old in the stark October sunlight. White paint flecked off the outside, and what remained had grayed over time. A bird's nest poked out of a hole in the steeple where the wood had rotted away. Fallen leaves littered the small hills around the building, its front walk, and its parking lot. The only nice part of the building was the sign out front, which Pastor Keller could be seen repainting every two months or so: BLACK CREEK CHRISTIAN CHURCH painted on fresh white in dark blue and gold.

Behind the church, the graveyard stretched into softly rolling hills until it met the line of the woods. Headstones ranged from unmarked rocks to seven-foot-tall monuments topped with stone angels. The only ghosts you really find in a graveyard are the ones there to look for other members of their family. Parents standing over the graves of their children. Ancestors searching for descendants. The dead don't hang around their own graves much; they have better places to be.

There were none here today. Too much firestarter activity in town.

We gathered at the edge of the graveyard near Black Creek Woods, our cars pulled off onto one of the dirt paths that wound through the graveyard.

"Okay," Hal said, leaning against the trunk of a maple, face screwed up in concentration, "tell me if I've got this. There are demons in Addamsville, Hermit Forester actually *did* commit the Firestarter Murders, and now he's in a turf war with a guy called Ludwig. He blackmailed you like a low-rent mob boss to find Ludwig so his enforcer"—he motioned to Bach—"can do some cleanup on behalf of the family. Oh, and also, you're the Ghost Whisperer. Is that about right?"

I stretched my legs out on the leaf-strewn ground and rested my head back against my own tree. "They're not demons and I'm not the Ghost Whisperer, but sure, close enough. Good analogy there, Hal. Does anyone else have questions?"

Artemis, Sadie, and Grim stood to my right. Lorelei haunted the space between Grim and Hal, and Mads had placed herself between Hal and Bach. I was the only one within arm's reach of Bach.

They'd all been staring at me for the last ten minutes, either too shocked or too overloaded to call me a liar.

Mads raised her hand, looking at Bach. "I'd ask why we should trust you, but Zora trusts you and we're here to help her. So: What's your plan? How do you kill him? Does it involve anyone else in Addamsville being put at risk?"

Bach shifted forward. "You don't kill him; you can only subdue him. I don't have much of a plan right now. The plan depends on where Ludwig is, and the risk depends on how much of a fight he puts up."

Sadie choked. "*Excuse me?* You don't have a plan?"

Bach actually had the audacity to look sheepish. I rolled my eyes. "*I* have a plan," I said. "Because I think I know where he is. I'll need Sadie's help to confirm it, but I think Ludwig will be at the junkyard."

"You need *me?*"

"The junkyard?" Artemis said at the same time.

"Think about it. Ludwig was trying to get rid of me, because he knows I can help Bach and Forester find him. I escaped, and now he doesn't know where I am. But he knows where my *car* is."

Sadie's head swiveled around on her neck like a possessed doll. "He's going to do something to the Chevelle?"

"Everyone in town knows we love that car," I said. "And they know it was Mom's car. It was her weapon of choice. If he wants to draw me out, he'll hold the Chevelle hostage. He's had to have seen enough of Buster Gates to know I'd never leave Mom's car with that pig. No offense, Lorelei."

Lorelei gave a wispy shrug, then said, her eyes huge and round, "But if Ludwig wanted you gone, he could have killed you at the motel."

"He doesn't want you dead," Bach said, and everyone turned to him again, like animals constantly aware of a predator in their midst. Bach let out a long sigh. "If he did, yes, he would have burned you on the spot. Don't be surprised if he makes a second try to win you over."

"So, hypothetical," Sadie said. "We find out he's at the junkyard with the Chevelle. He's got to be smart enough to lay some kind of trap."

"Right. Whether he's at the junkyard or not, he's going to know that I can find him, and he's at least smart enough to make a trap. That's why we don't go in. We draw him *out*." I pushed myself up and brushed off my pants. "He told me what he wants. Grimshaw House. He wants to find Hildegard. He thinks her entrance is there."

Bach made a noise. "Ah. He thinks if he owns the house, it will reveal something to him. So he's trying to drive Sammy out so he can get the deed from us."

"Why would ownership show him anything?" I asked.

"Possession is important to our kind. When we own something, it becomes part of us, and we perceive the world differently through that ownership of the thing. In this case, Hildegard made the Grimshaw will the necessary document to prove ownership; only the owner can find its secrets."

Sadie looked at Grim, who was staring off into the distance.

"Okay." My head spun. "Okay. So he wants Grimshaw House, and he knows you and Forester have ownership of it. If he thinks something is going to happen to Grimshaw House, he'll try to stop it."

"Something like what?" Sadie asked.

I glanced at Bach. "Something like fire."

The words rattled in my chest. Even suggesting setting a fire had my nerves on edge. "Not to burn Grimshaw House," I went on, "just a bluff. Enough to make him think you are. He comes to find you, you take him out, we get the Chevelle."

Bach crossed his arms and didn't say anything. The others looked between us, waiting.

"At least I had a plan," I snapped.

"I'll be making a scene," Bach said.

I met his stare. "Yes."

"You'd rather I do it in the street. In front of everyone."

"Right on the money."

"Someone will get video—" Artemis began.

"Lots of people will get video, I bet," I said.

Bach smiled a bit, flipped his sunglasses out, and put them on. "Well played, Novak."

"So you'll do it?"

"It was better than my idea. I should be able to subdue him without causing more damage to the town. Ludwig's not smart, but he's always been strong, even if he doesn't have as many dead as I do."

I looked around at the others. "The rest of you don't have

to do anything. Stay home. It'll be safer there."

"Stay home while you screw over the asshole who blew up my float?" Hal scoffed. "No way. I'm coming with you."

"And obviously I can't let all of you go without me," Mads said. "You need someone to make rational decisions."

"And I can help you get into the junkyard to get the car," said Lorelei, face flushed with color. "You have to take me with you."

"You're jerks," I said.

"Meet back here tonight?" Artemis said.

A round of nods.

Grim, as usual, looked like he was somewhere faraway, occasionally glancing northward, along the line of the trees. Now, as everyone went quiet, he turned to Bach. Despite having known both of them for years, the spheres they occupied had never touched, at least in my mind. Bach was always of the mysterious, even when he seemed like only a person. Grim was always only a person, even when he said or did something mysterious.

Now, Bach's shadows couldn't stand up against Grim's druidic concern.

"What about Tad Thompson?" Grim said.

Bach shook his head. "Tad Thompson is gone. When we possess a body, we destroy the person who once owned it. There's only Ludwig now."

Grim stared him down like he had some divine truth-sensing ability, and for a second I believed he did. He could see straight through the most mysterious of creatures, and his own strangeness kept them from harming him, as if he lived halfway between this plane of existence and another.

Finally he looked to the north again. Bach had told the truth. I felt a little twinge of regret: Tad Thompson hadn't been my favorite person, but possession seemed like a nasty way to die.

"Who was yours?" I asked Bach. "I mean, that body isn't yours, right? Was it someone from Addamsville?"

Bach dipped his head. Ran a hand over his stomach. "Ah. Yeah. A while back. So we're on for tonight?" He glanced around at everyone, then moved past the headstones that hid us. "Zora can check with Masrell first and text where Ludwig is. I'll go south. The rest of you head north. And stay out of his path once he gets going."

He shoved his hands into his pockets and made his way toward his car.

"Guilt gets the best of us," I said, then called to him, "Hey! What was his name?"

"Everyone in Addamsville knew his name!" Bach yelled over his shoulder.

"Dude is cryptic as hell," Hal said. The Mustang pulled out of the graveyard.

"What if Ludwig kills *him?*" said Mads.

"This is bonkers," Sadie muttered, rubbing her forehead.

Lorelei was talking to Grim in undertones. Artemis had gotten a strange look on her face and wandered the way Bach had gone, then stopped to look at a headstone. "Bach chose this spot, right?" she asked.

I shrugged. "Yeah. He got here first. Why?"

She motioned to the headstone. I went to stand beside her. Carved on its front was *Michelle Garrington.*

"She was one of the teenagers who died in the Maple Hills cabin," Artemis said. "The Firestarter Murders. Your mom had pictures of his car here. He's been coming to see them all this time."

She sounded so surprised. As if everyone who did bad things was a sociopath without thought for what they'd done and who they'd hurt. Classic Artemis. I knew guilt. I knew how it could hit you years later like a sucker punch. I knew how it could drive you to do things you normally wouldn't, to try to make amends for your past. Or for your family.

I knew how to exploit it, and if I had to exploit Bach's guilt to finish Mom's work and get rid of him and Forester, I was damn well going to do it. It was the Novak way: by any means necessary. I was done flying my own guilt flag in the hopes Addamsville would take mercy on me.

I was taking mercy on myself.

29

I had two options for getting out of Hillcroft House that night.

One: I try to explain to Dad what was going on and why I need to leave, and hope he doesn't do something reasonable like lock me in a room.

Two: I sneak out when it is time and hope I don't get caught, because I'd never be allowed to leave the house ever again.

I didn't want to have to lie to Dad again, but I didn't know if right now was the best time to tell him the truth, either.

Around five Dad got back with everything he could salvage from the trailer. It had landed where the waves lapped the shore, so it was technically flooded, but not underwater. He brought clothes, phone chargers, hygiene supplies, and framed pictures from the trailer. None of Mom's secret notes or pictures, but he wouldn't have known to look for them. Sadie nearly burst into tears when she found out Dad had saved her old combat boots.

Grim had come back to the house with her, and Aunt Greta didn't seem to mind him hanging around; when he offered to help her prepare dinner, she accepted with a genuine smile and let him taste test her potato salad. After nine thirty, when Sadie and Grim had to make up an excuse to leave the house so Sadie didn't fall asleep, I said good night to Dad and followed Artemis up to her room, where we barricaded ourselves in.

A terrible feeling roiled in my stomach. From a distance, every light was a small fire, and sweat had already started beading on my forehead. I had gotten tired enough of my guilt to free myself of it, but freeing myself of fear wasn't that simple. This fear wasn't a rational fear. It was bone-deep; it had wormed its way so far into me that prying it out would cause even more damage. It had to be coaxed away. Soothed. And it would take a lot longer than we had now.

"You don't have to do this," I told Artemis. She was opening one of the many windows in her room and peering out onto the roof. She turned to me.

"What are you talking about?"

I stood in the middle of the room, fully dressed, with the Chevelle's keys in my pocket and nothing else. "You don't have to come," I said. "He wants me, not you. You might get hurt. None of you guys have to come."

She dropped her arms to her sides. "Please. Enough with the altruism."

"Shut up, I'm being serious. I should call everyone right now and tell them to stay home—"

"I know you're being serious. You heard everyone earlier. We're doing this so you won't be alone."

"I won't be alone. Bach will be there."

She leveled a sharp look at me. "You might trust Bach, but that doesn't mean I do. And I don't care if I'm just a human, I'm going with you. You'd get yourself into too much trouble."

"Artemis—this isn't like playing pranks on a TV crew." I pressed the heel of my hand to my forehead, where a headache had begun. "Do you know what being hurt feels like? *Really* hurt, amputated-fingers hurt? It isn't fun. You don't do it to prove a point, or—hey!"

She'd climbed out the window, onto the roof. I hurried out after her. The night chill bit my nose. I pulled the window shut behind me before I followed Artemis across the shingles.

"Hey, hey! Listen to me!" I hissed.

She crept across the roof to a flat area where we'd stored a ladder earlier. Artemis carefully levered it over the side of the roof, struggling to keep it from scraping. I scrambled to help her.

"You're being stupid!" I whispered.

"Shut up, Zora." She grunted. The ladder slid into place. She rounded on me. Her eyes flashed. "I'm part of this. I'm your cousin, and I'm going with you. So be quiet, climb down that ladder, and get into my car before someone realizes what we're doing. Go. Go!"

With a jump, I climbed over the lip of the roof and down the ladder. We ended up in the shrubs. Artemis brushed herself off and pushed me toward the driveway and her car.

If you had told me two weeks before that Artemis Wake would tell me to shut up, push me around, and refuse to let me walk into danger by myself, I would've laughed in your face. I would've told you she didn't have the spine for it, and I didn't know anyone who would do that for me.

But I'd have been wrong.

Masrell's house hadn't changed. No one had cleaned it up yet, and I doubted anyone would. This side of town wasn't known for its money, and the money side of town wasn't known for its caring. The neighbors had gone about their business, and a clear line of demarcation showed where they'd cut their grass and Masrell's had kept growing.

We'd met up in the cemetery and brought Mads's SUV. Sadie and I were the only two who'd left the car for this first part of the plan. Sadie had worn her combat boots. I'd almost hugged her when I noticed.

"I almost hugged you," I whispered as we crept up to the house.

"Ew," she whispered back, the ire already up. Good ol' boots.

Sadie and I ducked through the ruined front door of Masrell's house and navigated a scarred linoleum floor littered with debris.

"So how do we do this?" Sadie asked, scanning the room. The sharp anger in her voice only became more pronounced as she fought her dislike of the dark and creepy. "Is he—is he here now? I can hear someone breathing."

"He's here somewhere. The first thing Mom taught me was not to be scared of the ghosts. They can't hurt us, and they know when we're trying to help them."

"What else did she teach you?"

"I'll tell you all of it." She stilled beside me. "You should have learned it, too."

"Thanks," she said, after a moment. Then, "Later. My brain's in freak-out mode right now."

I couldn't blame her. The smell of char made the hair on the back of my neck rise. We stepped between the doors to the kitchen and the living room. The wall had fallen where the sink had once been, and the lights of the junkyard were visible in the distance.

George Masrell stood in the fire-blackened living room.

"Hi, Mr. Masrell," I said as calmly as I could. Sadie gripped my arm. Masrell stood in the clothes he had been wearing when he died, white T-shirt and underwear. Eyes out. Face expressionless. "I—we need your help."

Still no response. "Is he saying anything?" I asked Sadie.

"Uh—I don't—he's kind of muttering." She paused, head cocked. "It's like someone trying to talk through layers of blankets." She frowned. "He sounds sad. A lot of them do, but this is like . . . it's like begging." Her grip loosened on my arm. "He stopped."

If Mom had known Sadie was capable of this, she never would have ignored her, and not just to teach her so Sadie didn't have to be angry all the time. If she could have heard what the dead were saying, she could have learned so much more. Maybe she wouldn't have had to go searching for answers in the woods.

I stepped forward. "I'm sorry I yelled at you, Mr. Masrell." I kept my voice clear but not too loud, my gaze fixed on the empty sockets of his eyes. "I'm sorry I made your life harder. I'm sorry my dad stole from you. And I'm sorry this happened. I'm sorry you have to be like this."

He floated forward. I made myself remain where I was, Sadie shuffling uneasily beside me. This was my responsibility. It wasn't my fault, but it was my responsibility.

"The thing that killed you is named Ludwig," I said. "I'm going to get him out of this town before he can kill anyone else. We need your help. You told me where he was before. Could you do that again?"

He took another step toward me. Sadie's hand landed on my shoulder. It felt shockingly like Mom's. Bracing, understanding.

Masrell's arm rose. He pointed past me, to the lights in the sky.

"Gates," Sadie whispered. "He said 'Gates.'"

3 0

Gates Automotive Scrapyard sat north of the mine. Ten years ago, Buster invested in a set of stadium floodlights, a bright glow of pollution for the northeast sky. Several buildings sat on the property—squat, warehouse-like structures with windows that reflected the gleam of Mads's SUV as we coasted along the edge of the parking lot, headlights off. A dirt area littered with cars and machinery stretched behind these buildings and past two layers of chain-link fence topped with barbed wire. The main building, a white one-story garage with a small suite of offices built into the side, sat out front, guarding everything. The ghosts who stayed here were mostly scrapyard workers who had died in machine accidents. They were all gone tonight.

Mads parked on the far edge of the lot. I figured it didn't

matter much if Ludwig saw us—he'd wait for me to come inside. We'd gone over the plan ten times on the way here, not because it was complicated, but because I had to make sure we got in and out as fast as possible after Ludwig left.

Artemis's phone screen lit up the back of the SUV. "Two minutes."

Through the fence north of the main building were the impounded cars. Buster kept them close to the front so their owners could look at them with longing. There was a red Toyota, a busted-up old Ford, and a Honda Civic. No Chevelle. A flush of anger washed over me. No one touched my mom's car.

"Thirty seconds," Artemis said, counting down to midnight. The leather seats creaked under Lorelei's white-knuckled grip. Hal's gaze stayed fixed on the junkyard. Beside me, Grim was holding both of Sadie's hands in his own, as if he had to stop her jumping out of the SUV right then. I gripped the haft of Dad's axe; the blade was balanced between my feet.

"Here we go," Artemis said, and turned to look south.

For a heartbeat, nothing happened. Addamsville was quiet. Bach could have gotten held up. Or he could have lied to us.

Then a plume of fire erupted far on the south side of town. It spread up and out, tongues of flame licking at the dark sky, roaring in challenge.

The first plume died, but a flickering light appeared over

the south side. Another plume, then a third, down by the Goldmine. Bach must have been setting trees on fire. My hand tingled. My fingers ached.

"Zora!" Artemis yanked on my jacket. The front doors of the junkyard had burst open and Tad Thompson came sprinting out, his eyes two glowing red embers, his lips curled back from his teeth. He didn't bother with any of the cars in the lot; he was running fast enough to meet the speed limit, anyway.

"Go, go, go!" I yelled.

We spilled out of the car and ran for the main building. Lorelei's keys got us in. Inside was an auto parts shop—aisles of wiper blades, seat covers, and detailing supplies. A long front desk housed a register, lines of file folders along the back wall, and a large sign that said, WE RESERVE THE RIGHT TO DENY YOU SERVICE. Beside the sign was a door with a plaque that read, OFFICE—EMPLOYEES ONLY.

Lorelei, Sadie, Grim, and Mads made for the desk to search for the impound records. Hal, Artemis, and I went for the junkyard.

Past the desk was a hallway that led outside. The scrapyard could have fit the high school football field inside its fences. Rows and rows of cars covered huge dirt lots. To the south, old tractors lined up next to three-tiered racks of cars with wheels stripped off and engines picked apart. To the north, rows of cars stood gutted and left to rust, motionless yet strangely animate, like sleeping animals. Before us, a pile of multicolored scrap metal loomed, underneath a floodlight at the center of the junkyard. No ghosts.

"He must have moved the Chevelle," I said as we hurried toward the Toyota, the Ford, and the Honda at the fence. We stopped several feet away, at the edge of two long, thick ruts gouged into the dirt. They were the width of tire tracks, but there were no treads visible in them.

The bastard had dragged my car.

We followed the tracks to the scrap mountain. Walls of metal surrounded an empty clearing; the floodlights burned away every shadow. The Chevelle sat in the dead center of it all, alone.

I huddled behind a truck with Artemis and Hal on either side.

"You both saw Ludwig run out of here, right?"

"Could we have *missed* him?" Hal asked.

"All right. If I catch on fire, just kill me. I don't care how, but make it fast."

"I'll throw a bar of soap at you," Artemis said.

"Fuck off."

I hopped out from behind the truck and jogged to the Chevelle. Ludwig must have known this was an obvious trap, but how could I resist it? It was the Chevelle. It was Mom. My skin crawled as I neared it. I was banking on the hope that Ludwig still thought I'd be useful to him. The car wasn't even turned on, but I could already hear the purr of the engine, the big old panther pleased that I'd found it.

I popped the door. Nothing happened. Sank into the driver's seat. Everything was quiet. Cranked the ignition. The Chevelle roared to life, its headlights flooding Hal and Artemis's hiding spot. Sweet relief.

I picked up Artemis and Hal and drove around to the back of the shop, where Mads was standing at the gate, fighting with a mass of keys on a key ring. "It's going to take me a minute to find the right one," she said. Behind her, a thick chain held the gate shut.

"I could try breaking the chain with the axe," Hal suggested.

"Not doubting your physical strength here, Hallybear," Mads replied through gritted teeth as yet another key failed. "I just don't think the laws of physics are going to be on your side."

"Try the gold one," Artemis said quietly. "That's a key for a Master Lock."

The key worked; Mads said, "Oh, nice eye, Arty," and Artemis's face lit up. Mads yanked the chain off and Artemis helped her push the gate open wide enough for the Chevelle to drive through. Gate closed; chain wrapped; lock back in place. Mads ran back inside to return the keys to Lorelei, who would put them back in the lockbox held shut with a six-digit code: Buster's birthday. The two of them returned with Sadie and Grim not far behind. Grim carried a thick file folder under one arm; Sadie was practically vibrating with excitement as she hopped past me.

"We're going to need a shovel," she said.

"What? Why?"

"Because Buster's office was full of *dirt*!" She cackled and threw herself into Mads's SUV after Grim.

"We weren't here to screw over Buster!" I hissed as I climbed into the Chevelle with Artemis. She was still smiling, just as jazzed as Sadie. "I hate everyone in this family."

"Oh my gosh," she said. "We pitted two firestarters against each other. We might get rid of Sam Forester. And we just robbed Buster Gates."

I pulled out onto the dirt road toward town. "Don't get too excited, criminal." I leaned forward to peer out the windshield at the fires brightening the sky. "Bach and Ludwig are still going at it. Look." Plumes of flame burst upward every few seconds. And they were moving north, past town center, in the direction of the high school. "That can't be good. Bach's having problems."

"Maybe it just takes a long time." Artemis's smile had faded. She, too, followed the progression of the fire. Mads's headlights glared in my rearview mirror as we turned south. "It's good that he's going north, though, isn't it? We can get home without anyone seeing us."

It was good for us *right now,* but Bach had never made any guarantees he could beat Ludwig. If Ludwig got the upper hand, then Addamsville would really be hosed. As far as I knew, Bach had been the only thing keeping Ludwig semi-controlled this whole time. I certainly hadn't been doing anything to help.

The Chevelle grumbled along the road, Mads on our tail. Fires leaped on the west side of town, snaking north like a dragon on a rampage. Sirens had gone up. Artemis's phone *ping ping ping*ed with notifications.

"There are videos of it," she said, the light from her phone washing her face a pallid blue. "You can see both of them. Bach and Ludwig." Tinny screams came from the phone speakers. "Neither of them look good. Oh my god— Bach's *arm—*"

My hands shook on the steering wheel. I could save myself, but what was the point if Ludwig destroyed Addamsville? This was my home. It had been Mom's home, too. She'd worked so hard for so long to keep it safe, not just to give her time to find her answers, but to keep her family safe. To keep everyone who lived here safe. She was able to help, so she helped.

For all her training, she'd never told me what I had to do or be. She'd helped me see what abilities I had and how to use them, and she'd let me decide.

Death or hunting.

"Artemis," I said, doing my best to keep my voice steady, "do you want out of the car?"

She glanced at me. "No. Why would I want out of the car?"

"Because I'm about to turn around and help Bach."

"Oh."

"Do you want out of the car?"

"I told you I wasn't going to let you go alone."

"Cool," I said, and swung into the wide dirt lane. Artemis screamed and grabbed her seat; the Chevelle's engine snarled as I floored the gas coming out of the turn. Then we were speeding north, leaving Mads and the others floundering behind us. Within seconds one of them had texted Artemis. "You can tell them what we're doing," I said, "but they'll have a hard time keeping up."

The Chevelle flew. It had been made for the hunt, this car. We raced past the junkyard, past Masrell's house, through the fringes of northern Addamsville, where the people were either hiding in their houses or had already ventured out to investigate the fiery disturbance. Those flames neared the high school now; if Bach and Ludwig kept on their path, we'd meet them there. The smell of fire permeated the car, and as we turned toward Handack, we saw it.

Walls of fire in the streets, leaping as tall as the houses. My hands faltered on the wheel. All I could hear was crackling, the hissed and pops, the small explosions. My fingers ached. My whole body ached.

"ZORA!"

Artemis grabbed my shoulder. I jammed my foot on the brake. The Chevelle roared as it curled onto Handack, through skeins of flame. We shot north, hot but not burning. I turned late, missed the entrance to the high school parking lot, and went flying over the curb. The bump onto the asphalt rattled my prosthetics loose. Black scars crossed the pavement in front of the school, erasing wide swaths of parking spaces, and a flaming hole had torn through the chain-link fence surrounding the football field. People—locals, *DMW* fans, ghost hunters—stood outside the fence, phones and cameras out. I aimed the Chevelle. They jumped out of the way at the roar of the engine. We crashed through the fence, and the melted links screamed against the doors and windows.

The Chevelle's wheels spun out on the field. It churned dead grass and dirt as I jammed the brakes. Small fires peppered the field and danced around the feet of the two combatants at the thirty-yard line.

The Chevelle's headlights flooded over them. Neither looked good. Half of Tad Thompson's hair was gone, one side of his face a twisted mask of burned flesh. His clothes were charred. He panted heavily. Bach's leather jacket was missing, his shirt hanging by threads. He still had all his hair, but he swayed where he stood, and his attention was now split between Ludwig and the Chevelle.

I gunned the engine. Ludwig leaped out of the way just before I drove through him. I spun the Chevelle around. Artemis groaned. Ludwig stood between Bach and me now, his attention on both of us. I couldn't hit him without running straight into Bach, too, and I needed Bach around until this was done.

"Stay in the car," I told Artemis, then twisted to grab Dad's axe from the backseat before kicking open the driver's side door.

"Hey, asshole!"

Ludwig's head swung toward me. I moved through the Chevelle's headlights and started making my way across the field. He followed me as I sidestepped to the left.

"Got my car back," I said. "Thanks for pulling it out for me. Really considerate of you."

Words seemed to fail him; his eyes were two red pinpricks in his eye sockets, and his breath came out in long rumbles. His expression was slack, but all his teeth showed. The longer he had to recuperate, the more life came back into his eyes. Bach, behind him, didn't seem to be regenerating nearly as well.

"Come on. I'm the one you want, right? No fire for me this time? Don't you want the rest of my fingers?" I spun the axe in my hands, drawing his eye. Behind him, Bach shook his head and regained solid footing. "Nah, you wouldn't have any left. I'm sure Bach has plenty, though. That's probably why Hildegard liked him better than you." A low hiss slipped between Ludwig's pressed-together teeth. "Oh, you poor *baby*. You're so easy to taunt. Can't get over the fact that Mom had a favorite." I was really glad Sadie wasn't around to hear me now. "Your answers aren't in Grimshaw House, and even if they were, you're never going to get them. You *lost*, you piece of—"

Ludwig lunged. So did Bach, at the exact same time, and Ludwig spun and unleashed a blast of fire that sent Bach rolling to the sidelines. I fell, too, with the streak of light imprinted in my vision. He still had fire. He stalked toward me now, leaving singed footprints in the grass. The smell of bonfires filled the stadium. An engine rumbled. The air in my lungs felt burned up, too. I couldn't breathe. Ludwig stood over me with his jaw tight and his teeth chattering.

The Chevelle roared. Ludwig turned as the front fender caught his kneecaps. Bones snapped like celery sticks; Ludwig screamed; the Chevelle bounced as it ran him over. I scrambled out of the way. The Chevelle roared backward, then shot forward again. *Crack-crack-crack-crack.* Rib bones, right in succession. The car swerved back again, and Artemis leaned out the driver's window.

"Is he dead?" she yelled.

I rose to my feet, scooped up the axe, and crept toward

Ludwig's motionless form. Mostly motionless. His legs were mangled and his chest was flattened, and one of his arms looked like pink taffy, but his eyes snapped to me and his lips curled away from his teeth.

You know why people generally have an easy time killing spiders? It's because spiders are not at all like humans. When a human body is smashed to a pulp, but the head is still staring at you and gnashing its teeth like it wants to eat you, you stop seeing it as a human body. It becomes some straight-up *Exorcist* nonsense, and that axe in your hand looks like a pretty good spider smasher.

The blade sliced squarely into his throat. Chopping through the human neck wasn't as easy as TV made it seem. They don't mention how much blood there's going to be, or how there'll be a little bit of whistling and a little bit of gurgling, and how the soft tissue will give way and the spine will hold out a little longer. Prosthetic fingers also don't help; Ludwig ended up with a neck like ground beef before it was over.

I wouldn't call it therapeutic. It was just necessary.

Tad Thompson's head rolled to the side. His smashed body writhed for another moment before smoke began rising from his jeans and a fire caught underneath him. It engulfed him in seconds, and then it was gone. All that was left was a sooty imprint on the ground where a body had once been. Even the blood on the axe flared and disappeared.

The head remained, motionless and bloodied.

Artemis stood by the hood of the Chevelle.

"That's going to be hard to explain," she said.

Bach had clambered to his feet and shuffled over to us, and now leaned down to pick up Ludwig's head by its remaining hair. Ludwig's own fire had cauterized the gaping neck.

I looked Bach up and down. "Are you—how are you still moving?"

"If you don't cut off the head, our bodies heal, no matter how bad the damage." He sighed. The skin was flaking off his lips. Even firestarter bodies could be harmed by fire. "Eventually."

"So he won't?" Artemis motioned to Ludwig.

"No. Just get him back through his entrance."

"Good luck with that," said Ludwig.

Artemis grabbed my arm so hard she almost broke it. I swung the axe up. Bach sighed again and turned the head around. Ludwig glared at Artemis first, then me.

"You think I'm going to let you get rid of me? I'll just come back again. And next time, I'll possess someone really important." He looked at Artemis. "Maybe your mother."

Without so much as a blink, Artemis punched Ludwig so hard his head went flying out of Bach's grip. It landed at the twenty-five-yard line with a heavy *thump* and rolled until coming to a stop.

Glancing approvingly at Artemis, Bach shuffled to retrieve the head again.

"Zora, do you have a bag somewhere? Something we can put him in?"

All I had was my school messenger bag inside the Chevelle. I dumped out the few papers and pens and the last remains of Aunt Greta's pruned mums, then held it open while Bach dropped Ludwig's moaning head inside.

"His entrance is in the mines." I turned to Artemis. "The chasm."

Artemis nodded. Then she looked toward the fence, where people were now climbing through the hole. "We have to go now, before someone stops us. This is going to be all over the news tomorrow."

Bach suddenly turned and looked out over the woods.

"What is it?" I asked.

"Sammy," he said. "He heard what's going on." He turned to me, a smile curling up his ruined mouth. "Can you two handle Ludwig?"

"That's what we're here for."

"Good. I'll take care of Sam." He started limping toward the far end of the field, toward the woods. As he walked, his stride lengthened, his movements stronger. "Go, now," he called over his shoulder. "And don't believe a thing Ludwig says."

31

Artemis and I stood at the entrance to the Hillcroft coal mine with an axe, a flashlight, and a human head in a bag.

"Do you remember the way?" Artemis asked.

"Kind of but not really," I replied.

"You're never going to find it again," Ludwig said, voice muffled. "Give up and let me out of here. I might get lucky and get eaten by a bear."

I punched down on top of the bag. Ludwig yelped.

Artemis grimaced. "If we're going to get lost, let's do it quickly. We lost the people from the school, but I don't think they'll stay lost for long."

Getting out of the high school was just a matter of driving the Chevelle back at the hole in the fence and watching another wave of people jump out of our way. They hadn't been able to keep up through town, and I was banking on having lost them long before the mine turnoff.

This time, we entered the mine through the main entrance. There were no fans around this time, no camera truck, no police cruisers. But there were ghosts. The most I'd seen in one place since the parade. They made way for us as we approached. Our steps echoed into the darkness, and water dripped from somewhere overhead. A few of the ghosts trailed behind us. Miners, all of them.

Artemis stepped around them. They watched her as much as they did me, and they were careful to keep from brushing against my bag.

"Hey," I said to Artemis. "I don't want to freak you out, but there are a lot of ghosts around us right now."

She only paused for a second. "I know. They feel cold. Like I might walk into a wall of ice."

Ludwig let out a low chuckle. "So many things neither of you know. And even Bach didn't tell you."

I pulled back the flap of my messenger bag. It was still Tad Thompson's head in there, cloaked in shadow, but Ludwig's eyes glowed out of the darkness like red Christmas lights.

"What kind of things?"

"Answers have a price."

I threw the flap back over him again. "Keep moving," I said

to Artemis. "Follow the cold. I think the miners know where we're going."

They made pathways for us, watching as we went. When Artemis's steps got shaky, I put a hand on her back to steady her.

"So, Zora," Ludwig said, "how does it feel to have something Artemis doesn't? Bet it feels good. You can't have the money, or the clothes, or the looks, the reputation, the status, the house, the *friends*—but you can see the dead. Does that ease the jealousy at all?"

"Don't listen to him," I said to Artemis. "I'm not jealous of you."

Ludwig let out a keening laugh that echoed down the tunnel. I gritted my teeth.

"Artemis," he said, still giggling, "how are *you* feeling, knowing that you're one of the few things keeping your dirtbag cousins from drowning? That they *use* you? They make you look bad just by existing, and you're expected to help them? You *have* to help them, because you don't have the tools to do this by yourself?"

"Shut up!" Artemis snapped at him.

"And now both of you know there's more out there, and the answers are slipping through your fingers faster than you can ask the questions. Who is Bach? Who am I? Who was Hildegard? Why were we here? What is this town? You'll never find the truth without me. I know all the questions and all the answers. The dead might help you find my entrance, but you'll never really get out of here. Without the answers, you'll be lost in the dark forever. Lost like your mothers."

The farther we went, the louder he got.

"When you die, you'll be stuck down here, too. No light. No air. And a century from now, when new teenagers come to see if the legends are true, you'll ask for their help, and they'll run screaming. They'll tell everything they saw, and no one will believe them, but they'll use it to bring tourists. They'll hold ghost tours here. You'll be the main attraction. And you'll plead and beg to be let out, but no one will listen. You'll be trapped in hell together, and no one will ever know the truth."

"Here," Artemis said, voice shaky.

We had turned a corner and come to a short ledge, and past the ledge, the flashlight beam spilled into a wide, dark area. The light revealed the cave in sharper relief than the camera viewfinder had before, but there was the deep chasm that cut the area in half, and there was the old, short bridge where Ludwig had stood when we first saw him.

Except now the space was full of ghosts.

Miners and children. Facing us, watching us, clearing the way to the bridge, where an impenetrable darkness waited. We stepped past them, up to the bridge, where the chasm yawned beneath us.

I opened my bag. Artemis shined the light inside. Ludwig flinched as I reached in and pulled his head out. Already he looked pallid, except for the bottom of his neck, which was a dark purple blue. He blinked at me and bared his teeth.

"Think hard before you do this, Zora Novak," he said. "I've seen things you could never imagine. I know things you have no way of finding out on your own."

My fingers tightened in his hair.

"What's the one thing you want?" he went on quickly. "More than respect, or friends, or freedom? I could give it to you. I could give you the truth." He paused, and so did I. He smiled. "I know what happened to your mother."

"Zora." Artemis put her hand on my arm. A soft squeeze around my elbow. She watched me in silence.

"Is it that obvious?" I said.

"You take me out of this cave," he said, "and I'll tell you everything. I'll tell you what happened to her that day in the woods. I'll tell you where she is now. I'll tell you how to *find her.*"

Was it that obvious that I wanted to find her? Was it that obvious how much I missed her, obvious enough that Ludwig could tell? I couldn't even get angry at him for trying to use her to trick me. There was only an emptiness inside my chest, an understanding that there was a good chance I'd never know what happened.

"Zora."

A second hand rested on my other arm. It flickered at the edges. Another hand on my shoulder, and one on my forearm. Bodies pressed in from all sides. They smelled like the dank must of the mines. Ludwig's gaze darted over and past me. Dozens of them pressed in.

There was a good chance I'd never know the answer to Mom's disappearance. But I also knew that if that answer existed, I already had everything I needed to find it, and it didn't matter if other people knew I was looking. I was allowed to hunt.

It was my job.

Ludwig began backpedaling. "Don't you at least owe me the benefit of the doubt? You know better than anyone that doing bad things doesn't make you a bad person. You gave Bach a pass. I can do good, too. I know the truth."

He wasn't wrong, but here's the thing: no one owes you the benefit of the doubt when your actions have shown, repeatedly and without reparation, that you do not deserve it.

Ludwig would not have me or anyone who lived here. He wouldn't have Addamsville. It wasn't for him. It was for me and Sadie and Dad. It was for Artemis and Aunt Greta. It was for Hal, Mads, Lorelei, the chief and her officers. It was even for Buster Gates. It was for George Masrell.

It was for the dead.

It was for my mom.

"You always think you know the truth," I said. Then, with all the disgust I could muster, "Fucking *tourist*."

And I hurled his head across the bridge.

He disappeared into his entrance. The darkness and the pressure sucked inward, like his head had hit a curtain and the curtain was collapsing on the spot. A stale wind roared past us, kicking up dirt, dragging on clothes and hair. I grabbed Artemis, and the ghosts braced us, and we huddled there against the force of the entrance closing until it was over.

Dust swirled through the flashlight's beam. I raised my head first. Artemis lifted hers a second later. The hands holding my jacket let go, one by one, until there were only Artemis's, slowly unclenching from my arm.

As we exited the mine, the only sounds to be heard were the rustle of the wind in the trees and the scraping of leaves across the ground. The Chevelle waited for us by the fence.

Artemis's phone buzzed. She glanced at the screen.

"Sadie," she said. "She wants to know where we are."

"Yeah," I replied, exhausted but wide awake. "We should get back."

Artemis started toward the Chevelle. I grabbed her arm. She looked back, puzzled.

"Thanks for doing this with me," I said. "I don't think I would've lasted very long on my own."

"Oh, it was just—"

Before she could finish, I pulled her into a hug.

"Ope," she said, surprised. Then she hugged me back.

"Is this the weirdest thing that's happened to you all week?" I asked.

"It's up there." She squeezed tighter. "And you're welcome."

32

By morning "Addamsville's Firestarters" had aired on every news channel from New York to LA. Hundreds of videos flooded the Internet, some more believable than others. Tad Thompson, founder and leader of *Dead Men Walking*, had fought the assistant of Hermit Forester in a battle of fiery fisticuffs that scorched the streets of Addamsville from the Goldmine to the high school. Their trail led to the black silhouette of a body burned into the football field. The fight only ended when two shadowy figures driving an old muscle car came onto the scene to take Tad's head and flee into the night.

Tad Thompson was gone, and the rest of the *DMW* crew fled Addamsville shortly after, retreating to Indianapolis to escape the crush of fans and news crews. The footage they had on Artemis's memory card was now proof the *DMW* crew had known about the threat and done nothing, and I suspected that was why they said nothing about it. The producer claimed in one interview that they would search for the truth of what happened to Tad, but they would rely on the police first. Leila gave a very different story.

"I'm done with this," she said to a reporter over the phone. "I don't care what anyone else does. I'm out of here. I'm going somewhere warm. Ghosts are bullshit. Indiana is bullshit. This whole thing was Tad's idea anyway, and he's a demon now. I'm getting my money, and then I'm out of here."

That morning I sat outside Happy Hal's with half of Addamsville, watching a swarm of police, firefighters, and reporters mill up and down Handack and Valleywine. Everyone from Addamsville knew it was me and my car in the videos, but they watched me now with wide-eyed wariness. They didn't know what I was, but at least now they were aware of it.

Dad was perched over me like a watchful hawk. Aunt Greta was there, vouching for my whereabouts and fighting off as many of the rumors as she could. So were Sadie and Grim, on the opposite side of the table. Hal was arguing with his dad about opening the shop. Mads had escaped her parents to swoop in and rescue Lorelei from hers; Buster was being led out of the crowd, bellowing his head off, by Officer Norm. Pastor Keller was standing where the town council ghosts had once been, decked out in full religious regalia and gripping his moth-eaten Bible in both hands. To pray the evil away, I guess.

Like the town council ghosts, all of Bach's corrupted spirits had disappeared after last night. So had Masrell, after we put Ludwig back through his entrance.

Next to me, Artemis said quietly, "I feel like we should have told the *DMW* crew what happened to Tad. What if they wonder about it for the rest of their lives?"

"If they wanted the truth, they would have asked," I said. "They know who to talk to. But they didn't, and they're still getting their money. So let's leave them that way, huh? Leave them happy with their money."

"Don't you think knowing the truth might make them happy?"

"Hell no. You don't go looking for the truth to be *happy*. You go looking so that you *know*."

Clusters of ghosts drifted amongst the onlookers. A girl in a floral dress watched Chief Rivera cut a path through the crowd. The ghosts that always watched Pastor Keller root through his trash for his glasses was following him around now.

Artemis said, "I think part of happiness is contentment. And knowing this, you can't be content, because it creates so many more questions. How do ghosts exist? What does this mean about the afterlife? Who are we, that we can sense them? Ludwig was right. We don't even know all the questions to ask yet."

"Mysteries on mysteries," I said.

Chief Rivera made her way up to our table. "Novaks," she

said, nodding to us. "Greta. Artemis. Mr. Grimshaw." Sadie was pointedly holding her expression in check. "I found an interesting set of packages waiting for me at the police station this morning. The first contained several documents of dubious purpose relating to Buster Gates's business practices. I found it interesting that this package appeared the morning after Buster reported the doors to his shop unlocked and some of his things rifled through, not to mention the Chevelle missing. I stopped by to see if it had any relation to what happened on this side of town."

"I don't know who would've done that," Dad said, resting one hand on my shoulder and one on Artemis's. "We were all at Greta's last night, as my sister-in-law already explained to Officer Newall."

"It seems," Aunt Greta added, "that Tad Thompson had something against Zora. He could easily have made a stop at the junkyard on his way south."

"Mm-hmm." Rivera surveyed us from behind her aviators. "And I guess I should chalk the documents up to fiery shenanigans?"

"Hey," I said, "at least the fiery shenanigans are over."

She focused on me. "Are they now?"

"Forester's gone."

"That he is." She took a deep breath, held it in, then let her shoulders relax. "That brings me to the second package. In it was what appeared to be the very legitimate will of Malcolm Grimshaw, the previous owner of Grimshaw House."

We all stared at her.

"Who sent it?" Sadie asked.

"If I knew that, I'd already be questioning them," the chief said. "Unfortunately the package was unmarked except for a very large letter *B*. Mr. Grimshaw, I'll need you to come down to the station with me to talk about this document. And actually, Greta, it might be good if you come, too."

"Happily," Aunt Greta said.

"Can Lazarus come?" Grim asked, shaking as he stood from the table, even with Sadie's hands to brace him. "I'm not very comfortable with legal issues."

Dad jumped to Grim's side. "All above the board, Abby, swear to God."

"Fine," Rivera said. Then to me and Artemis, "Don't get into trouble, all right?"

I held a hand to my heart. "Scout's honor."

They disappeared. Sadie shifted around to our side of the bench and tightened her grip on her afghan. She'd been less on edge this morning, but still tense, and I hadn't realized why until I remembered that the ghosts had all come back.

"Was it better quiet?" I asked.

"Not really," she replied. "I've heard them my whole life. Without them, it felt wrong."

"It felt wrong not seeing them, too."

"So, let me get this straight." She spoke quietly enough that no one nearby would hear. "You had to . . ." She mimed cutting her neck. "Does that bother you? I know you needed therapy before, but at least before it was something you could actually talk about."

There were a lot of things that bothered me, and severing a human head was probably top of that list. It hadn't been the same as the swift slice to sever a firestarter's natural head. It bothered me that I could still remember the feel of the axe in my hands and the warm blood misting my face. But that I had beheaded Ludwig didn't bother me, probably because he'd kept talking, but also because I knew cutting his head off hadn't killed him. He was still alive out there, wherever *there* was, and if he could find his way back to Addamsville to search for Hildegard, he would.

"Nah," I said. "But you're right, I gotta get some kind of therapy for . . . everything. You should probably come with me."

"Why? You're old enough to take yourself."

"I meant you should *also* go to therapy. She was your mom, too. And thanks to Dad, you've basically been a single parent for most of your twenties."

Sadie cooled. "Oh. Well . . . yeah."

"And we can work on the ghosts, too. Maybe together we can become two halves of a whole functioning psychic. Or"—I glanced at Artemis—"three halves."

Artemis turned long enough to say, "Three-thirds."

"Whatever."

Sadie rolled her eyes. "Oh. Yay. Just the glamorous, high-paying job I've always wanted."

I punched her. She kicked me with a combat boot.

Mads and Lorelei found their way over to us, causing Artemis to freeze halfway through applying fresh lip balm. Lorelei was beaming; Mads looked solemn.

"Lorelei, shouldn't you be more upset?" I said. "Your dad got dragged off in front of the whole crowd."

"It's his fault anyway." She practically radiated joy. "And Gavin told me about the will! He's getting his house back!"

"Don't be too optimistic," Sadie said. "They could still say the will isn't legitimate. Or that Forester still owns the place. *Or* the town will keep it as another tourist attraction."

"Yeah, but we've got Aunt Greta on our side now." It felt nice to say. "And I don't think she's going to need it for the tourists."

I wasn't entirely happy about that point—tourists would never leave Addamsville now—but if tourism was how we kept Addamsville alive, then so be it. Keeping them from destroying our buildings and our homes would be a constant, slow, grinding struggle, but it was better than facing a firestarter.

The only person who still didn't look happy about this was Mads.

"What's wrong with you?" I asked her.

"Midterms," she said. "They're next week."

"Oh, *eff.*"

Artemis snorted. Mads nudged her with a leg and said, "Do you want to study for AP chem together?"

Artemis looked up at Mads. "Me? Uh—sure. Uh—when?" She fumbled for her phone. "Uh—I have tomorrow free, the next day, all weekend—"

As they compared schedules, Hal joined us. He was healing, slowly but surely. I hoped the lasting effects of the firestarters—on him and on the rest of Addamsville—wouldn't be too bad. Or, if they were, that my friends would talk to me about it. Hal started poking around Mads and Artemis, making Artemis flush again and Mads step in to her rescue.

Sadie and I watched Pastor Keller in silence. He was preaching about how Hermit Forester and Bach would suffer retribution for what they'd done. Tourists, *DMW* fans, and newspeople passed him by. Only the locals stopped to listen.

Tad's disappearance was a draw for the rest of America, but for Addamsville the mystery was the disappearance of Bach and Forester. Scraps of Bach's ruined clothes had been found trailing from the football field to the edge of Black Creek Woods. Come early this morning, Sam Forester was unreachable, the Forester House abandoned, and Forester's car still in the driveway. They had gone, like Mom five years before, and there was no knowing where they were now or if they'd ever be back. The disappearance of the Firestarter Murder ghosts meant, I hoped, that Bach had taken Sam back through his entrance.

"Death or hunting?" I said to myself.

Sadie frowned at me. "What?"

"Hypothetical situation: you can know there are answers to your questions but ignore them in order to be happy, or you can spend your life hunting them down. What do you choose?"

She thought for a minute. "I choose both."

"You can't have both."

Sadie smiled, and something about it—her amusement, her resignation—made me realize I hadn't been the only one thinking of this. "Sure you can. I would hunt, but only for so long. There are too many questions, and too many answers; if you don't draw the line, you'll lose yourself to it. I think it's important to find the answers you need, but at some point you have to stop and ask yourself if you really need them."

I followed her gaze to the hazy gray sky over Black Creek Woods. Sadie bumped me with her shoulder, then put her arm around me, shrouding me under her afghan. "We deserve to be happy," she said.

A long moment passed while all of Addamsville moved around us. Living and dead, locals and tourists, the known and the mysterious.

Sadie gave me an obnoxious squeeze and added, "But if you want help looking for Mom first, I won't say no."

33

The old Victorian loomed over Grim as he waited for us on the curb. Grimshaw House's windows reflected the gray sky and the bare trees as the wind tugged at the last of their leaves. As always, the ghosts kept their distance.

"About time!" Dad said, smacking Grim square between the shoulder blades. Grim fumbled to keep hold of his manila envelope. "How does it feel?"

Grim smiled. "Cold."

"You have the key?" Sadie said, gathering him up in a big hug and kissing him on the cheek. "What are we waiting for?"

We followed Grim up the front walk and ascended the porch steps. Grimshaw House groaned like someone woken too early.

"There's a lot of work that has to be done on it," Grim said. "Mrs. Wake said she'd help out, but I told her she didn't have to."

"Do you think there's really treasure buried in there?" I asked.

"That railroad fortune had to go somewhere," Sadie said.

Grim shook his head. "I think the real treasure is that we all have a place to sleep tonight."

"He's a smart one, Sadie," Dad said. "You made a good choice."

While Grim dug around in the manila envelope, I stepped back and looked up at the face of the house, the cracked paint, the weathered siding. Even with Bach and Forester gone, it looked as empty as the day it had been built. Ghosts should have been in every window, patrolling every hallway, relaying a message through the house that there was someone new here, a new owner, a Grimshaw come back to the nest.

Maybe, like Artemis's shoe ghost, they were just very good at hiding. It didn't make me want to go inside any more, but that was a comfort. Maybe they would get used to me and show themselves. I could tell them this was my first time ever living in anything other than a trailer, and though I would have given almost anything to have the trailer back, I was excited about this, too.

They'd understand. They were used to it. Life in

Addamsville was, after all, just a prolonged cohabitation between the living and the dead.

Grim found the key, a surprisingly shiny thing for a house so old, and slid it into the keyhole. The lock made an audible *chunk* sound. Legally entering the house felt a lot better than picking the back door.

The entrance opened into a dusty foyer. Thick cobwebs hung from a metal chandelier. A staircase ran up one side to a darkened second floor, and luckily there were too many footprints disturbing the dust for ours to be recognized from the night we snuck in. To the right was a parlor. To the left, a dining room. Oil paintings still hung in their frames, warped from the weather. The chill seeped through the walls, and the musty air hung stagnant. The size of the house could be felt in every inch of it.

"It's *beautiful*," Sadie breathed.

"Why would anyone need to bury treasure beneath this place?" I said. "Look at it. It *is* treasure."

Dad and Sadie went into the dining room to look at the china cabinet and the long dining table. Grim held me back and dug around in the envelope again. "I found this in the mailbox when I got here. I didn't recognize the handwriting, but . . . well." He pulled out a smaller envelope with *Zora* printed on the front in sharp handwriting. The flap was sealed, but the whole envelope was browned and crisp, like it had been tossed in an oven for a few seconds. Inside was a letter signed with a jagged *B*.

"I'll leave you to it." Grim stepped into the house.

Zora,

L was wrong. He wanted the house because he thought H hid her entrance to Addamsville there. But a house isn't big enough to hide something like that. H is much stronger than us, and her entrance would have to be huge. L isn't the sharpest knife in the drawer.

I think I might know the location of H's entrance. It took even me a while to find it. I'm not positive yet, but we'll find out once I get Sammy there. I'm telling you this because I think it might answer your question. And I'm not telling you what it is in case someone else reads this letter. The entrance is hidden for a reason.

I don't want to get your hopes up. If you see what I did—and I know you will, eventually—you can decide for yourself if you want to check it out.

Just don't forget, not everyone out there is as nice as me.

B

P.S. I included one answer with this letter. I made sure no one else was able to find it a long time ago. I hope it's the first of many.

Folded in with the letter was an old black-and-white photograph of Bach, looking eighteen, standing before the entrance to the mine in its heyday. He wore a light suit with a vest beneath, and his expression was sullen. On the back of the photo was the year *1883* and the letters *S. H.*

Feeling strangely hollow and light, I went back to the letter.

My question. I'd asked Bach a lot over the years, but it was the obvious one, the one I would ask everyone if I thought someone could give me an answer. He had disappeared into Black Creek Woods in almost the exact same place Mom had because he thought he knew where she'd gone. Hildegard's entrance, whatever it was—whatever it meant. Something bigger than a house, but not yet found by anyone in Addamsville. Artemis might have some ideas about that, and Sadie could ask the dead if they knew. It was a starting point, at least.

I wouldn't go so far as to say Bach was a good person. After you've murdered people, even in service to someone else, it's tough to regain that title. He was trying to do good things, though, and if another crumb about Mom came out of that, I'd take it. I tucked the letter and photo back in their envelope, along with the picture of Mom and Aunt Greta I'd kept in my pocket, then hid it in my jacket..

Grim had drifted from the foyer into the parlor, for once looking like part of his surroundings. A ghost in a ghost house. Sadie and Dad had disappeared upstairs, so I followed Grim. The place was beautiful, but I didn't want to think of the property taxes or the amount of money it'd take to fix it up. Thankfully, the house wasn't the only thing Grim had inherited from his parents. The Grimshaws were mostly gone, but their money—some of that railroad fortune Sadie had mentioned—wasn't.

"This place is great, Grimmie," I said, turning back to him. "Way better in the daylight. We're going to have to find some furniture, though. I think you should get a piano."

Grim didn't respond. He was busy wiping grime off the front window with his sleeve. After a few moments of futile cleaning, he gave up, unlatched the window, and gave it a sharp yank upward. The window groaned, jerked halfway open, then went the rest of the way. Grim kneeled in front of it and looked out. He'd crushed his envelope.

"Grim."

Still no response. Grim could space out sometimes, but he almost always answered after the second prompting. I kneeled beside him. He stared to the northwest like he always did, past the houses and the shops, past the high school, past the place Mom had left the Chevelle, over the trees where Mom had *found* the Chevelle, where the clouds had broken and an eerie glow lit the horizon.

"What's the matter, Grimmie?" I said. "It's got to be a shock. Getting the house. Bach sent Rivera the will—I think Sam Forester had it this whole time. They were trying to keep ownership of it. They had this thing about ownership, how it let them see things differently—"

"I figured out what it is," he replied. "The thing that's been bothering me for so long. The thing that's wrong with the world."

He pointed to the horizon. There was Black Creek Woods, whispering with mysteries. There was the radio tower, its pinprick red lights blinking in the growing dark. There was the peak of Piper Mountain, standing alone against the dimming night sky.

"There are no mountains in Indiana," Grim said, and smiled like a great burden had been lifted off his shoulders.

ACKNOWLEDGMENTS

This is the second book in a row I have to give the biggest thank-you to my agent, Louise Fury. Thank you for being so perceptive, and thank you for telling me it was okay to say no. It was exactly what I needed to know. I will never forget it.

Thank you to Kristin Smith—I hope this wasn't too spooky for you—and all of Team Fury.

Thank you to Virginia Duncan, who provided me the time and space I needed to write this book; Katie Heit, once-assistant, now editor herself!; Sylvie Le Floc'h, amazing designer; and Tim Smith and his team of copyeditors. Big thank you to Chad W. Beckerman for the absolutely *kickass* cover art.

Thank you to my dad for patiently answering all (ALL) my questions about Indiana cops, laws, and prisons. Thank you to Darci Cole, Brett Werst, Marieke Nijkamp, and Rebecca Coffindaffer for reading the mess that was early drafts of this book and/or keeping me alive with talks of fantasy and science fiction and tabletop gaming. As always, thank you to Christina Bejjani for listening to my woes, talking to me about books and writing, and generally just being an awesome person. Thank you to Colin Dickey for writing *Ghostland: An American History in Haunted Places*, the book that gave Addamsville its heart.

Thank you to Gus, the best boy, a paragon of dogs.

And finally, thank you to my parents and my siblings. You're all jerks, and I love you.